Florence Montgomery

Seaforth

Fifth Edition

Florence Montgomery

Seaforth
Fifth Edition

ISBN/EAN: 9783337267896

Printed in Europe, USA, Canada, Australia, Japan

Cover: Foto ©Andreas Hilbeck / pixelio.de

More available books at **www.hansebooks.com**

THE LONELY CHILD IN THE OLD PICTURE-GALLERY.

SEAFORTH

BY

FLORENCE MONTGOMERY,

AUTHOR OF "MISUNDERSTOOD," "THROWN TOGETHER," ETC.

THE POPULAR EDITION.

WITH A FRONTISPIECE BY

MADEMOISELLE ADRIENNE LOUDON.

LONDON:

RICHARD BENTLEY AND SON,

NEW BURLINGTON STREET.

Publishers in Ordinary to Her Majesty the Queen.

1885.

SEAFORTH.

BY

FLORENCE MONTGOMERY,

AUTHOR OF "MISUNDERSTOOD," "THROWN TOGETHER," ETC.

FIFTH EDITION.

LONDON:

RICHARD BENTLEY AND SON,

NEW BURLINGTON STREET.

Publishers in Ordinary to Her Majesty the Queen.

1885.

TO

MY FATHER

THE FOLLOWING PAGES

ARE DEDICATED.

CONTENTS.

BOOK I.

SEAFORTH.

CHAPTER I.

THE LONELY CHILD IN THE OLD PICTURE-GALLERY.

EVERY old house, it is said, has its haunted chamber and its flitting ghost.

Seaforth was no exception.

Flitting about its rooms and corridors went a lonely little spirit; but it was not sprite, nor shade, nor fairy. The ghost that haunted the halls of Lord Seaforth was his own and only child.

She lived a little life of her own, which none cared to inquire into, among the relics of past ages, of which the old house was full.

She knew no fear of the long, dark corridors and deserted rooms; the grim knights in armour were her boon companions, and the cold, silent picture-gallery her favourite resort.

Here she would spend hours by herself, playing with the pictures.

Every picture was a friend to her, and she treated them as though they were alive, and talked to them, laughed with them, and quite believed they answered her, and were in sympathy with her varying moods.

The lonely child had no companions, and so made playmates of grandfathers, and great uncles, and great-great aunts, who had all been dead and buried years and years before she was born.

But they had been children *once*, and their pictures seem to have been mostly painted when they were merry little boys and girls.

For very smiling faces looked down upon little Joan from the walls, and in the games that some of them were playing she would have been very glad to join. There were groups of children playing on the grass, making daisy-chains, and twining them round each others' old-fashioned hats; groups of children chasing butterflies and dancing on the smooth lawn, or standing by the lake, feeding great white swans.

Then there were separate pictures of companionless children like little Joan : a little girl with a kitten in her arms, another leading a pet lamb crowned with flowers, a little boy clinging round the neck of a great Newfoundland dog.

But the favourite of all was a half-length picture of a youth of eighteen, with a thoughtful face and dark, earnest eyes.

Under this picture was written, " Godfrey, Earl of

Seaforth; painted 1763." All the other Earls of Seaforth in the gallery were called Harold, and she often wondered why this was the only one who was called Godfrey. She would talk to this picture by the hour. There was something about the grave, earnest expression of the beautiful face which seemed to invite her confidence.

She never had this feeling for any of the children's pictures. They looked at each other, or at their pet animals or flowers, not at her.

"Godfrey, Earl of Seaforth; painted 1763," was the only one who looked straight at her, with his kind, understanding eyes.

She had the greatest faith and trust in this picture. She would put down her dolls and other treasures in front of it, when she was called away from the picture-gallery, and say, "Take care of them till I come back. I know I can trust you;" just as a happier child might have confided its little possessions to the care of an elder brother; and, of course, they were there when she returned.

"I *knew* I could trust you," she would say ex-ultingly when she found everything exactly as she had left it.

She would not for a moment have thought of entrusting her treasures to any of the other pictures. She would play with them in her gay moods, holding out her hands in imaginary claspings, or twining fancied daisy-chains with the Harolds and the God-freys, the Joans and the Bridgets, of long ago; but only to him did she tell out her childish thoughts and fancies, the mournful regrets and wondering lamentations of which her little life was full.

"You think of nothing but play," she would say sometimes to the laughing groups of children, "and I want a grave talk to-day."

And, unhappily, the days when little Joan wanted "a grave talk" came round very often. For she knew well that she was an un-wanted, unloved child.

She had had early instilled into her that she was a disappointment and a mistake; and that as such she was regarded by every one, servants, tenants, and parents included.

For her nurse used often to tell her (and the story fascinated while it saddened her) of the circumstances which had attended her birth; of all the preparations which had been made to welcome the heir; and of the terrible disappointment she had occasioned.

"Tell it me again," she would say, when the tale was finished; "tell me more and more about it."

And then the nurse would begin again, and paint a vivid picture of the unlighted bonfires, the silent joy-bells; of the tenantry separating in silence and returning to their homes in gloom; of the depression and disappointment that seemed spread all around, and the mournful silence that reigned in the house; how that it was her father himself who had sent all the crowds away, and forbidden any sign or sound of rejoicing; of how her mother had said, "Take it away; I do not wish to see it."

The nurse would proceed to point a moral to her tale by telling her how good she ought to be, how submissive, how obedient, to try and make up to her father and mother for the great grief she had caused them. And, poor child! she was as obedient and as submissive as possible to her parents; but all this made her shrink from them—made her wish to keep out of their way, to be by herself, and to see them as little as possible.

The nurse was not aware of the deep effect her tales had upon the child, nor of the lasting impression they were destined to make upon her, for little Joan never said anything at the time. But in the silence of the picture-gallery she would pour out all her feelings to the picture she loved so well.

And "Godfrey, Earl of Seaforth; painted 1763," always seemed to understand and to be in sympathy with her. Every feeling seemed to find an answer in his earnest eyes. He looked sorry, or tender, or pitying, according to the mood she was in and to the demands she was making upon him.

So infinite was the expression the master-hand of the painter had thrown into the work !

There were times when the sense of being a disappointment overwhelmed the child.

"Godfrey, Earl of Seaforth; painted 1763 !" she would sometimes say; "how I wish I had been you ! How happy *your* father and mother must have been when *you* were born ! How the joy-bells must have rung and the cannons fired ! There was no hushing of chimes and sending away of tar-barrels *then!* And *your* mother did not say, ' Take it away; I do not want to see it!'"

Poor child! this was the hardest part of all, and her little voice would be choked with sobs as she repeated the cold, cruel words, and they be lost in a passionate burst of tears.

But even in moods like this the beautiful eyes in the picture would smile down sympathy and comfort.

She often wondered what the past events of the family history could have been, that made it so all-important that she should have been a boy, and her advent so disastrous to her father and mother.

Her young spirit cried out sometimes in a sudden rebellion against the injustice of her lot.

" Could I help it? " she would passionately cry, kneeling in an agony of grief before the picture, and raising her streaming eyes and clasped hands to the calm face above her.

The picture could soothe and quiet her, but it could give no answer. No! It could throw no light upon the past; could not tell her why a shadow should have rested on her young life from its beginning, nor why on her fair young brow should be written the cold, cruel words, " Not wanted."

Had the little heart not been so tender, had the passionate longing for love not been so great, who shall say what evil might have come out of such a childhood? Who shall say what a cold, crushed, and hardened being might have been made at last of a child who bore such a brand on her brow?

CHAPTER II.

THE TWO BROTHERS.

THE family of Seaforth was one of the most ancient in Great Britain, and the property had been in its hands, and had descended in direct line from father to son, unentailed, for generations.

And it had been the glory and pride of the family that it should have been so.

No *vaurien*, no graceless spendthrift had ever darkened the pages of the family history; and the property had always been as safe and as sure to be handed down to its legal heir as if it had been entailed and tied-up to the utmost limits of the law.

About thirty years before the opening of our story, in the first chapter, the possessor of Seaforth was a widower, with two sons. He was a great invalid. This fact, and the great distance of Seaforth from London, kept him quite stationary, and rendered the boys' home-life an isolated and monotonous one. In due time they went to school and college, like other boys, and returned three times a year to spend their holidays at home.

Harold, the eldest, was a self-contained and silent boy, of a proud and overbearing disposition, with an iron will, an overweening sense of his own importance, and a great love of power; but a boy of rigid integrity and unsullied conduct. From his boyhood he was trustworthy, and his father could always rely on his word and on his sense of duty and honour.

Godfrey, the younger, was as careless and light-hearted as his brother was grave and stern.

He was weak, yielding, and easily led; with no sense of responsibility, no reverence for any one or anything, and very little principle.

To please himself and to enjoy the passing hour was to him of far greater importance than all the honour and duty in the world.

At school and at college he was as idle, as thoughtless, and as extravagant as his brother was strict and conscientious.

Between two natures so opposite there could be but little sympathy, and the brothers were from childhood always at variance.

As years went on mutual indifference deepened into mutual antipathy. For, as his sons grew on into manhood, the old Earl failed yearly in health, and lived more and more the life of an invalid.

He felt himself daily less able to cope with a wild and troublesome youth, and was thankful to delegate his parental authority to his eldest son, who was so able and so willing to exercise it.

Godfrey cháfed against and resented the perpetual espionage his brother kept up upon him, both at college and at home. He hated the austere virtue of Harold's character.

Harold, on his side, had a profound contempt for Godfrey's vacillating disposition, and lived in perpetual dread of his bringing disgrace upon the family name. And in Harold's eyes there could be no crime less venial.

He loved his name, his home, and his family traditions with a proud and absorbing affection. To him there was but one place in the world, one house, one name; and it angered him to know his pride of birth and family were totally unshared by his only brother.

To Harold a life spent at Seaforth was a dream of all that was perfect. He asked for nothing better than to establish himself there so soon as his college life should be over, and to nurse the estate for his invalid father until such time should come when it should be all his own. Life he had no wish to see; travel and adventure formed no part of his plans. His programme of life was an irreproachable career at college, a brilliant coming of age, a happy marriage with some beautiful and high-principled woman, and then a useful and honoured life in a place every stone of which he idolised, and every tree of which he held dear.

The younger son's day-dream was altogether different.

He held the monotonous life at Seaforth in abhorrence. To him it was the acme of dullness, pomp, and formality.

His great desire was to escape from it as soon as possible, to enter the army early, and so become his own master at once, and to pass his life as far away from his brother as could possibly be.

Within a few months of Harold's coming of age (which in the Seaforth family was not till five and twenty), both brothers had succeeded in carrying out the first part of their respective programmes.

Harold was established at Seaforth, the prop and support of his invalid father, and the recognized master of all.

Godfrey was a captain in a cavalry regiment, in every way removed from his brother's control. His career, so far, had been just what might have been predicted. He had plunged headlong into a life of reckless extravagance, had developed a passion for gambling, and already had he three times applied to his father to pay his debts, and give him a fresh start.

He was on the eve of a fourth application, when he was summoned to Seaforth to attend his brother's coming of age.

Godfrey's career had, of course, been pain and grief to Harold. Antipathy had ripened into dislike; but an event now occurred which converted antipathy and dislike into bitter, undying hatred.

CHAPTER III.

THE FIRST CHANGE IN THE PROGRAMME.

It was within, as we have already said, a few months of his coming of age that Harold took up his permanent residence at Seaforth.

It was at about the same time, too, that the old rector of the place died, and the living changed hands. A young college friend, whose character closely resembled his own, was chosen by Harold to fill the vacant place.

This young man, Edward Stanhope by name, brought with him to the rectory his newly married wife and his orphaned and penniless sister.

Beautiful, high-principled, and full of character, the young girl was just the kind of woman Harold had dreamed of in his wife. Before he was aware of it himself, indeed, from the hour of his introduction to her, he fell deeply in love with her. The rector and his wife were not slow to perceive it, and did all they could to assist and encourage him.

An intimacy sprang up between the hall and the rectory. Almost daily was Harold to be found there; and, for a time, the hard, stern man forgot his duties at home, neglected his usual avocations, and gave himself up to winning the beautiful girl who exercised so powerful an influence over him.

The situation was patent to all. The only person unaware of it was Hester herself.

So far was it from her thoughts to connect any-thing of sentiment with the cold, stern man, who she looked upon solely as her brother's friend and patron, that the idea of his being in love with her, or, indeed, with any one, never entered her mind for a moment. Herself in the heyday of youth and hope, gifted with tender feelings, quick susceptibilities, and strong powers of affection and devotion; Harold, with his rigid integrity, untempered by tenderness, and total want of sympathy and imagination, was the very last man in the world to interest her.

All unconscious of the meshes which were being woven round her, she pursued her way unthinkingly; and, unfortunately, her way was such that Harold's hopes strengthened day by day.

Her natural goodness made her kind to every one, Harold among the rest. She always did what she could to please others and make them happy; and, at his request, would sing or play at any moment, and for any length of time, as she would have done for any one who asked her.

Moreover, she took pleasure in doing it, for she

had a beautiful voice, and an inborn delight in music
for its own sake.

It was quite as much to please herself as to give
pleasure to him that she would sing song after song
all through the soft summer evenings.

She would have done just the same had she been
quite alone.

She was quite unaware of him, as he sat silent
and enthralled, her voice going through and through
him, and raising feelings within him never experienced before. And Harold, meanwhile, deceived by
her kindness and her willingness to comply with his
every request; deceived, also, by her *manner* of doing
it; mistaking her delight in the performance for its
own sake for delight in the performance of his wishes,
began to fancy his feelings were returned.

And on all this his future hopes now hung. He,
for the first time, felt himself completely in the hands
of another, and realised that that other had the power
to withhold or bestow that on which his heart was set.

His whole future life, he soon realised, its happiness and its success, was dependent on his securing
her for his wife.

And with this knowledge there crept over him
also, for the first time, a feeling of inferiority. He
lost sight of himself as his admiration increased for
her.

At length the crisis came; and one summer evening he made his declaration, and placed his future in
the young girl's hands.

Completely taken by surprise, alarmed, and slightly indignant, Hester instantly and without a moment's hesitation told him that what he asked was impossible, and begged he would never mention the subject again.

The *dénouement* caused a terrific *fracas* at the rectory. Edward Stanhope and his wife were at first incredulous, and then furious. Harold himself staggered under the blow; and in justice to him we must say that the disappointment far outweighed the astonished mortification.

But his friend the rector told him to wait, and not suppose for an instant that Hester's resolution was final. The girl, he said, had been taken by surprise. She was young, she was inexperienced, she was ignorant. She did not know what she was doing. Give her time, and it was almost certain she would come round.

Harold suffered himself to be guided by his friend's advice, and was once more filled with hope. He made up his mind to wait till the eve of his birthday, and then renew his suit; so that he might on the same day be welcomed by his tenantry as their future master, and present the beautiful girl to them as their future mistress.

Meanwhile great pressure was put upon Hester by her brother and his wife. Arguments, entreaties, even threats, were by turns brought to bear upon her.

At last she was taunted with her dependent

position, and given to understand she was *de trop* in their home.

Till this last means of coercion was tried, Hester's resolution had never faltered. Her answer had always been the same : gentle but decided.

But they had gone too far. Her independent spirit rebelled against such an implication ; her pride rose, and she plainly told her brother that sooner than be the wife of a man she did not care for, or a dependent in a home where she was not wanted, she would go out as a governess and work for her daily bread.

Edward Stanhope was alarmed. He knew how fearless and determined his sister was, and he was afraid she would act up to her intention.

He knew, too, how fully competent she was to undertake such a post, for she had always been the sharer of his studies, and was almost as good a classical scholar as himself, and well-informed and well-read to a remarkable degree. So that he felt it was no idle threat, but one which she was as well able to carry out as she might become determined to fulfil.

He saw that it was best to be silent for the present ; and he told his wife they had overdone their part, and must let the subject drop for a time. They agreed, therefore, to leave matters as they were, and to maintain a kind of armed neutrality.

It was at this juncture that there arrived at Seaforth the younger son.

2

He had been summoned, as we have already said, to attend Harold's coming of age. He would willingly have refused the invitation; but being about to make a fourth application for money, he did not dare disobey; more especially as he thought a personal interview with his father would be more to his own advantage than a correspondence, which he felt sure was always overlooked by his elder brother.

The sequel is easy to guess. The beautiful girl at the rectory exercised the same fascination over him as she had already done over his brother, and her position woke up all his best feelings, and roused his pity and indignation. Certainly no one could have been found who could enter more fully into Hester's feelings than Godfrey Seaforth.

Sympathy, cordial and hearty, he would have accorded to any one who shared in his dislike to his elder brother; but when a young and beautiful girl was in question, every chivalrous feeling was called into play, and he could not stop at sympathy: he must come to her help.

The present moment was, and had ever been, all-important in his eyes.

No thought of the future, therefore, nor of the responsibilities he was incurring, troubled his thoughts when, filled with pity for the forlorn damsel, he offered to play the part of the knight-errant and to rescue her from the meshes in which she was entangled.

He never reflected for a moment on his own

position, harassed as he was by difficulties, and plunging deeper and deeper into debt.

Neither—to his credit be it spoken—did he consider what an additional burden a wife would be to him.

Rash and uncalculating as ever, he invited another to share his already fallen fortunes, and to go with him to poverty and ruin.

And in Hester's eyes he contrasted so favourably with his elder brother. He had all the youth, spirits, and sentiment that Harold lacked, and the chivalrous sympathy he showed towards herself roused all her gratitude.

There was nothing about him of that hardness and rigid love of duty that her knowledge of his brother, and her recent experience of her own, had taught her to dislike.

Of his real character she, of course, knew nothing. Stories against him she had heard, but in her present state of feeling she was quite ready to believe he had been mismanaged, and was a victim to his brother's austerity. She magnified him into a hero. He was, no doubt, an ill-treated younger son, whose father had been prejudiced against him. Woman-like, she took the part of the injured and oppressed—believed him, pitied him, and loved him.

Everything was privately arranged by Godfrey; and on the day previous to the coming of age—the day on which Harold was intending to urge his suit again—she became Godfrey's wife.

The marriage took place in London, and a telegram announcing the event reached Seaforth in the evening.

*   *   *   *   *   *

This, then, was the event which made Harold's cup of wrath and hatred brim over, and changed the whole programme of his life.

The brilliant coming of age, the happy marriage, the honoured life spent among his own people, with a beautiful and beloved wife at his side—all these dreams faded away.

Stunned by the blow, he was not even able to appear among his tenantry on that long-looked-for day.

It dawned in silence and in gloom. The rejoicings were postponed, and it passed without festivity or mark of any kind.

Postponed at first, they never afterwards took place.

From that time Harold became more rigid, more hard and stern, than ever.

He isolated himself entirely, shrank from society, and gave himself up to the management of the estate and the care of his invalid father.

He formed for himself a sort of mill-wheel of tasks and duties. Round and round it went every day, and he with it.

Every hour had its work allotted to it, every day brought with it its special occupation.

One act testified to the soreness and bitterness of

his feelings, but he never opened his lips on the past to any one. This was to procure, through his father's influence with the party then in power, a Crown living for Edward Stanhope, so that with his departure all association with his bygone sorrow and mortification should be swept away.

His property became his idol, and upon its improvement he expended all his time, all his care, all his devotion.

In this life he became, to all intents and purposes, completely absorbed.

Years went by, and still found him living the same life, still shrinking from society, and drifting by degrees into that eccentricity which seems inseparable from want of contact with our fellow-men.

CHAPTER IV.

LORD SEAFORTH'S DEALINGS WITH HIS YOUNGER SON.

At the time of the marriage the old Earl had been as furious with his younger son as it was in his nature to be; more especially as Godfrey's conduct towards himself on that occasion had been marked by more than his usual duplicity. The evening before his elopement he had so far imposed upon his father by a feigned interest in his brother, and even in his brother's hopes concerning his marriage, as to induce the old man to promise once more to pay all his debts, on condition of an improved behaviour, and to forestall his promise by the immediate gift of a cheque for five hundred pounds.

The utter want of principle, of a common sense of honour even, in this transaction, in view of subsequent events, had finally disgusted the old man; and as he afterwards brooded over the falsehoods of which, in that one short interview, Godfrey had been guilty, he had lashed himself into fury, and had sworn he would withdraw his allowance, cut him off with a shilling, and, to use his own expression, "allow him to go to the dogs as fast as possible."

But here Harold had interfered. True to his character, his rigid sense of duty would not allow him to countenance any measures that partook of the nature of revenge.

True to his family pride, he would not allow the name of Seaforth to be degraded.

True to the one affection of his life, he could not be a party to the sentence that would entail suffering on the woman he had loved, who must share in her husband's disgrace.

But by-and-by, though no communication had been held with Godfrey, rumours reached Seaforth of the reckless career in which he was plunging. Numberless bills were forwarded to Seaforth, and it became necessary for Harold and his father to lay their heads together and to resolve upon a course of action.

For the crash they saw must come: the day could not be far distant when Godfrey would be obliged to leave his regiment, and perhaps have to fly the country.

To avoid such disgrace being brought on the family name, Godfrey must be got out of the way, must be made to sell out at once, and be bribed, by the promise of a settlement of all his difficulties, to go and live abroad for a time.

Harold easily made his father see the wisdom of

this plan, and the proposal was made. But it came too late. A letter from Godfrey to his father arrived in the mean while, coolly announcing his having sent in his papers, and his own precipitate flight from England; alleging, as an excuse for his "misfortunes," that the promise of payment of his debts, made to him on the eve of his wedding-day, had not been fulfilled; and urging his present state of utter destitution, and that of his wife, as an argument in favour of a speedy remittance.

The disgrace sat heavy on Harold's soul.

The thought of the gossip at the clubs, of the family name in every mouth, was sheer pain to him; and he registered a solemn vow that Godfrey should never return to his native country. He who had disgraced the name of Seaforth, and brought upon it such dishonour, should re-enter its walls no more. Henceforth Godfrey Seaforth should be as one dead, and his name should never be mentioned.

Still, for the sake of one whose fate could not be dissevered from his, Godfrey should not starve. An allowance should be made him, but on certain conditions.

A yearly allowance, therefore, should be his still, on condition that he never returned to England.

The moment he set foot on English soil the allowance ceased, and would never be renewed.

To these stipulations Godfrey agreed with the utmost *sang-froid*. He seemed lost to all sense of shame. He settled himself at Homburg, moving to

Ems and Spa at his own convenience; and in the end, when the gaming-tables in Europe were closed, establishing himself for good in the neighbourhood of Monaco.

No more letters passed between him and his father. His allowance was regularly paid; and but for that half-yearly reminder of his existence he was, to all intents and purposes, forgotten by his father and brother.

For, the stipulations agreed upon and the necessary arrangements concluded, his name, in all the years that followed, was never again mentioned between them.

CHAPTER V.

THE STRUGGLE WITH FATE AND FORTUNE.

It would seem, then, that Harold had been the victim of fate, and had been forced to relinquish the programme which he had carved out for himself.

To the outside world it appeared so. What it saw was a misanthropical and slightly eccentric man—a man with no thought beyond the management of his property, to which the devotion of his life was given.

And the world wondered at what it saw ; for it was apparently an aimless and purposeless expenditure of time, since the only heir to those wide acres was an outlawed gambler. But the world did not understand the solitary man.

There was not, there could not be, anything purposeless in the life of a man like Harold.

Running through all those years was a fixed and settled resolution, and a pre-determined course of conditions of mind, which none knew but himself.

None but himself knew what he had suffered, as

none could guess how, year by year, he did battle with his feelings, with the resolute intention of overcoming them.

No trial that God could have sent could have driven the iron so deeply into the proud man's soul.

To have staked his life's affection and happiness on one throw, and to have lost, was in itself as the bitterness of death to him.

But that in his one venture the brother whom he despised and hated, of whose character he had a scorn almost amounting to horror, that *that* man of all others should have rushed in where he had feared to tread, and have borne off the prize before his very eyes—this it was which had been to him as gall and wormwood, and had well-nigh, at one time, driven him mad. And yet he was determined to overcome it.

Come what might, do what violence he might to his feelings, never should Seaforth descend to his spendthrift and vagabond brother.

Nor should Seaforth, his idol, suffer. Without a mistress it was shorn of half its glories—turned into a sort of magnificent shooting-box and hunting-lodge for two solitary men.

It always had, it always ought to take, its place as one of the greatest houses in England. And take it it should still.

On these two pivots his life turned; on these two points his mind was fixed; and through all those years, apparently aimlessly passing, they underlay every thought, every act, and every intention.

And to pave the way for their accomplishment, he stood aside, as it were, and looked on at himself, and treated that self as if he were treating and providing for another person.

A nature like his, he saw, must not be hurried.

Time—much time—must be given to make the past a dreamy long-ago; and then, *then*, perhaps, there might be a chance of the admission of a new future, and a fresh programme of life. Others had lived through the wreck of their life's hope, and from the ashes of the past risen into greater strength than ever. Then why not he?

Others had conquered by the force of time, and he would do so too.

Triumph over circumstances he must and would.

Never should it be said that he had been a victim to fate or to evil fortune. Time he stooped to use for his own ends. Fate and fortune he scoffed at. In the power of time and habit he fully believed.

So many years, then, he gave himself in which to forget, and in a round of occupations he hoped to hurry the moment of oblivion.

A change in his feelings must thus, he thought, be wrought.

Year after year, with their unceasing mill-wheel of duties, *must* at length obliterate the one year, or rather the few months, which had been laden with so much joy and sorrow for him; and every day, bearing him further and further away from what he was pleased to call the era of his weakness, would restore to him the mastery over his feelings, which for those brief and happy weeks he owned to himself he had partially, if not entirely, lost.

Then, thus much accomplished, he hoped by degrees to be disposed to re-enter society, and by slower degrees still to turn his thoughts once more to marriage.

Not for love. Not the old dream of a happy marriage and a beloved wife. No! *that* part of his programme could never be ; therein he had been wholly vanquished ; and he knew in himself that in that nor time, nor habit, nor will, nor self-respect— these gods to whom he bowed, and in whom he trusted —could do anything for him.

Victory the first for fate and fortune, but victory how complete and final he knew too well.

But he would have the outline of the programme still. With but that one exception, it should be, to all intents and purposes, the same.

He would yet find some beautiful woman whom he could esteem and regard, albeit she might never kindle in him the feelings with which he had once been inspired.

And with the tie of mutual interests, mutual hopes and fears, with children growing up around them and sharing their affection, who should say that esteem and regard would not ripen into affection, and the greater part of the programme be carried out still ?

Still might he laugh at fate and fortune, and defy

adverse circumstances to make any radical change in the life he had carved out for himself.

So from the ashes of his life-wreck his will sprang, phœnix-like, in greater force than ever.

The thunderbolt of heaven had fallen hot and heavy, but he would not recognise God's hand. There was in him no thought of submission, no bowing to a higher will. He was determined still to carve out his own future, and to make it what *he* deemed it ought to be.

But he could not escape like this. For when the time he had allotted to himself in which to forget had expired, fate had scored another victory; for, to his own dismay, he realised that his wound was as fresh as ever, and that he still shrank from the idea of any woman in his home, any face at the head of his table.

Once more the old prescription, the old remedy— time. Another year must now be added, and another, and another; and so the years rolled on.

Yet in one sense was he worsted in the struggle, for, as it wore on, Time, who was to have been his friend, became in a way his enemy also.; and Habit, who was to have been his help, turned out a hindrance too.

For the one laid her hand upon him so heavily that all the little youth he had ever had slowly departed from him; and the other rendered his mode of life so completely second nature to him, that every day he shrank more from the thought of any altera-

tion. The two, banded together, were making him
a premature old man, in appearance, in ways, and in
feelings.

Grave and stern he had always been, but now he
rarely smiled. His keenness for sport departed; the
good-fellowship of the hunting-field went against him;
he lived more and more alone.

He was himself startled to find how the habit of
unsociability was growing on him; to realise how it
was his instinct to turn his horse's head into a bye-
lane when he saw in the distance any one he was likely
to know.

By-and-by, he told himself, he would have grown
so old, so morose, so unlike other people, that even
with Seaforth at his back he would offer but little
attraction to any young girl. And he actually began
sometimes almost to wish to give the struggle up—to
own himself defeated; to leave Seaforth to take care of
itself in the present and in the future, and to live for
ever in the memory of the one love of his life.

But these were his moments of weakness, when the
cry of his soul was, "Vanquished, vanquished!"

Quickly following upon them would come the
fierce reaction, and Will be predominant again. "She
shall *not* spoil my life for me! Overcome these feelings I must and will. Vanquished once, victor I will
yet be. The triumph shall be mine still!"

Little did the world as it saw, and grew used to
see, the solitary man, with his set stern face going his
daily rounds, his long, monotonous rides, guess of the

wild battle that was raging within him, above the din of which rose ever the resolution of which no man dreamed.

We are dealing with a character over whose life no softening mother's love or sister's influence had ever rested, no hallowing religious power had ever shone. Of a strength outside himself he knew nothing, nor of the power of a Voice that could still the raging of the storm within him.

Napoleon's " *Je me suffis* " was ever the motto of his life.

And what was the end of it ?

That after all those years he was in just the same position as at first : still struggling with his own strong feelings, still determined to overcome them, and still unable to forget Hester Stanhope, or to banish her beautiful face from his mind.

CHAPTER VI.

THE OLD EARL'S DYING REQUEST.

THE next event in the family history was the death of the old Earl; and a conversation which Harold held with his father a short time previously did for him that which all his own resolutions had been powerless to accomplish.

The evening of the day on which the doctor had announced that the Earl's hours were numbered, the old man called his son to his bedside, and somewhat suddenly asked him the following question:

"Has it ever occurred to you, Harold, that when I am gone there is only one life between your brother and the property?"

"Do not disquiet yourself," was Harold's reply. "I shall certainly marry some day."

"Some day!" repeated Lord Seaforth. "Ah! Harold, I have been waiting patiently these many years in the hope of it, but there seems to me even less chance than there was at first of your making up your mind to do so."

3

"I shall certainly marry some day," repeated Harold, in exactly the same tone as before.

"But supposing you die in the mean time?" said the old man, excitedly.

Harold raised his head.   He seemed struck by the idea.

"Supposing you die," the old Earl went on, eagerly following up his advantage, "what happens?   The whole of this ancient estate, upon which you are daily bestowing so much care and attention, falls at once into the hands of an unprincipled spendthrift, who would put it up to auction to-morrow."

A sound that was half an execration, half a cry of pain, escaped from Harold's lips.   He rose from his seat and began to walk up and down the room.

"There are two ways of avoiding this terrible misfortune," Lord Seaforth went on.   "One would be, of course, your having a son of your own; but failing that, there is a plan in my head which I have for some time past been revolving, and for which I have long waited an opportunity of propounding to you."

Harold came nearer to the bedside and listened with some curiosity.

"We must do that which it has been our family's glory *not* to do.   We must entail the estate."

"Entail the estate!" exclaimed Harold.   "And upon whom?   Except myself and my heirs, there *is* no one but that vagabond himself."

"You   mistake, Harold," said the old man.   "Godfrey has a son."

There was a long silence after this. Harold walked up and down the room slowly, without speaking, and the old man lay back on his pillow and watched him.

"I am very feeble, Harold," he said at last. "Bear with me while I put the case before you, and then tell me your objections if you will."

Harold instantly resumed his seat and gave all his attention.

He went on to explain that he intended to cut Godfrey off with a shilling, thereby leaving him entirely in his brother's power, to whom he should look for continuing the stipulated allowance, on the same conditions as heretofore. That the estate should now be strictly entailed on Harold and his heirs; and failing them, on Godfrey's son, Godfrey himself being omitted altogether.

By these means the worthless younger son should never have the chance of making ducks-and-drakes of the property.

He concluded by an earnest entreaty to Harold to marry at once, and to let him die with the feeling that he was pledged to do so.

And standing there, by his father's dying bed, Harold felt it was not worth while to disturb the old man's mind by any objections. So certain was he of his own resolution that he felt the matter to be quite unimportant. The only argument in its favour that struck him was that of the possibility of his own death before he had carried out his intentions. So he first pledged himself that within a year there should be a mistress reigning in the halls of Seaforth, and then gave his consent for the summoning of the lawyers, with a view to the entail being made.

But he took no part in the lawyers' arrangements. He looked upon the whole transaction as simply the humouring of a dying man's fancy; and his only feeling with regard to it was thankfulness to see the old man's mind at rest before he passed away.

CHAPTER VII.

HAROLD FULFILS HIS PROMISE TO HIS FATHER.

WHEN the year of mourning for his father had nearly come to an end, Harold, for the first time for many years, left Seaforth and went up to London, nominally to take his seat in the House of Lords, but in reality to re-enter society and seek for himself a wife. But, once in society, he realised what he had before suspected, that it was too late. He was too old and too unsociable for society, too confirmed in his old-fashioned ways.

He could not exert himself sufficiently to make himself agreeable, and he felt that the girls he danced with looked upon their solemn, bald-headed partner as quite an elderly man. He had literally no conversation, no small-talk of any kind, and even his manners he felt to be somehow different to those of the young men to whose attentions these young girls were accustomed.

They were very kind, but their manner was such as they would use to an uncle, or a father even.

There was a respectful tone in their talk, and he knew that both he and his conversation was a strain to them, and that they breathed a sigh of relief when the quadrille was over. How he hated and loathed it all! What a fish out of water he felt in the gay scenes in which he found himself!

Dinner-parties suited him a little better, if by chance he got any one next him who did all the talking for him; but he could not start a conversation. He did not know *what* to say. He had no idea how to begin or what to talk about, and he would sometimes gaze hopelessly first at the lady on his right, and then at the lady on his left, wondering what kind of subject would be likely to please or interest them. He had almost made up his mind to go back to Seaforth, when he came across Lady Helen Fraser, a young widow of good family and no small share of personal beauty. She was clever, agreeable, and attractive. Her conversation was such that he could join in with it with ease, and he altogether got on better with her than with any one he had yet met.

She was just the sort of person, he told himself, to adorn a great position, and to enjoy and appreciate it. Thus far he had made up his mind the first evening he met her, and as time went on he discovered other qualities, which all tended to increase his approbation.

She was a woman of the world, with a great deal of *savoir-faire.*

She would know how to value the glories of Seaforth, would do the honours well, and entertain the county in a way which would redound to his credit.

Though still quite young, she was old enough and experienced enough to look after herself, and not to give him any trouble. And this was a great point. He did not wish to have to do husband and father in one, nor to have his wife depending on his companionship.

He wished to be allowed to go his own way still.

Of her character, as far as he could judge of it on so short an acquaintance, he approved.

She was sensible, energetic, and apparently straightforward.

That she was worldly and ambitious he either did not see or, seeing, did not object to. It was altogether the very thing. His mind was soon made up.

What should he wait for?

Lady Helen was not slow to perceive his intentions, and met his advances more than half-way.

At the end of a few weeks he made her a formal proposal, which was instantly accepted.

Then, and not till then, did he discover that she had two little boys by her first marriage. Whether or no the fact had been purposely kept from him he could not tell, and it was too late to inquire or to draw back.

His word was given, his proposal made.

He probably would never have asked Lady Helen to be his wife had he known the circumstance; but having committed himself, he made up his mind to make the best of it.

He resigned himself to the infliction, and did not say a word.

But deep down in his heart, that heart which never forgot and never forgave, was planted a feeling of distrust towards his future wife, which in all the years to come she will never be able to remove.

It was a fatal mistake on Lady Helen's part; an irreparable false start with a man like Lord Seaforth, who loved truth and uprightness above all things. It gave him a hold over her from the very beginning, and it laid the foundation of a lifelong distrust.

It had been to her a sore temptation, and she had yielded to it.

Left a widow at an early age, with two boys and a scanty dowry, she had had a hard time of it, and every day that her boys grew older it became harder.

Contact with the world single-handed, experience of poverty, combined with the sense that her boys' future depended entirely upon her, had made her worldly, practical, and mercenary.

She was ambitious for her boys, and for their sakes she had toiled and slaved to make herself a position in society, and to what is called "get on in the world."

Taking all these circumstances into account, we may imagine what it was to Lady Helen to see such a brilliant prospect opening before her as a marriage with Lord Seaforth.

It seemed the answer to all her anxious inquiries as to the future, the end of all her difficulties, the beginning of a new life for her and for her boys.

The three weeks' courtship was a time of intense excitement to her, and to the last she never felt quite certain whether the prize might not slip from her grasp at the eleventh hour. How she stilled her conscience with regard to the non-mention of her boys it is not for us to inquire.

That the end justifies the means is the creed of some consciences, and perhaps Lady Helen's was not so sensitive as yours or mine.

As we sow so we must reap, and she was laying up retribution for herself in the days which were to come.

But the end of the reaping is not seen at first, and to her mind it was a glorious harvest that she gathered in when Lord Seaforth laid himself and his worldly goods at her feet.

The wedding-day was fixed, the settlements drawn up, and preparations on a large scale commenced at Seaforth for the reception of the bride.

Outwardly, as we said before, all went well; and Lord Seaforth was apparently well satisfied with everything.

But one morning, when the engagement was about a fortnight old, he called upon Lady Helen at an unusual hour and requested a private and serious conversation.

He had, he said, been thinking matters over with

regard to her sons, and thought it best to have everything cut and dried. He had come to stipulate that
he personally should have *nothing* to do with them;
that the responsibility of their training and bringing-
up should rest entirely with her, and the management
of their affairs with their guardians.

Considering Seaforth's love of power, it was a
curious contradiction in his character thus to put it
from him.

Two reasons had led him to this resolution.

First of all, with the experience of the past lying
like a dead weight on his breast, he shrank from
having anything further to do with the training of
youths; and what were Colin Fraser's sons to him?

But, more potent reason still, he was determined
not to have responsibilities thrust upon him which he
had not knowingly incurred.

It was his only way of in some degree showing
that he considered he had been unfairly dealt with.

It was his only way of declaring against and
defeating the ends he suspected Lady Helen to have
had in view.

It was, in fact, his silent protest against what in
his heart of hearts he considered the deceit which
had been practised upon him.

Lady Helen readily agreed—gladly too; she would
not have liked him to interfere. She felt quite
capable of managing her own boys, seeing she had
always done so, and she promised Lord Seaforth he
should never have any trouble in connection with
them.

"They will be going to school soon," she said, "and shall never be in your way. At twenty-one Colin will come into his little property in Nairnshire, which is let till then; and little Andrew—— "

She paused a minute.

She knew little Andrew's future to be exceedingly vague, and in her own mind intended him to be provided for out of Seaforth livings or interest.

"Andrew," she promptly resumed, "is a clever boy, and will push his way. Neither of my boys shall ever be any trouble to you, dear Lord Seaforth, I assure you. Why are you so concerned about them? Boys always turn out well in the end."

Irritated, perhaps, by the confidence born of inexperience betrayed in these words, he then, for the first time, spoke to her of his brother, and gave a short sketch of his career and banishment. Lady Helen listened with deep interest. She would fain have heard more, and put a question when Lord Seaforth had ceased speaking, in the hope of eliciting further details.

"Is he your only brother?" she inquired. "And is he unmarried?"

But his answer effectually put an end to any further inquiries.

"My only one," he answered very shortly, and he began at once to take up his hat, with a view to departure. "This is a most painful subject," he added, as he rose from his seat, "and I beg it may never be mentioned between us again. It was necessary that I should allude to it before you entered the family, but it is for the first and last time."

So saying, he took his leave.

"At any rate," thought Lady Helen to herself, as soon as she recovered from the shock of his sudden set-down and as sudden departure, " at any rate he has no poor relations to provide for, and so there will be all the more chance for Colin and Andrew."

A few weeks after this conversation the marriage took place, and the bride and bridegroom went straight to Seaforth.

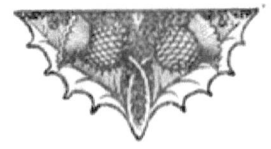

CHAPTER VIII.

LIFE AT SEAFORTH UNDER THE NEW RÉGIME.

For a little while the place was alive with rejoicings, and the house full of society.

Lady Seaforth proved all and more than her husband had expected as a perfect hostess.

He gave her *carte blanche* to invite who she chose to the house, to spend as much money as she liked on entertaining, and she took full advantage of his permission and liberality, and did it all thoroughly well. Harold took it all as a matter of course. It ought to be, and so it was.

Seaforth was keeping up its ancient character as the great house of the neighbourhood; the "princely hospitality" of which he had always dreamt, was being dispensed freely, and he was satisfied.

But he soon tired of it personally, and retired a great deal to his own rooms, leaving it all to his wife.

He resumed imperceptibly his solitary life, and

she relieved him of all his social duties. And Lady
Seaforth was at first delighted with her position and
with her husband. He was so liberal, so easy to live
with; he left her so entirely free, he interfered so
little with her plans and wishes, he gave her such
complete power to ask who she liked to the house,
and to do with her guests as she pleased when they
were there, that she had not one wish unfulfilled or
one whim ungratified. Her boys had ponies to ride,
little gardens to work in, and the stablemen and
gardeners were as ready and eager to attend to their
behests as if they were the masters of the place.

She had only to ask Lord Seaforth leave for them
to have this or that, and it was accorded immediately.

Every one about the place was glad to have
children to attend upon once more, and there were
so many old possessions of Harold's and Godfrey's
which it was an interest to utilise for Lady Seaforth's
little boys.

The aviaries and rabbit-hutches were done up, the
little ponds restocked with gold and silver fish. The
old coachman volunteered to "teach Master Fraser to
leap against the hunting season came round;" the
keeper offered to initiate him into the mysteries of
rabbit-shooting and ratting. He also gladly brought
out long-unused fishing rods, and declared himself
ready to take the young gentlemen out fishing and
punting whenever they liked to go.

Everything at Seaforth had been dormant so long
that all hailed with joy the advent of a new state of

things, and the cheeriness and movement which young lives bring.

And can we wonder that the poverty-stricken, struggling mother of penniless boys was carried away by all this, and, dazzled by the new state of things in which she found herself, failed at first to see a great deal that she saw only too clearly afterwards?

She must certainly have been a little blinded, for she was a clever woman, and not likely to be slow to see.

But still it was a long while before she realised that Lord Seaforth held himself entirely aloof from her boys, and never took the smallest interest in them. Indeed, he never saw them.

She had herself been careful that they should never be in his way, and had arranged their school-rooms and bedrooms as far from his rooms as possible. But she had not expected that he would ignore them like this, and never take any notice of them at all.

She was slow in allowing to herself that it was by the gardeners, keepers, and stablemen themselves, and not by Lord Seaforth's orders, that so much was done for them.

He assented, certainly, to everything she asked; but when she came to think it over it was more as a politeness to her—"Just as you please; pray give what orders you like; you have only to speak to the keeper," etc. He entirely disclaimed any personal interest in the boys or their pursuits.

But it was not only as regarded her boys that, as time went on, she began to ask herself questions, and to find the answers unsatisfactory.

It was not till the novelty of her new position had worn off, and she was beginning to tire a little of the life of perpetual society, that she began to perceive that her relations with her husband were not quite what she had expected.

Gradually she began to realise how entirely he kept her at a distance, and how little their daily lives ran together; how little impression her presence or opinion ever made upon him, and how little power or influence she was acquiring over him.

She was a long while finding it out, and was at first more astonished than mortified.

She had had complete power over her first husband, and she had never doubted that she should speedily acquire it over her second.

No sooner had she thoroughly convinced herself that she had not this power than she set to work to try and gain it. But she made no way at all. Some things, as we have said, Lord Seaforth made over to her entirely, and of these he never asked an account; but in matters of mutual interest he was supreme, and his own private affairs he never mentioned. There was no confidence between them, no interchange of thought or opinion. He never consulted her nor talked things over with her.

He simply told her when he had made up his mind about a thing, and there was an end of it.

There was no wish on his part to hear her view of the subject. Her objections, if she made any, he listened to with a formal politeness, and then quietly reiterated his first words, as if she had not spoken at all. It was very galling to a woman of her disposition, and she began to resent the way in which he treated her very much.

For she was growing much interested in him, and interest combined with respect and a kind of mysterious awe with which she regarded him were leading her on to a deeper feeling.

It was impossible to live with Lord Seaforth without learning to respect him, and to admire his integrity, his high-mindedness, and all his really grand qualities. And she was deeply mortified to feel she got to know him no better; and that, respectful and courteous as he always was to her, there was not a shadow of affection, of intimacy even, in his manner. The silent, reserved man was a mystery to her, and a mystery he remained.

The worst of it was that she had an intuitive conviction that he had strong feelings and deep powers of affection, and she could not bear to think that she had not the power of drawing them out.

. She began to long for a quiet domestic life with him—a life in which she might grow to know and understand him, and get at what lay beneath that cold and silent exterior. But it was not to be. Supreme, as usual, he had decreed otherwise. The wheels of society were to be kept turning.

That was not the kind of life he wished to lead; and she found that if there were not guests present he retired to his own rooms directly after dinner, and she was left to spend the evening by herself. How she wondered what he did in those rooms all the evening long alone!

One night, moved by irresistible curiosity, she followed him to his room, and to her surprise found him unoccupied: sitting with his head buried in his hands, his whole attitude expressing the deepest dejection.

But at the sound of her step he rose from his seat, and a look of great displeasure came over his face. "I have to beg," he said formally, "that my privacy may not be invaded."

After this rebuff she naturally never repeated the experiment.

But these were matters of inward feeling, and Lady Seaforth knew how to conceal her feelings. Outwardly, therefore, all went well, and the neighbourhood, admitted once more into the long-silent halls of Seaforth, saw nothing in the demeanour of husband or wife to take hold of or comment upon. She grew in a measure accustomed to this state of things as time went on. Besides, she had a great deal in her life to make her happy, and also she did not despair of matters improving. His home, she told herself, would not be a perfect home till there were children of his own in it. She could not expect her boys to be anything to him.

But boys of his own round him would develop all the affection that she felt sure was hidden within him, and very likely change him entirely. She made every excuse for him. It was difficult for him to shake off the habits of so many years, and his long, solitary, bachelor life had made him self-contained and unsociable. And, his affections once brought out, she would share in them too.

As the mother of his children she *must* be consulted and advised with; and mutual love and interest in a son and heir would draw them more closely together. She herself often found her thoughts travelling proudly on to that son and heir in whom her pride and her ambition would both be so fully satisfied.

But, alas! that son and heir never came.

Years went by, and the Frasers were still the only children about the place.

And when at last a child appeared, it was only a little girl, who was, perhaps, a more bitter disappointment to her father and mother than no child at all.

And that was all!

She was the first and she was the last. So no boys played on the green lawns of Seaforth save the two who could never inherit its broad acres nor bear its ancient name.

Lord Seaforth, as was his wont, kept his feelings to himself, and thereby gained the character of bearing the disappointment better than his wife, who could not overcome her grief, and made no effort to

conceal her mortification. But none save the solitary
man himself knew what it was to him. None could
guess what a hard and bitter and cruel trial this final
failure in his programme was.

He did not care for children as children, only as
heirs, and he took not the slightest interest in his
little daughter. She was to him what Florence
Dombey was to Dombey and Son—"a bad boy:
nothing more."

And the disappointment hardened and embittered
him. He grew more silent, more morose, more un-
approachable.

The disappointment hardened Lady Seaforth too.
She openly declared her indifference to little Joan, and
pointedly overlooked her.

I think she thought to curry favour with her
husband by doing so.

For very early in the child's life she had perceived
there was something more than indifference in the
way he regarded her.

There was some feeling behind which she could
not fathom. But we, who know him better, will
understand it at once when we hear that, though little
Joan was a pretty child, there was in her whole
appearance, in all save her dark eyes, a most striking
resemblance to her disgraced and disinherited uncle.

It was a most natural likeness, since Godfrey had
inherited his mother's features, fair hair, and colouring, and had never been the least like a Seaforth; but
in Lord Seaforth's eyes it was a terrible aggravation
of all poor little Joan's offences.

As she grew the likeness grew, till at last he could hardly bear the sight of her.

Lady Seaforth, of course, could not guess all this; but, taking her cue from him, she studiously kept the child out of his way; and excusing herself, on the plea that she knew nothing about girls, left the child very much to the servants.

Little Joan had her luxurious nurseries, and in due time her luxurious schoolroom; and with her nurse and governess her little life was chiefly spent, for she saw very little of either of her parents.

Lady Seaforth devoted herself more than ever to her boys, and in their affection and in the interest of their opening lives she found some consolation for all her troubles and disappointments.

Lord Seaforth had no such distraction from his brooding thoughts, no such refuge from his own society.

Alone he brooded over his life and its failures, and alone he did battle with the bitter thought that now, after all, Godfrey and Hester's son was the indisputable heir to Seaforth.

BOOK II.

.

CHAPTER I.

A SUDDEN DETERMINATION.

THE reader will now understand why the little ghost who haunted Seaforth was so desolate and uncared for.

It was a curious household.

Three distinct lives were lived under one roof.

There was that of the mother and sons in one part, that of the neglected child in another, and that of the solitary, brooding man in a third.

Brooding, brooding more than ever—brooding as the years went on, on a new subject, in which all the broodings of his whole life met and were intensified.

That second Godfrey, that uneducated son of his "ne'er-do-weel" brother—to him his thoughts were always turning. Gnawing ever at his heart was the feeling that he ought to do something for the boy—something to save him from the life he must be leading.

Conscience perpetually told him that he ought to

have him over to England, and bring him up as an English gentleman should be brought up, so that he might properly fill the position he must one day hold.

Growing up as he probably was, among gamblers and the scum of the earth, he must be imbibing every day all that was most pernicious—living a life which must inevitably bring him to tread in his father's footsteps.

Yes, he ought, no doubt, to adopt him and to bring him up as his own.

But he could not make up his mind to open the long-closed communication with his brother, and to stoop, as it were, to ask a favour of him; and so, as in the case of his marriage, he let the time pass on, and could not bring himself to stir in the matter.

Bitter, too, as was the thought that Seaforth should, at his death, pass into the hands of such a one as Godfrey's uneducated son would be, more bitter still was the thought of the presence of that son at Seaforth—that son who was Hester's as well as Godfrey's—the sight of whom would bring back and parade before him all the joys and sorrows, the hatreds and mortifications, of former years; who united in his own person the sum and substance of every feeling he had ever known, be it joyful or be it bitter.

How could he bear the sight of the son of the man he hated, the woman he had loved?

But one day his broodings ended in a sudden and

abrupt determination, and the letter was written and
sent. Not with his own hand. No, it was a purely
business-like transaction, written by the family
lawyer, and couched in formal, business-like terms.

The offer, like all Lord Seaforth's money trans-
actions, was as handsome and liberal as possible;
the conditions, like all his conditions with his brother,
were hard and stern to the last degree.

He charged himself entirely with the boy's education and all future expenses, profession, and settlement in life, treating him exactly as his own son;
but Godfrey was to renounce his parental authority
altogether, and to abstain, both in the present and
in the future, from any sort of interference.

For the answer to this letter he waited with a
feverish impatience, hardly knowing whether he most
wished or most dreaded a compliance with his tender.

And while he sits there waiting and brooding,
painting dark pictures of his heir's surroundings, let
us follow the letter to the sunny South, and enter
with it the gambler's home.

CHAPTER II.

THE GAMBLER'S HOME.

"M'AIMES-TU—un peu—beaucoup—passionnément—point du tout ? "—

"I think the daisies *must* have made a mistake," said a plaintive little voice, "for I know I *do* love Godfrey so *very* much ; and three times they have told me that I don't."

"Try again, Venice," said a laughing voice; "three is an unlucky number, you know."

"But three times three are nine, and nine is the luckiest number of all, papa says," said the first speaker.

"Well, **try** again," reiterated the laughing voice. "Faites votre jeu, messieurs; faites votre jeu."

"Hush, Olive ! " said a third and very soft voice. "You know mamma does not like you to go on like that."

"Papa taught me," said Olive.

The speakers were the three little daughters of

Godfrey Seaforth. They were sitting in an orange grove, playing with the wild flowers they had been gathering, which lay in their laps and on the ground beside them in rich profusion.

Pretty little girls they were all three, and there was about them that air of refinement and distinction which bespoke them at once the children of an English gentleman. Their dress was scrupulously neat and fresh, but of the plainest and cheapest material.

They wore the broad-brimmed straw hats of the country, and their long fair hair streamed down their shoulders.

The mother's hand was clearly discernible in the care with which their pretty complexions and white little hands were shielded from the destroying effect of the sun, and in the punctilious neatness of their whole appearance.

Unknowing exiles, they made a pretty group as they sat there chatting and laughing.

The laughter was at its height when a shadow fell across the grove and footsteps were heard approaching.

Flowers, wreaths, and chaplets were thrown down, and all three sprang to their feet and ran forwards, calling out "Papa! papa!"

Can this wreck be really the gay and handsome Godfrey Seaforth?

Can this prematurely bent figure, this slatternly appearance, this sullen, discontented expression be his?

But his face lights up for a moment at the sight of his little daughters.

"How are all you ragamuffins this morning, and what are you doing?" he says, as he bends down and kisses each in turn.

He is a late riser, and this is his first appearance.

The children gave various and laughing answers, to which he does not appear to listen particularly, for he asks the same question again a few minutes after; and then, lighting his pipe, he says absently, "Come for a stroll."

Like little dogs they follow him, laughing, talking, and skipping about him.

He holds very little converse with them, but "moons" along, his hands in his pockets, his pipe in his mouth, absorbed in his own gloomy thoughts.

"Hold up your head, papa!" says the laughing voice of Olive, the second girl; "you want to be drilled, I think."

Her merry voice rouses him, and he smiles.

Then he stopped short suddenly in his walk, and taking his pipe out of his mouth, he said, "Big Bear, Middle Bear, and Little Bear, who is coming with me to Monaco to-day?"

This question came regularly every day, and was as inevitable as the morning salutation or the invitation to come for a stroll.

He called the children the Three Bears, and the name had its origin in this ceremony.

The answers generally took the following form :—

"I'm not," from the Big Bear, decidedly.

"I'm not," from the Middle Bear, softly.

"I'm not," from the Little Bear, in a whisper.

But this morning, something possessed Olive to make a different answer, and, to the surprise of her sisters, she said, when her turn came, "I am."

Godfrey looked at her and laughed.

"What would you do with me, papa, if I came?" she said.

The father's absences from home and occupations in that unknown Monaco were a source of the deepest mystery to the children.

"Turn you into gold," he answered.

He never took the trouble to talk sense to them or to explain things properly.

"How silly that is!" said Olive.

"I'm quite serious," he said. "You might be as good to me as a lot of gold. You'd bring me luck, perhaps."

"What *is* luck, papa?" asked Olive. "You so often talk about it, and I never *exactly* understand what it is."

"Don't ask *me*," he said bitterly. "I'm the last man in the world to tell you anything about it. I'm the most unlucky dog that ever lived. I never had a bit of luck in my life, Olly—except one," he added, half to himself.

"And what was that?" inquired Olive eagerly.

"Oh, never you mind," he said more gravely; "that's no business of little girls."

"Well, you won't tell me anything I want to know," she said, rather poutingly, not liking his tone, with the hurt feeling of a child who will not suffer a word of reproof from an unwonted source.

"I *can't*," he said, with a laugh which was half hard, half bitter. "How can I tell you what I don't know myself?"

"You're not half such a good answerer of questions as Godfrey," she said discontentedly; "*he* always tells us what we want to know. So I shall just ask *him* what luck is."

"You'd better," he said, with a sneer, and with such a frown on his handsome face that he looked for a moment positively diabolical; "you couldn't ask any one who knows more about it."

"You're very cross, papa," said Olive, half crying. "Why do you frown at me like that?"

He recovered himself at her words and pulled her hair laughingly. "I wasn't frowning at you, my little woman, only at my own thoughts. But come, Olly," he said, more lightly, "here's a bargain for you. If you'll come with me to Monaco I'll explain to you what luck means."

Olive clapped her hands. "Oh, papa! do you really mean it?"

"Oh yes, really and truly," he answered.

"Oh, what fun!" she exclaimed; and she turned back to her sisters, who had fallen behind and were picking flowers. "Hessie! Venice! what *do* you think? Papa says he'll take me to Monaco!"

The two little girls looked much astonished.

"We must go home and ask mamma first," said Hester.

"And change your frock and boots," added Venice.

Olive looked down at her brown-holland pinafore and dusty boots. "So I must," she said.

"I say, Hester, do you think mamma will say 'Yes'?"

"No," said Hester, demurely; "I'm sure she'll say 'No.'"

"Then I shan't go home and ask her," said the impulsive child.

Hester looked too horrified to speak, and little Venice burst out, "Oh, you naughty Olly! I'm quite shocked at you."

"I don't care," said Olive. "Papa said I might, so that's quite enough."

"You don't generally think it enough," said Hester.

But Olive was now reckless, and she dashed after her father, calling out, "I'm coming, papa; wait a minute for me."

Godfrey Seaforth turned round, laughing. "I didn't really mean it, you know, Olly; I was only joking."

Poor little Olive fairly burst into tears. She knew she was doing wrong. She had sacrificed a great deal for him in the war of conscientious scruples—lowered herself in the eyes of her sisters; and now he told her he was only joking!

"You shouldn't tell stories like that, papa," she sobbed; "it's very, very wicked."

Godfrey laughed more than ever.

Nothing amused him more than "getting a rise" out of the impetuous Olive.

Hester and Venetia now came running up, and by tender words and caresses sought to soothe their little sister.

But she would not be consoled. Her feelings, her pride, and her conscience were all wounded; and the disappointment, too, was more than she could bear.

"I wish Godfrey was here," said Hester, half to herself; "he always knows how to comfort Olly."

Godfrey caught her words and turned sharply round. "Leave her to me, both of you," he said roughly. "*I* can comfort her as well as any one. Look here, my little Olly; I couldn't take you with me. Mamma would not like it, you know."

"No," put in little Venetia; "no more wouldn't Godfrey like it, neither."

Godfrey looked furious, and muttered something to himself in very strong language.

"Look here, Olly," he said, suddenly springing to his feet: "I *will* take you; so dry your tears, and come along. Hessie, run home and tell mamma I have taken Olly with me, and will bring her home by the early train. Look sharp, Olly! Give me your hand. We must run to catch the train. There! your best leg foremost, and ' après nous le déluge ! '"

So saying he started off, with Olive flying at his

side; leaving the other two children quite speechless with astonishment.

Hester looked grave, but little Venetia's pretty eyes were sparkling with excitement.

"He had no business to do it," said the spirited Hester, "and she had no business to go."

The little girls retraced their steps, very much sobered, till they came to the orange grove they had lately quitted; and here Venetia's attention was distracted by the sight of her daisies scattered about on the grass. She sat down among them, and was soon immersed in "M'aimes-tu?—un peu—beaucoup," etc.

Meanwhile Hester passed on, across the grove, through the garden, up a flight of stone steps which led to a balcony, and entered the house by the drawing-room window, exclaiming, "Mamma! only think! What *do* you think? Papa has taken Olive to Monaco!"

CHAPTER III.

HESTER'S MARRIED LIFE.

NEARLY twenty years have passed over the head of Hester Stanhope since the day when she fled with Godfrey Seaforth, and yet she is not very much altered. She was a beautiful girl then, and now she is a beautiful woman. Time and trial have but deepened the lovely expression of her eyes, and the soul of a noble woman looks more fully through them.

She has grown accustomed to sorrow, and has ceased to expect anything from life; but her natural hopefulness and buoyancy are not quite beaten down yet, and so, though a saddened, she is not what many a wife in her place would most infallibly have become —a broken-down woman.

Gone, indeed, the bright hopes of youth and the expectation of this world's gladness; but their loss has only driven her more closely to God, and caused her to put all her hopes in a happier world.

Let us glance at the events of those twenty years and see what her life has been.

In the heyday of youth and hope she married Godfrey Seaforth, and youth and hope carried her through a great deal. At first, too, she was very happy. The joy and relief of having escaped from her troubles, and the gay freedom of her new life, were enough for her, combined with the love and gratitude she bore towards the man who had so unhesitatingly sacrificed himself for her.

He had made her believe—and he did all he could to foster the belief—that he was ill-treated and un-justly used by his father and brother, who, for some reason unknown to him, hated him, and had always done so. He took pains to instil into her that he was sinned against, not sinning—unfortunate, not in fault —and that all his money troubles arose from his allowance being inadequate to meet his expenses and to enable him to live like a gentleman.

What that allowance was she never exactly knew, for Godfrey took care not to tell her. Probably in her eyes it would have seemed a large sum.

She was ignorant about money and its manage-ment, and did not, therefore, realise how recklessly Godfrey lived, nor how extravagant he was in every way.

Her only sorrow was that she had brought him no fortune of her own, and that his marriage had but increased his expenses.

To such lamentations Godfrey had always the

same answer to make : that her expenses were a mere
drop in the ocean as compared to his (which, indeed,
was true), and that his marriage with her, far from
adding to his difficulties and troubles, had given him
courage to bear them !

In justice to Godfrey we must say that such
speeches had more meaning in them than was generally to be attached to his words.

For his marriage *was* a source of the greatest
pride and satisfaction to him.

He was so proud of having gained a victory over
his brother, and at having scored one to the good in
the race of life they ran together.

It was a never-ending matter of triumph to him
that Harold, with all his worldly advantages at his
back, should have been worsted when they came to
struggle hand to hand ; and that this beautiful girl,
noble and high-principled as he knew her to be,
should have preferred him, the black sheep, to his
immaculate brother, thereby proving that he was not
such a castaway as that brother considered him.

He *must* be worth something, after all, if a
woman like Hester could trust and prefer him.
Besides, he did really love his young wife with all the
depth of feeling of which his nature was capable.
He loved her and was proud of her.   And, indeed,
she was a wife of whom any man might be proud.
Her beauty and her brightness carried all before her.

Then, too, he enjoyed her good opinion, and would
not for the world have had her faith in him shaken.

She was the first person who had ever believed in him, and the sensation, from its very novelty, was exceedingly pleasant.

He resolved, in so far as anything so weak *could* resolve, that she should never repent the step she had taken, and that Harold should never be able to glory in her wretchedness as the unhappy wife of a bad man.

He was determined to **try** and act up (outwardly, at any rate) to her idea of him, so that she should not know how unprincipled and bad he was.

And so, partly by concealment, partly by deception, and partly by trading on her youth and her ignorance of the world, he did for a very considerable time continue to blind his wife's eyes to the real character of the man she had married.

But this ideal state of things could not last.

As the shadows deepened and the inevitable crash drew near, fresh qualities appeared in his young wife to increase yet more his love and admiration.

But, alas ! the very circumstances that drew them forth, and raised her higher in his estimation, lowered him in hers.

Slowly but surely her eyes opened.

He saw, with surprise and delight, her courage rise above all their troubles ; her dauntless behaviour when at last the blow fell, and they had to fly like thieves in the middle of the night ; the calmness with which she submitted to his father's conditions, and saw herself condemned to a life of enforced exile.

She, meanwhile, saw a great deal which he had endeavoured to conceal from her.

As soon as the conditions were agreed upon, and the first advance of the allowance paid, they went for a tour in Italy, and then settled for the summer at Homburg.

By that time they had been married nearly eighteen months, and Godfrey's character was no longer a secret to his wife.

I do not mean that she had fully realised his total want of principle; but her faith in him was thoroughly shaken, and she knew how frail was the barque in which she had set sail on life's sea.

She had found that he was not to be trusted, and that he did not speak the truth; had learnt that she must depend upon herself, and act always without help or counsel from him. Nay, more, that on some occasions she must conceal her intentions from him, lest he should make her act in a way her conscience could not approve.

Her character, happily, was a strong one; and these lessons once learnt, she grew firm and self-reliant. Not in the independence that is born of pride and self-sufficiency, but in that which has its source in something higher and holier. Not Lord Seaforth's "Je me suffis," but St. Paul's "Strong in the Lord and in the power of His might."

She needed such strength sorely, for she was never certain from day to day what her husband was going to ask her to do, nor whether he was giving her the real reason for his actions and intentions; never sure how much he was telling her and how much he was concealing.

Often and often she had complied with his wishes because he had alleged a reason she considered sufficient; and then, having secured her compliance, he would laugh and tell her it was for some quite different reason—one for which she would never have yielded had she known what it really was.

He would thus trade upon the uprightness of her character and upon her sense of wifely duty, causing her to make promises from which he knew well she would not withdraw, while he reserved to himself the right of breaking his word.

He himself would be faithful to nothing, true to no promise, bound by no laws.

God knows how earnestly she tried to influence her husband for good, and to do a true wife's part, by trying to lead him into the right path; how ceaselessly she sought to bring to bear upon him all the influence which she knew she, to a certain extent, had over him.

In vain! He could admire, but he could not imitate. There are some natures on which everything is thrown away. Light, shallow, and worthless, it is but casting pearls before swine.

She lavished a wealth of thought and care upon him. He never retained, though he seemed to listen.

Sometimes she would imagine she had at last made some faint impression; the next day he would talk and act as if she had said nothing the day before.

He never exercised the powers of his own mind on what she said; till she was forced to own that it was all waste of time and mind and thought and strength.

His moral sense was not to be reached, his conscience not to be touched, nor any real feeling to be got at even for a transient fit of earnestness, except on very rare occasions, and even then the fit would pass away as quickly as it had come, and all that had been undertaken under its influence be scattered to the four winds again.

The promises of to-day were lightly broken to-morrow, the resolutions of the morning dismissed with a laugh before night. And hopelessness would take possession of her, wondering how it was all to end.

A shrinking fear would come over her that the work of reforming him must be left in the hands of God, and that some terrible lesson would one day be given. Her heart would be wrung with the desire to save him ere that time should come, ere God himself "took the pruning knife into His hand."

Perhaps it was well that such sad yearnings should wake and live within her, for, as she more fully realised how terribly the want of truth, depth, and principle tells upon the smallest detail of every-day life, a blow was dealt to her affections, and, had not Pity pinioned it so firmly, Love might have soared away.

CHAPTER IV.

THE POISONING OF HESTER'S HOME-LIFE.

WHEN they had been married two years a son was born to them, and though Hester's aching heart was filled with joy in his possession, yet, in so far as her husband was concerned, the child's birth only added to her troubles; for the sight of the boy was a perpetual reproach to Godfrey. It brought home to him how he had thrown away his life and its advantages, and so done his son an irreparable injury. Till now his exiled life had been no grief to him, the thought of the future no trouble, the memory of the past no pain. But now he began to feel what he had done, and what was worse, to fancy Hester felt it too, and would begin, for her boy's sake, to deplore the loss of advantages she had never regretted for her own. Then he was very jealous of her affection for the child.

For two years he had had her entirely to himself, and been accustomed to look upon himself as the

pivot round which her every thought turned, and he
could not bear to see her interest straying from him
to another.

He was injured and angry when he saw what a
large share of her love and attention was given to the
baby, and he would try to persuade himself and
her that the love which was given to the boy was
taken from him.

His son was a thorn in Godfrey's side from the
moment of his birth; and if in the most indirect
manner he came in his way, or anything went wrong,
he would put it all down to the baby, and say they
had never been so happy since he was born.

Hester was naturally deeply hurt at all this. It
grieved her to find her feelings unshared, and to see
that Godfrey had no fatherly love or pride in him.
Unfortunately, little Godfrey was a regular Seaforth,
utterly unlike either father or mother, except that he
had her smile. Being like a Seaforth, he naturally
bore a strong likeness to his uncle; and this was a
fresh offence. Godfrey would harp upon it, declaring
the child was his brother's living image, and asking
Hester how she could expect him to like the child,
such being the case.

In vain Hester pointed out it was not his brother
in particular, but the family in general that the child
resembled.

Godfrey would not listen. He persisted that the
boy reminded him every day more and more of what
he remembered his brother as a child, and he even

went so far as to say he had the same cold, grave way of looking at him.

No doubt the personal likeness was very striking, and as little Godfrey grew out of babyhood into boyhood he began to develop something of the same character.

Grave, conscientious, and trustworthy, both in disposition and appearance, he might have been Harold's own son.

Then why did not Hester dislike him too?

Alas! poor Hester!

What in the intolerance of youth she had despised and held in contempt, bitter experience had taught her to appreciate. She had learnt how an earnest nature must suffer when thrown with, or, worse still, allied to, a light and shallow one; and she had suffered so much from the want of those firmer and more enduring qualities in her husband, that she no longer regarded them in the same light as formerly.

On the contrary, she found in her boy's disposition, whether it resembled his uncle's or not, a deep rest and refreshment.

But she did not dare show her love before her husband; for Godfrey's anger and jealousy were dangerous things to rouse. He would say, if she ventured gently to remonstrate with him, that she was regretting her marriage, and thinking how the child might have been Harold's son, heir to everything.

Or he would tell her plainly that he could not

stand a rival, that her affection held him straight,
and that if he thought her love for him was waning
or passing to another, be that other who he might, he
would "go to the bad" altogether, and give himself
up to all the temptations from which for her sake he
refrained ; mysteriously affirming that he could make
a fortune at play, if reverence and love for her did not
hold him back.

And, terribly alarmed, she would hardly dare ask
him what he meant, but would only reiterate her
assurance of her never-dying love and devotion.

As the years went by, Godfrey began to grow
restless and discontented with the life he was leading,
and to long to return to his native land.

The point before him was his father's death,
when, as he imagined, his younger son's portion
would accrue to him, and his exile come to an end.
And a new idea, too, was filling his mind.

His brother's long-delayed marriage raised fresh
hopes in his breast. The heirship seemed brought
very close to him.

Gaming became a necessity to him, that the
excitement might a little distract his thoughts and
allay his impatience. When his father was dying he
expected every day to be sent for and forgiven, and he
grew suspicious that something was wrong when the
summons never came. But little was he prepared for
the news that reached him after his father's death.
That he should be cut off with a shilling was a most
unexpected blow, but that his father should entail the

estate over his head and divide the property from the title was a thing he could not have believed possible.

It was the ruin of Godfrey for ever. He saw himself condemned to end his days in exile, with no hope in the future, no chance of retrieving the past. Nothing before him but poverty and expatriation to the last day of his existence. It was a bitter punishment, and it exercised the very worst effect upon him.

He grew reckless, and from that day steadily deteriorated. Hitherto he had only played moderately, though always more than his wife had any idea of; but now he plunged into play deeply, to drown his troubles in excitement.

By this time, too, he was a good deal in debt, and the most rigid economy had to set in.

They removed into a smaller house, and discharged nearly all their servants.

Godfrey made his poverty an excuse for neglecting his dress and personal appearance, and began to have an untidy, "going-down-hill" look about him.

He avoided his equals, and sank by degrees to a lower class of companions, living almost entirely with professed gamblers.

Hester felt all this deeply. She herself retired altogether from society; but she never relaxed her efforts to keep herself, her child, and her home what a gentleman's wife, child, and home ought to be.

When the gaming-tables in Europe were closed, Godfrey removed to the neighbourhood of Monaco;

and Hester, only anxious now to hide herself and her
troubles from the world, persuaded him to build a
little châlet among the hills between Nice and
Monaco, where she might lead as retired a life as
possible.

This isolated spot became their home.

Here Godfrey's life settled itself into that of the
regular and professed gambler.

He spent part of almost every day at Monté Carlo,
not returning home till evening; and sometimes remaining there for the night.

Here, in course of time, three little daughters
were added to the family.

The eldest was the image of her mother, after
whom she was, of course, named, and she became her
father's darling at once. The other two also resembled her, but inherited Godfrey's features and
colouring; and he received them also into his affections.

The advent of these little girls made a great and
happy change in the gambler's home.

Bright, happy little creatures, and lovely withal,
the orange grove was kept alive with their merry
voices from morning till night. And the grave boy's
smile grew less rare, and the mother's heart grew
lighter, and the prematurely aged gambler grew
young again as he listened to the gay prattle and
laughter, and joined in the gambols of his pretty
little daughters. The two youngest were called Olive
and Venetia.

Hester had tried to revive family names, for she had a faint hope that some day her children would be restored to their native land and their forefathers' home ; and she did not wish them to be quite aliens from family associations.

But Godfrey would not hear of it. He would have no connection with Seaforth. The home, he said, from which he had been banished, should never have a chance of opening its doors to his daughters, and they should grow up ignorant of any family associations whatever, believing themselves to be, what to all intents and purposes they were, foreigners.

So he called the one Olive, after the olive trees by which their home was surrounded, and the other Venetia, in memory of the visit he and Hester had paid to Italy in their early married life.

The little girls created a distraction in Godfrey's mind, and his attention became more diverted from Hester and her son.

She was therefore more able to attend to her boy, and began to devote all the time and care she could to his education. She was, as the reader will remember, well fitted for the task ; and thankful she felt that she had shared her brother's classical and other studies, so that she was able now to be useful to her son.

Matters between the father and son did not improve as time went on, for when the birth of little Joan put the boy in the position of direct heir to

Seaforth, jealousy of his son's prospects became mixed with Godfrey's other feelings towards him. He grew positively to hate the very sight of him, and took to persecuting him, picking holes in him, trying to catch him tripping; his object chiefly being to lower him in his mother's eyes.

Hester had to contrive to keep him out of his father's way more than ever, and to explain matters to the boy as best she could; but she dreaded the effect it might have upon him, and feared it might either harden and make him reckless, or else confuse his sense of right and wrong and justice. To see so young a creature's life saddened by neglect and un-kindness, to have him live in such an atmosphere of jealousy and suspicion, and not to be able to shield him from injustice, was almost more than she could bear.

But what could she do? She could only try to give him the means of being happy in himself, and hope that habit might perhaps enable him to take his life as a matter of course, and to grow used to things without understanding why they should be.

His natural thoughtfulness was deepened by the studious, contemplative life he led. In the long hours during which she was obliged to send him out on the hills by himself to keep him away from his father, his books were his sole companions, and reading became the great solace of his existence.

This she did her very utmost to encourage, knowing how far love of study goes to make any one independent of outward circumstances and present surroundings.

She longed to send him to school in England or in Germany, away from the saddening conditions under which his young life was spent. But Godfrey would not hear of it. He would do nothing for the boy, make no sacrifice, deny himself no luxury for his sake.

She found herself sometimes even wishing Lord Seaforth would adopt him, and bring him up as his own; and almost grew to expect that some such offer would one day be made. She was beginning to be alarmed about his education, in view of the position he would one day fill. But this was an argument she did not dare use with her husband. The very faintest allusion to his son's prospects sent him into a furious rage, followed by days of brooding and persecution.

The contrast between the way Godfrey treated his son and the terms he was on with his little daughters was very marked. To Hester's mind it brought out his unkindness in a stronger light. To them he was charming. He was fond of them and proud of them. Their light hearts and high spirits suited him exactly. Personal authority or influence, as the reader has seen, he had none; and respect or reverence on their side he neither exacted nor received. He did not wish for respect. He liked to be on equal, easy terms with them, and to have them ready and willing to be dancing round him whenever he felt inclined for their society. He was proud of their quick answers and merry retorts, and would not for the world have had them checked. Of course he had no trouble in connection with them. Shirking all responsibilities, as usual, he merely treated them like toys, and left everything else to their mother.

He liked them to be as free with him as they were with each other, and Hester found it best to let it be so. Anything was better than the danger of his ceasing to care for them.

Only on a few points she was firm; and one of these was a distinct refusal whenever he asked permission to take any of them with him to Monaco.

As with her boy, so with her little girls, she found the only way was not to let them know anything about the life their father lived; on all such matters to keep them entirely in ignorance.

With the boy, of course, she had had also in her mind the desire to preserve him from imbibing any of the tastes which had proved so fatal to his father, and to keep him from being in any way mixed up with the people with whom her husband associated. With the girls, though it was less important, she had greater difficulty, on account of Godfrey's desire for their society.

But still he had, so far, respected her wishes.

And so, in ignorance of the troubles around them, the gambler's little daughters grew and flourished. Their lines were cast in pleasant places, and amid flowers and beauty and sunshine their gay and careless childhood was being spent.

Light-hearted, high-spirited, loving and beloved, three happier creatures did not exist than Godfrey Seaforth's little daughters.

And yet their mother's heart was often sore with pity for their fate. For their future she was often anxious, wondering what would befall.

A mighty dread would seize her, with a sharp pang sometimes, at the thought of how it would all be if she should ever be taken from them, and they be left to the tender mercies of their father.

This dread almost always, more or less, haunted her; but in moments of sadness and depression it was a weight almost heavier than she could bear. It required at such times the exercise of all her faith to put the thought away and to resign her children's future into the hands of God.

It was only that she did not see what other trial would teach her husband the lesson that she felt he must at last be called upon to learn, that the thought of her own death and of all that it would entail was so ever present to her.

And when this dread was thus upon her, she was terribly, feverishly anxious that her boy should have some settled prospect in the future, not only for his own sake, but for the sake also of his little sisters.

Surely, surely Lord Seaforth must at last do something for him!

This day the weight of years has been lifted off her mind, for the long-expected letter has arrived this morning, and driven all her fears away.

The letter which had cost Lord Seaforth so much time and thought has done this for the woman he had loved.

She had longed for this letter, looked for it, prayed for it, and now here it was!

A terse and business-like production truly; the family lawyer the writer of it, the terms of the letter lawyer-like indeed. Her boy was bidden for as any other part of the family estate might be.

And yet she was thankful, joyful, filled with gratitude.

And thus it was that, lost in thought, oblivious of time and of what was passing round her, the voice of her little daughter broke in upon her wrapt meditation : "Mamma! only think! What *do* you think? Papa has taken Olive to Monaco!"

CHAPTER V.

HOW WILL HE TAKE IT?

"WHAT do you say, dear?" she inquired as little Hester, surprised at getting no answer, advanced nearer and laid her hand on her mother's shoulder. The child eagerly repeated what she had said before.

"To Monaco, Olive?" exclaimed the mother, surprised out of her usual caution on the subject of their father before the children.

Her calm expression has changed all in a moment, and a troubled, anxious look has come over it.

God help her! it is the look the sight or hearing of her husband has ever been wont to bring.

He has never slighted all her wishes and broken through all her rules on this subject before, and she is wondering what sudden impulse has caused him to do so to-day.

"Papa said Olly would bring him *luck*," said little Hester, "and something about being turned into gold. And we asked him what luck meant, and he said he could not tell us. Can you, mamma?"

"Luck is a kind of chance," the mother answered. "So I do not wonder papa said he could not tell you what it meant. For we know there is no such thing as chance; don't we, Hessie?"

"Yes," said the child; "I wonder papa didn't think of that. Don't you?"

"Perhaps he was joking," said Hester, quickly; " he is always joking, isn't he?"

"Yes," said Hester, doubtfully; "but I don't think he was this time. He got quite cross about it. You're not angry with Olly, mamma, are you?" she added anxiously; "you look very grave. But it was not quite her fault, you see."

"No, dear," said her mother, "not if she didn't ask to go."

"She didn't," said the child eagerly. "Papa asked us, like he always does, 'Who's coming with me to Monaco to-day?' and Olly said, 'I am.' Papa was only joking at first, as usual; but he changed his mind, and said he really meant it, though we said you would not like it, nor Godfrey either."

A quick look of intelligence came into the wife's eyes, and then she sighed. She quite understood now why her wishes had been set at nought, and Olive taken to Monaco.

She knew her husband to be in a most curious mood ever since the receipt of that letter; all sorts of feelings surging in his breast as to his brother in the past, and as to his son in the future. He was hardly responsible for his actions to-day.

She told little Hester she might run out into the garden again. She wanted to be alone.

She read the precious letter again and again, till she was roused from her absorption in it by the dearly loved voice of her son in the garden, talking to his little sisters.

" Where is mother ? " she heard him say.

" In the drawing-room," answered one of the children. " She's got a letter from England to-day, that she keeps on reading over and over again. She is so interested in it that she has not called us in to our lessons yet ! I really think she must be going to give us a whole holiday ! "

There was no answer to this, and the mother wondered whether a faint suspicion of the truth had entered the boy's breast.

She would fain hope it might be so, for she dreaded announcing it to him, feeling so very uncertain how he would receive the news she had to tell.

The subject of his prospects was one which was always mutually avoided between them. More on his side than on hers, for she had wished sometimes to talk them over with him, and to draw his attention to his future position and its attendant responsibilities ; but she could not get him to talk of it.

She fancied sometimes that he looked upon his heirship as the source of all his troubles—the remote cause of his father's behaviour to him. But she was not sure. Questions originally she had never encouraged him to make, dreading the subjects to which they might lead; and now that he was older, he was more reserved on these points than she was herself. Her difficulties with regard to him had always been very great. To keep up his filial reverence for his father, and to prevent his finding out what that father was, had been two great objects in his education, and to them she had sacrificed a great deal. She had had scruples in her own mind sometimes about it, as to whether she had not overdone it, and confused right and wrong in his mind. But she had no means of knowing what effect her training had had.

That he deeply felt his father's dislike and unkind behaviour she knew; but in what spirit he took it she had no idea, nor how much he blamed his father for it. All such subjects were tabooed between them.

Now that he was nearly grown up, it was more difficult to approach subjects so long mutually avoided, and he almost always turned the conversation if she tried to introduce them.

She had thought it her duty latterly to speak to him on the probability of his uncle's sending for him to England, and a peculiar look had come over his face.

She had pressed him to tell her what was passing in his mind, but he had answered it would be time enough when the summons came.

She felt that the reserve of years might now be going, to a great extent, to be broken down between them, and she shrank a little from the prospect.

She heard his step on the balcony, and nerved herself for his entrance.

"Could I help it?" was the cry of little Joan in her lonely life, and "Could I help it?" seemed to be echoed in the grave, sad expression of the beautiful youth who now came into the room. We see standing before us, in flesh and blood, the picture at whose shrine the lonely child so persistently worships. The same features, the same colouring, the same mournful, beautiful eyes. Almost do we expect to see the kneeling figure, and to hear the appealing cry, "Godfrey, Earl of Seaforth! how I wish I had been you!"

There was not a trace in him of his father, sisters, or mother, till, meeting her glance, he smiled, and then the likeness of expression drove even the likeness to the picture away.

"It has come at last, Godfrey," she said very softly.

He did not start or wince, but he turned white to the very lips, and compressed his hands together firmly.

"I thought so," he answered in a low voice, which he strove with all his might to render steady.

She trembled a little inwardly at his unwonted display of emotion, but she said nothing.

She only raised her pleading eyes to his face, as if to pray him to spare himself and her.

"Let me see the letter, mother," he said quietly.

She handed it to him without speaking, and he read it through twice, and then returned it to her.

"Well?" she said anxiously.

"Well, mother," he answered, "what answer is to be given?"

"What answer?" she repeated, while her heart sank within her. "Oh, Godfrey! you surely do not mean to say you thought there could be a doubt. What answer *could* there be but one?"

He turned quickly away, and went and stood by the window.

Hester watched him anxiously. "Godfrey dear," she implored, "come back to me."

He came directly, but his face wore such a peculiar expression that she took alarm, and begged him to tell her at once what was passing in his mind. She shrank from the idea of hearing even while she made the request, and could hardly breathe as she waited to hear what he would say.

"I was only thinking," he replied, in a low, concentrated tone, "of the answer *I* should send, if it all depended upon me."

"What would it be?" she whispered, more and more alarmed at his manner.

"No! a thousand times no!" he exclaimed, with a vehemence that she had never seen in him before. "I would fling back to him all his high-flown offers and so-called advantages, and say, "You have exiled and disgraced the father, and the son will share in that unjust and unmerited punishment!"

He paused for a moment, breathless with the excitement under which he was speaking, and then went on: "Tyrant that he is, and always has been, is no

one ever to say him nay ? At his bidding family ties
are to be snapped asunder, and whatever he chooses
to ask for is to be instantly granted. At his command
I, the son of the brother he has so cruelly wronged,
am to be separated from all I hold most dear, and to
make my home with the very man who inflicted that
cruel wrong! The very man," he went on, with
increasing excitement, " who has poisoned our family
life at the root, and, by making my father hate me,
been the cause of the unhappy division in our home.
What are all the things he offers me matched against
those he has cost me ? And is it for my sake or my
father's sake that he makes this proposal? No ! he
turns to us when everything else has failed, for his
own ends, for the sake of his family, his name, his
property. And I would gladly tell him that I would
never touch a penny of his money, and I wish that I
did not bear his name ! "

Poor Hester ! As he spoke all the old scruples
woke up in her breast with greater force than ever.

Had she done well to let him grow up with such
a false view of past events ? Ought she to have
allowed him to make this false hero of his father ?

Ought she to have shown him a little what manner
of man his father *was ?*

What ought she to have done ? *How* ought she to
have acted ?

Her own sense of justice almost made her long to
clear his uncle to him—to hold up the curtain that
overhung the past and unfold to him the history of

the two brothers' early lives: to show him how severely that uncle had suffered, how blow upon blow had descended upon him, till this last but not least heavy had fallen—of having to sue humbly at the feet of his brother for the heir who, though indisputably his, was not his own son.

She could not answer; could not trust herself to speak. She sat silent, wondering if by any means she could clear the innocent without blaming the guilty. But no; she saw it could not be done. She could not justify the one without showing how deeply the other had been to blame; could not enlighten the mind of the son without blackening the character of the father; could not tell a part; it must be all, or none.

Once more Harold must be sacrificed to Godfrey. She must hold her tongue for ever. It was too late.

The silence of years could not be broken now.

But the effort it was to her was so great that she sat like a statue, her hands tightly clasped together, and her heart beating wildly.

Godfrey was the first to recover himself.

"Does my father know of this letter?" he said, with his usual quiet manner.

"Yes," she answered; "he read it before he started."

"And his wish is——"

"That the proposal should be accepted."

"When is he going to answer it?"

"He has done so already," she forced herself to

answer; but her voice trembled and shook. "The answer is written and sent."

He started and turned away. "So soon! Without one word of consultation with me!" escaped from his lips in the surprise of the moment. "But, of course," he added bitterly, "he is too glad to be rid of me. It is only natural he should wish me out of his sight."

"Oh, Godfrey!" she cried, "do you want to break my heart?"

He was at her side in a moment, calm and tender.

"Oh, mother! mine is almost broken at the thought of leaving you."

"But still you will go, darling?" she pleaded, raising her face, streaming with tears, to his.

"Still I will go, mother," he answered sadly, as he bent over her and touched her forehead with his lips.

A step outside made them both start. She hastily disengaged herself from his embrace, almost pushing him from her; and he started back, and tried to appear as if he were intent on some newspapers which lay upon the table.

And the next moment the husband and father walked into the room.

CHAPTER VI.

FOR OLD SAKES' SAKE.

GODFREY SEAFORTH gave a quick, suspicious glance at his wife's agitated countenance, and his eye rested on his son for a moment with an angry scowl. "I want to speak to you, Hester," he said; and the boy took the hint and left the room.

"What is it, Godfrey?" she said, rousing herself eagerly. She had a faint hope that some twinge of conscience had brought her husband home, to talk over his brother's letter and to show some little interest in his son's affairs.

"It's about that little goose, Olly," he said, with a light laugh.

"Olly!" she said, her surprise and disappointment showing themselves in her voice.

"Yes, Olly," he repeated. "Why, Hester, what an odd woman you are! I have been expecting a tremendous 'rowing' from you, and you seem quite unconscious that anything unusual has occurred. Didn't Hessie tell you I had taken Olive to Monaco?"

"Oh yes, Godfrey," she said reproachfully. "I did not think you would have done such a thing."

"Well, it has not affected you much," he said; "you seem to be thinking of something else."

"I have had a great deal to think of to-day, dear," she said wistfully, "as you know."

He frowned, and went on talking as if she had not spoken. His mood, too, changed, and he became tiresome and teasing.

"It's been a failure taking the child for luck," he said, stretching himself and yawning. "But don't you scold her, Hester, for coming. I've guaranteed her a peaceful home-coming, for she's frightened to death at the thoughts of a row. So vent your indignation on me."

Hester looked at him in surprise.

She wondered what he could be driving at. The relationship between herself and her children was such a perfect one, and he knew as well as she did that there never were any "rows" between them, and that there was no such thing as a possibility of Olive being "frightened to death."

That there was something behind she felt sure.

"What do you mean?" she said wearily.

He was delighted, and rubbed his hands together. "I thought I should get a 'rise,'" he said.

Poor Hester! she was not equal to his trifling to-day. With her boy's earnest voice and fervent words

ringing in her ears she felt she could not bear it.
And a feeling of anger against her husband rose in
her heart that he should go on like this when he
knew how full her thoughts were of something else.

Consideration for her, she thought, apart from
any feeling about the circumstances, ought, at any
rate, to have some effect upon him. She glanced at
him for a moment, and averted her eyes quickly.

We must not attempt to fathom the thoughts
which were passing through the wife's mind; but for
ourselves we may say that Godfrey Seaforth, sitting
there, was a sorry object.

His whole appearance had a "going-down-hill"
look; his hair unkempt, his dress untidy, a short pipe
in his mouth, and a " devil-may-care " expression on
his still handsome face. How ill he filled the place
just vacated by the beautiful youth, his son! What a
contrast he was, in every way, to him!

Did some such thought flit through the wife and
mother's mind ere she turned so quickly away?

Ah! but Hester had loved him once, and that
was the keynote of her lifelong patience with him.

Whatever he might be now, once he had been her
girlhood's hero, and traces of that hero remained
still. With all his weaknesses, all his unprincipled
ways, he was still the same Godfrey who had loved
her when she needed love so much, and generously
came to her aid when she wanted help so sorely.

And for the sake of old sunny days of love and
happiness, for " old sakes' sake," much can be borne
with and forgiven.

Something in the glance she gave him did not please him, and he asked her why she looked at him in that contemptuous way.

"I did not mean to, indeed, dear Godfrey," she said gently; "only when you are in this teasing mood I know it is no use asking you questions, and I felt rather out of heart, as I wanted to hear about Olly."

"She's quite safe," he said, "and in the orange grove with the others. She brought me no luck, the little wretch—not a five-franc piece."

"I am glad of it," said Hester, gravely. "It will not encourage you to take her again."

He chuckled to himself, and then said, "You don't ask what train we came back by, or how we managed to be home again so soon."

"To tell you the truth," she answered, "I have not an idea what o'clock it is. I have been sitting here ever since you left, and have no notion how time has been going."

"What have you been thinking about?" he asked.

Then, without waiting for an answer, he added, with a sneer, "I need not ask, though. Such concentration and absorption could have but one object. Few thoughts could detain you idle, save those connected with that immaculate son of yours, that young Admirable Crichton."

"Oh, Godfrey!" she said earnestly, "he is going to leave me. Do you grudge the poor boy a few hours of my attention?"

"Poor boy, indeed!" he retorted; "the luckiest young dog that ever lived. What nonsense you talk, Hester. If ever any one was born with a gold spoon in his mouth it is this 'poor boy,' as you call him."

Hester knew she was on dangerous ground, but the prospect of her boy's departure made her bolder than usual, and she tried to make a little effect on her husband. "Godfrey," she said, "won't you talk over his affairs a little? There will be so much to settle and arrange, and so many things to get. Won't you sit down and talk over ways and means with me, and interest yourself in him just for once? It won't," she added, while her voice faltered, "be for long that you will have a chance."

"Not I!" he said, turning on his heel; "I'm going up to change my coat, and then I want you to come and take a stroll with me. I shan't go to Monte Carlo to-night. Olly's upset my luck. And as to ways and means, why, good gracious, if Harold wants things done properly, he must send the money. *I've* got none to spare. And I can't be bothered about the boy's kit. Let him see to it himself. Why, when I was his age I looked after myself, and ran up my own bills, and had got into a hundred messes and out again. You forget how old the fellow is getting."

So saying, and with a light laugh, Godfrey Seaforth stepped out on the balcony and lit another pipe. "Here!" he shouted. "Big Bear, Middle Bear, Little Bear! come up with me while I dress."

Hester sat very still after he was gone, while

thoughts passed through her mind, as so often in her long married life they had passed before, always leaving behind them the one dominant feeling—hopelessness!

She was roused by the consciousness that she was not alone in the room. Some one was either sitting or standing on the balcony, half inside the room, where her husband had been a little while before.

She turned her head towards the window, and there she saw a little huddled-up figure, with downcast head, shaking with suppressed sobs.

"Olive!" she exclaimed.

The sobs burst out at the sound of her name, and the repentant child flew across the room, sprang into her mother's lap, and hid her face on her shoulder.

"I'm so sorry, mamma, so sorry!" she murmured through her sobs.

Hester put her arms round the little girl and kissed her fondly. "I forgive you, darling," she whispered; and by degrees Olive's sobs ceased, and she told her story.

Hester now learnt for the first time that the child and her father had never been to Monaco at all.

Either the child's entreaties to take her home had moved him or else he had got bored at the idea himself, or some conscience towards his wife had restrained him at the last from carrying out his intentions. Anyhow, he had not been, and both she and poor little Olive might have been spared much unnecessary suffering.

Hester sighed deeply as she listened. Olive was the child whose character gave her the most anxiety. She had all her father's light, careless ways, and unconcern for the future for the sake of the present.

Only with it all she had what he never had, a very tender conscience and a very truthful disposition.

On this child Godfrey worked terrible mischief; and his dealings with her were always a painful anxiety to Hester.

She often had to stand as a wall of defence between Olive and her father.

She sent the little girl away happy, and then gave herself up to the deep rest of the thought that her children's future was not altogether vague and indefinite now; that one at least was amply provided for and in safe hands; and that in the days to come he would be an able and worthy protector for his little sisters.

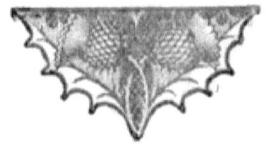

CHAPTER VII.

MEAN TO THE LAST.

THERE was but little time between the arrival of Lord Seaforth's letter and the boy's departure.

Mother and son saw but little of each other in the interval, for Godfrey the elder seemed determined to keep them apart as much as possible.

He hardly went to Monaco at all, and was more tenacious than ever of his claims on his wife's companionship. It was hard to say whether this was most trying to Hester or his unconcealed joy at his son's departure, which showed itself continually in ill-timed high spirits. She particularly wanted to have a great deal of conversation with her son on the subject of his behaviour to his uncle. She had been alarmed about this ever since his outburst of feeling had shown her in what light she regarded him ; and she wanted to extract a promise from him that he would for her sake preserve outwardly, at any rate, a proper demeanour towards him.

Just so much and no more did she contrive to

accomplish. She was not able to enlarge upon the
subject as she had wished.

Godfrey the elder was certainly in a most curious
mood. For sometimes there would be sudden reac-
tions from his high spirits, and it would be evident
that the thought of the future opening before the boy
had revived all his old bitterness of feeling with regard
to his own fate. His manner to his son was odious,
and constantly betrayed his ill-will and jealousy.
Then, also, he was angry and resentful at the sight
of the sorrow that reigned in his home at the prospect
of the boy's loss. It irritated him to see the love of
the little girls for their brother so undisguisedly
brought out; to hear them crying themselves to sleep
at night, and to find them less ready and eager to
run after him than usual.

These feelings culminated in an act of despotism
on the day of the departure, and he prevented his
little daughters at the last moment from accom-
panying their brother to the station, saying he wanted
them to remain with him.

He would fain have detained his wife also, but a
look in her eyes told him that his efforts would be
fruitless.

But he could not prevent the children sobbing
round their brother in the orange grove, clinging to
him with many tender words and caresses, crying
their little hearts out at his departure, though
beguiled, childlike, by the fancy that he would soon
return.

And he turned his back upon the touching picture, scowling as he went, without ever dreaming of taking farewell himself of the son he might never see again.

The mother's hands were pressed upon her beating heart, torn with conflicting feelings.

Anger against her husband struggled in her breast with sorrow for her son and grief at the pained look she saw gather on his face. Should she interfere? But what could she do?

The little girls settled the question. "Papa! papa!" they cried, rushing after him, and seizing him by the coat-tails, "come back. You have not said good-bye to Godfrey."

"Hands off! Let me alone!" he said pettishly, shaking them off.

The children fell back alarmed, but the boy, with a desperate effort, came forward, holding out both his hands. "Won't you say good-bye to me, father?" he said mournfully.

I think Godfrey would have refused the boy's proffered hand even then, had he not met his wife's fixed gaze. It probably expressed more than she was aware of. For a feeling of shame seemed to come over him, and he just touched his son's hand for a minute with the tips of his fingers, saying lightly, "*Bon voyage!*"

Then, as if with a sudden revulsion of feeling, a look of hatred came into his face, and he turned on his heel, muttering what sounded very like an imprecation.

"Come along, dear," said Hester faintly to her son, hoping he might not have heard; "we shall be late for the train."

And the boy obeyed, casting as he did so a lingering glance at his father's figure, disappearing rapidly in the direction of the house.

*   *   *   *   *   *

Half an hour later Hester returned alone.

Her husband was leaning over the balcony, smoking.

"What a time you have been!" he said as she approached. "The poor children are quite tired of waiting, and I wouldn't start without you."

"I cannot walk with you to-night, Godfrey," she said wearily.

Her heart was too full, and his light manner and evident forgetfulness of his recent conduct jarred painfully upon her overwrought feelings.

"Why not?" he exclaimed. "Why, I thought you would be in the highest spirits now. Haven't you got the very thing you've been wishing for all these many years?"

She met his eye fully, for her spirit was roused and gave her courage for an instant.

"Yes, Godfrey," she said firmly, "I have; and God knows how I thank Him that my boy should be removed from a home where his young life has been saddened by neglect and unkindness. I *am* thankful —more than thankful—*filled* with joy and gratitude—— "

She broke off suddenly, for her voice shook and faltered, and was choked by a rising sob.

"Nevertheless," she added, with a bitter burst of weeping, as she turned hastily away, "nevertheless the light of mine eyes is gone from me!"

BOOK III.

CHAPTER I.

LADY SEAFORTH'S PLANS.

THE setting sun of an autumn afternoon is shedding its glory over the wide-stretching park and richly wooded surroundings of Seaforth, and deepening the tints of the decaying leaves till the foliage looks one rich mass of gold.

Every window of the stately old house shines and flashes as the glass catches the rays of the sun as it sinks to rest. The sunset is followed by a very chill twilight, and there is a suspicion of frost in the air.

Nevertheless, the drawing-room windows are still open, and entering by them we will pass through a suite of grand old rooms till we reach the snug little boudoir, where Lady Seaforth with one of her sisters is sitting at tea.

Lady Seaforth, somewhat stouter than of yore, but handsome still and energetic as ever, is presiding over the tea-table, and her faded, careworn-looking sister, Lady Margaret Cartwright, is knitting by the

fire. "I am sorry you have missed the boys,
Maggie," Lady Seaforth is saying. "It is so unusual
for them ever to go away in the holidays ; but on this
occasion I was obliged to send them up to London to
spend a few days with their aunt. They return on
Monday."

"In time for the first of September, I suppose,"
said Lady Margaret.

"Yes," said Lady Seaforth with a smile. "They
would not miss the first for all the aunts in the world ;
and so they begged this visit might be paid now
instead of later. You must positively, you say, go
to-morrow ? You could not stay over Monday to see
them ? "

"I am afraid it would be quite impossible,"
answered her sister. "William must be home by
Saturday night."

Lady Margaret Cartwright was the poor sister of
the family. She had married a hard-working clergyman in the coal country, and had a large family.
Few and far between were her visits to Seaforth ;
she and her husband could so seldom be spared from
home. Now that her children (they were all boys)
were older and getting out in the world, she was more
at liberty, but only for between Sunday and Sunday.
This was one of these occasions, and the visit was to
end the following day.

Boys were naturally her chief interest, **and** her
favourite topic of conversation.

"When does Colin leave Eton ? "

"This will be his last half. He will be very loth to leave, and I do not wonder at it. I can fancy no life pleasanter than an Eton boy's, when he has nearly reached the top of the school, and is quite a little king in his way. Can you ? "

"No, indeed," answered Lady Margaret, rather bitterly.

She liked to hear about her sister's sons, and encouraged her to tell her of their Eton life, prospects, etc. ; but she often sighed as she listened, and mentally compared their circumstances with those of her own penniless boys.

Eton *versus* cheap grammar schools, and unlimited shooting in the holidays over the whole estate of Seaforth *versus* an occasional rabbit by the kind permission of some parishioner.

"And what is he to do after leaving Eton ? "

"The University comes next," Lady Seaforth answered. "I mean Colin to go in for a parliamentary life from the very first. I intend, after his university career, to get him made private secretary to one of the ministers—— "

"The Prime Minister preferred, of course," put in Lady Margaret, with a little laugh.

"—— and then, at two or three and twenty, a seat in the House of Commons. You see that by that time our present member will be getting very old, and will, I am sure, be ready to retire. I feel certain he will not offer himself again at the next election. And Colin, having lived here nearly all his life, is quite a son

8

of the soil, and immensely popular with all the people about. He is just one of those pleasant-mannered, easy-going, high-spirited boys who is sure to be a favourite among the tenantry and labouring classes. So I consider it quite a foregone conclusion that he should one day represent the county."

"But, Helen!" exclaimed Lady Margaret, "he will be very poor. How can he afford to live without a profession?"

"Of course," answered her sister, "I mean him to make a profession out of it. When I talk of his going in for a political life, I mean him to make a living by it, and to go in with a view to office some day. Taken by the hand early by a minister, he is sure to get it *in the end.* And in the mean time——"

"In the mean time," thought poor Lady Margaret to herself, "I suppose that generous Lord Seaforth will give him a handsome allowance."

Lady Margaret had arrived at that stage of poverty and realisation of its difficulties through bitter experience, that generosity was almost *the* one virtue in her eyes.

She could forgive her brother-in-law everything in consideration of his behaviour, or rather what she imagined to be his behaviour, to her sister's sons.

"And Andrew?" said Lady Margaret.

"The University also," said Lady Seaforth, "with a view to Holy Orders."

"I see," said Lady Margaret with a smile; "the family living!"

"It is worth 1200*l.* a year," said Lady Seaforth, "and the present incumbent —— "

" Will take himself off just in time, like the member, I suppose," interrupted Lady Margaret, with a laugh which she could not suppress.

But Lady Seaforth was much too full of her plans to see the vein of sarcasm in her sister's manner. She had no sense of the ridiculous, and could not look at herself from another's point of view. She was always quite unsuspicious of being laughed at.

Besides, it was all too serious. These plans, which she had just divulged to her sister, were the great interest of her life. She had worked steadily up to their fulfilment for many years. The gratification of her ambition for her sons was her great hope and consolation, and a balm in a life which was sore with many vain regrets, and seared with one bitter disappointment. She had never mentioned her plans to her husband, but felt pretty sure of his co-operation when the time came.

" Well! " sighed Lady Margaret, " you are a fortunate woman, Helen. When I think of everything being so plain and easy before your boys, who were born as penniless and as prospectless as mine, and then think of my Charlie farming in Australia, and Johnny in India for his whole life, and poor Frank in a counting-house at 100*l.* a year, and the other three quite unprovided for in the future, I can't help feeling the good things of this life are very unequally distributed."

The conversation was interrupted by the entrance of a servant, who advanced to Lady Seaforth, and said in a low voice—

"His lordship will be glad to speak to you, my lady, in the library."

The summons was as unusual as it was unexpected.

Lady Seaforth coloured for a moment, and then, in as matter-of-fact a way as possible, said, " Tell his lordship I will come directly."

Lady Seaforth was very reserved on the subject of her relations with her husband. She would not, therefore, allow her sister to see how surprised she was at the unusual summons. Leaving her cup of tea untasted, she rose from her seat, and with an excuse for leaving her, and a promise of a speedy return, left the room.

Lady Margaret sat knitting for a long time after her sister was gone, lost in meditation. Lady Seaforth's agitated manner had not been lost upon her, and ere the heel of the sock was turned, a new phase of thought had been wrought into the socks that were on their way to Australia.

The half-bitter look which her face had worn during her conversation with her sister had faded away, and some inward thought brought a glow to her eyes and softened the lines of her mouth.

The contrast between her boys' lives and her sister's might be very sharp, but there was a contrast in their own lives which was sharper still. A careworn face rose before her, a face worn with toil and care and poverty, but wearing a tender smile.

It was the face of William Cartwright, and the inward thought was, the memory of the happy life they had lived together; a life which, in spite of poverty and anxiety and struggles, had been ever brightened by the love they bore one another, and the perfect sympathy which existed between them.

"No!" she said almost aloud, as the music of her soul kept time to the click of the knitting-needles; "no, the good things of this life are *not* so very unequally distributed, after all."

She had time for plenty of reflection on the subject, for the sock was finished and the stitches cast off, and still her sister did not return.

CHAPTER II.

IN THE LION'S DEN.

WE will follow Lady Seaforth into her husband's private apartments, and enter with her the presence of the solitary man, sitting as usual in front of the fire, buried in gloomy thought.

He rose at her entrance, and in the most courtly manner placed a chair for her, and then resumed his seat.

"I wished to speak to you, Helen," he said, "on a matter of great importance to myself, and one which will not altogether be without its effect on you."

Lady Seaforth's heart beat quickly, and she wondered what could be coming.

"I don't know if I ever explained to you the manner of the entailing of this estate, in the event of my dying without a son."

Lady Seaforth murmured something in the negative. This was a most unwelcome subject, and her breath came quick and short.

"It is soon told," he resumed. "My father cut off my brother with a shilling, and entailed the estate over his head upon my brother's son. That son," he added emphatically, "is my heir. You were perhaps not aware," he added, "that my brother had a son."

"I was not even aware," she said, "that your brother was married. If you remember, you told me before our marriage that the subject of your brother was a painful one, and that your wish was that it might never again be mentioned between us. That wish I have respected, and I have never," she added, with a little warmth, "inquired of any one else what you did not see fit to tell me yourself."

"You have done well," he said. "The subject is still, as it has ever been, a most painful one, and it is only necessity that makes me allude to it now. But certain conclusions, to which I have lately come, force it upon me, and render silence on the subject no longer possible. It is my intention, as it is clearly my duty, to adopt my nephew, and to bring him up as my heir. I must do my best to counteract the impressions which I fear such a life as he must have led with such a father may have made, and to try and fit him for the position he will, at my death, hold. My only fear is it may already be too late. But be that as it may, I can no longer delay the execution of my duty; and matters between his father and me having been arranged, it only remains for me to inform you of my intentions, and to fix the day of his arrival. I have named next Monday."

Lord Seaforth ceased speaking, and paused, as if expecting a reply.

But none came.

Lady Seaforth's breath was coming in such short gasps that she could not steady her voice to speak, and feelings had succeeded each so quickly in her breast while he was speaking, that his abrupt pause found her quite unprepared with a word.

Astonishment, dismay, resentment, vain regrets, and bitter feelings had by turns had possession of her, habitual fear of her husband dominating and overpowering all.

The old, old grievances were swelling in her heart —the old, old feelings of resentment at the way in which she was treated; at the way her opinions, her very feelings, were overlooked; at the way she was never consulted, never advised with; that he just revolved matters in his own head, and then informed her when his mind was quite made up.

Time had, to a certain degree, accustomed her to this in all small matters, or in matters only affecting himself; but that on a matter of such moment as this, on one so closely affecting them both, he should treat her just the same!

He might at least have asked her if she had any objections or distaste to the plan, might at least have considered her feelings a little, might at any rate have given her a little time to consider.

But no; she was no one, and nowhere. She and her feelings equally disregarded in his arrangements.

The old, old passionate regrets were smiting her cruelly that she had no son of her own. New feelings of hatred and jealousy were rising within her towards this unknown one who was to fill the place *her* son would have had.

The pent-up torrent of years was swelling within her, and threatened to bear her self-control away.

Let that torrent burst its bounds, and come rushing out in speech, and it will sweep everything before it. Let her give way to feeling or temper, and she will degrade herself before her husband, and it will be all over with her. Truly silence was her only safeguard, and she stood silent, with her hands pressing down her throbbing breast.

"I can allow something for your astonishment," Lord Seaforth went on, finding she did not answer; "for myself, the subject has been in my mind for years. Do not, therefore, force yourself to express any feeling on the matter. And, indeed, it is not necessary. The advent of this boy will make little or no difference to you. I intend to keep him under my own strict surveillance until I find out how far he is to be trusted. For this purpose I shall give him a suite of apartments not far from my own. His leisure hours will be spent with me, and he will be given over during the rest of the day to a tutor, whom I have already engaged. You see clearly, therefore, that the new-comer will not be in your way, and that this change will in fact be nothing personally to you."

Nothing to her! This was the sharpest pang of all; these concluding words the cruellest in all his cruel speech.

As if their interests *could* be divided. As if, man and wife as they were, anything that affected him *could* be without its effect upon her. As if, loving him as she did, she could bear to see him endure anything that she knew would be a trial and a mortification to him. Was it nothing to her to feel that a sharper regret at having no son of his own would be added when he came to see the graceless son of an outlawed spendthrift in his home as his recognized heir?

Was it nothing to her to have this boy in her presence, daily parading before her her grief and disappointment? Oh, she could have borne it all better if it had not been for those unfeeling words.

With all this the wife's heart was so painfully smarting that the mother's feelings had as yet had no place.

But suddenly, with a fresh pang, came the thought of her own boys! Their present position! their future prospects! How would all this affect them?

For *their* sake came the anger she had not felt for herself, for *their* sake she was nearly speaking out, and indignantly asking if it was fair they should be thrust thus suddenly into such baneful society.

But before she could use this weapon in her own defence, it was wrested from her.

Ere she could steady her voice to speak, her husband went on. "I do not know who—my nephew's associates may have been, nor what kind of life he may have led. It will be well, therefore, that there should be no communication between him and your sons at present. I shall not, therefore, at first ask you to invite him to your drawing-room, nor shall I bring him in to dinner among your guests. I intend, however, that he shall be treated in every respect as my father's grandson and my heir. It is in those two lights that I wish to regard him. I wish to forget that he is my brother's son. I shall myself inform the household of his intended arrival, and of the position he will occupy in my house. I shall give orders that all shall look upon him as, and treat him with the respect due to, their future master, for, were I to die to-morrow, he would infallibly become so."

So saying, Lord Seaforth rose from his seat and advanced to the door.

And before his wife could recover from the confusion of thought into which she had been thrown, she found he was holding it open for her, and that the interview was over. She went to her bedroom as in a dream, feeling as if she had been for hours in her husband's presence, and entering hastily, locked and double-locked the door.

Mr. and Lady Margaret Cartwright dined alone with Lord Seaforth that evening ; for when the gong sounded, a message was brought to the drawing-room that Lady Seaforth had such a bad headache that she would not be able to appear.

CHAPTER III.

FELLOW-TRAVELLERS.

King's Cross Station, and the mid-day train for the north getting near its time for starting.

A tall, handsome youth is settling himself in a second-class carriage, arranging his luggage, etc., with all the independence of a poor man, used to shift for himself.

The train was very full, for it was a travelling time of year, and this particular train a great favourite.

Just two minutes before it was time to start, two tall, fair boys came tearing down the platform.

Thorough types of the luxurious, helpless young Englishman they appeared to be. They had nothing in their own hands but their umbrellas; even their great-coats and railway rugs were carried by the porters who were hurrying after them.

Their luggage they appeared to leave to look after itself entirely; their only object was to find seats in the train.

In this, however, they were not successful. Every first-class carriage was full. In vain they protested; in vain they declared places must be found, or a new carriage added to the train. The train was off, and the guard, opening the door of a second-class compartment—the same in which the first traveller we mentioned had settled himself—told them it was all but empty, and that there was just time for them to jump in. There was nothing else to be done. Railway-rugs, overcoats, gun-cases, and hat-boxes were pitched in, and the two boys took their seats just as the whistle sounded.

Then began hunting and shouting. "Hullo! where's my hat-box?" "Are you sure the long gun-case is in?" "Is there a bag there with an F on it?" "I say! call the paper-boy. I want *Bell's Life* and the *Sporting Gazette!* Look sharp!"

Tips were freely held out; porters and paper-boys running in every direction, and the newspapers flung in at the windows just as the train slowly glided out of the station.

Eldest sons of millionaires any one would have supposed the lads to be, and yet these were the penniless sons of Colin Fraser. So much for education.

Their fellow-traveller, rolled up in his corner, book in hand, watched them with some astonishment; but, after a time, he became absorbed in his book, and thought no more about them.

The two brothers yawned, sighed, stretched themselves, and then began to talk. Their conversation was all of sport, dogs, keepers, coverts, and speculations on the coming shooting season.

The stranger read on quietly, till a sentence caught his ear in which the words " the coverts at Seaforth " occurred.

He coloured slightly, turned his head for a moment towards the speaker, and then resumed his book. The action was not lost on the eldest of the two brothers, who glanced that way for a moment. By-and-by he and his brother took up the papers, and began reading extracts to each other, as long as the light lasted, of the shooting on the Scotch moors, and what bags different people had made.

It was getting too dark to read, and the stranger put down his book, sat up, and looked out of window. As he did so he caught the eye of the eldest brother fixed upon him with a most inquiring expression, and soon after he said something to his brother in an undertone about an " extraordinary likeness." But the whispered conversation was put an end to by the arrival at a great junction, where they all got out.

The train which went on to Seaforth Station was waiting on the branch line. Quietly removing all his things, the stranger transferred them to another second-class carriage, and went to see after his luggage. Meanwhile his late companions were rushing about, absorbing the attention of all the porters. They were treated here with great consideration. Every one was looking after them and their luggage, most of which they appeared to have left behind.

As the stranger was moving towards his carriage, he stumbled against the eldest brother. Instantly, in a very foreign fashion, he raised his hat and apologised. Young Fraser half raised his, and, as he did so, he met the stranger's eye, and the same look of astonishment passed over his face as had come into it before.

He ran after the station-master, and apparently made some inquiry. But the station-master shook his head.

The brothers then got into a first-class carriage, the train started, and they lost sight of their fellow-traveller.

"Seaforth! Seaforth!"

And the train steamed into the station.

It was almost dark, but just light enough to show a neat little brougham drawn up in waiting, and a cart for luggage. There was also a fly. A footman standing on the platform began at once to peer into the first-class carriages.

"His lordship's own brougham, I declare!" said Colin to his brother.

"Here we are, William!" he shouted to the footman. "You can look after the luggage, and we'll go on without you."

So saying, the two brothers entered the brougham and drove off immediately, amid a general raising of hats from all the *employés* at the station.

The footman, meanwhile, had not heard what was passing, and was still going down the line, looking into all the carriages. When he returned from an apparently fruitless search and found the brougham gone, he looked rather discomfited, and went up to the guard, and began making some inquiries.

After that he went and fetched the luggage, and had it put on the cart, and, calling out to the fly that it would not be wanted, took his seat by the coachman on the luggage-cart, and drove off.

Meanwhile the young stranger had been gathering all his things together, and getting his boxes out of the train.

He now came down the platform, and, going up to the station-master, asked if he could hire anything to take him on to Seaforth.

The answer was doubtful. The fly was too far gone to be called back; there *was* a spring cart at the inn, but nothing much in the way of a horse. The inn itself was some way off; it would take ten minutes to get there. The stranger was huddled up in a great-coat, and no guess at his station could be made.

He had his luggage put upon a truck, and walked off by the side of the man who wheeled it in the direction indicated, till he reached the inn, where he succeeded, after some trouble, in getting the horse and cart harnessed, and in securing a driver who knew the way.

The drive was long, the stranger very silent.

They reached the gates of the park at last; and, after driving two miles up an avenue, turned off to the right, and went by a side road to the stables, and through them to the back entrance.

A maid, with a light in her hand, peered curiously at the stranger as he got out of the cart; and, bearing all his own bundles, walked up to the kitchen door, and seemed about to enter.

"Who did you please to want?" she said.

"Lord Seaforth," was the answer.

The girl looked closer at him, and more suspiciously, but consented at last to lead him through the stone passage to the steward's room, where she handed him over to one of the men-servants, who was standing at the door, and to whom the stranger gave his name. "This way, sir," said the man, respectfully.

And thus the future master of Seaforth entered the home of his forefathers.

CHAPTER IV.

THE MEETING OF UNCLE AND NEPHEW.

THE scraping of the carriage wheels on the gravelled sweep had made more than one heart leap within the walls of Seaforth.

The mother, longing for her boys, and yet shrinking from what she had to tell them.

And, in his own room, the solitary man, sitting before his fire, brooding as usual. He is trying to realise that in a few minutes Godfrey and Hester's son will be before him. He is telling himself that he hardly knows what a task he has imposed on himself. He is wondering if he has sufficiently realised what a daily cross that presence in his home will be. It will bring in its train every sort of association and recollection; and names, long silent and dead, will sound upon his ears again.

What will be the effect of this bridging over the gulf that divides him from his buried youth, of thus calling up the ghosts of the past, and the joys and sorrows of former years?

*   *   *   *   *   *

A bustle—an arrival—and he rose slowly and took his way to the hall door. He arrived in time to meet the two tall lads, his stepsons, tearing wildly in. At sight of him, they stopped short, and pulling themselves up, came forward, and shook hands respectfully. He returned their greeting formally, and then went on to the door.

The carriage was gone; there was no other arrival! Puzzled and alarmed, he made some inquiries of the servants who were at the door, and learnt that no one else had arrived by the train.

He retraced his steps, chilled and disappointed; with the feeling, which so many know, which follows on having braced oneself up to the performance of something dreaded, and finding the performance delayed, and the duty still hanging over one.

The revulsion of feeling made him angry, and he revenged himself on the innocent cause.

"I thought as much," he muttered; "run away on the road—strayed. I ought to have sent some one over to fetch him—a bear-leader of some kind."

He regained his room, full of bitter feelings; wondering what course he had better pursue. To telegraph to Nice to know if he had really started, or to employ a detective to find out on what part of the road he had strayed? He sat down to think it out; bitter thoughts of the renewal of old disgraces filling his mind—placards and handbills, describing a creature like that Godfrey of old. He began involuntarily to compose the advertisement. "A tall, fair youth, light curly hair, eyes rather bloodshot, loose shirt-collar, short pipe in his—— "

" Mr. Seaforth, my lord."

Lord Seaforth started from his seat, and advanced a few steps; just in time to come almost up against the tall, dark youth, who had followed the servant into the room. At the sight of this youth, Lord Seaforth started back, uttering an exclamation of astonishment. The youth, startled, fell back a few paces too, and there they remained, gazing at each other.

The butler retired, closing the door behind him, and Lord Seaforth stood still, gazing at the figure in front of him without saying a word, his eyes glowing with some unusual feeling, and his hands nervously clasped together. Was *this* the gambler's son ? *This* the to-be-suspected *vaut-rien?* For the moment he forgot Godfrey, forgot Hester even ; absorbed only by the feeling that before him was his own son. Yes ! the long dreamed of, often dwelt on ; fondly imagined and fully realised—here he was ! The face and figure which at one time had been always rising before him, he who was to make up for so much, to do away with such lifelong regrets ; in whose opening life, and young future, all the pain of the past was to be merged and lost ; his son ! his very own son, was now standing before him !

Recovering himself with a desperate effort, he once more advanced, and with courtly gravity held out his hand, bidding the new-comer welcome to Seaforth. He then motioned him to a seat, and sitting down opposite him, with his searching eyes still fixed upon him, he made a few inquiries as to his journey, his non-arrival at the right time, etc. And Godfrey began to explain. But he had not finished his sentence before Lord Seaforth sank back in his chair and covered his face.

The voice, the manner, the strange indescribable likeness of expression, half natural, half caught from constant companionship, transported Lord Seaforth back to the fair past, and, violently agitated, he shut out the picture from him with his trembling hand.

His son was gone, and Hester Stanhope was before him.

But when he uncovered his face again, Godfrey was sitting gazing quietly at the fire, and the likeness had faded away.

But he addressed him no more; he felt he must be alone awhile. He could not trust himself to conjure up again the voice, the manner so dearly loved, so clearly remembered; and rising slowly, without looking at him, he said, "Come with me. I will introduce you to Lady Seaforth, and then take you to your room."

CHAPTER V.

LADY SEAFORTH'S RECEPTION.

A VERY different meeting was going on in the drawing-room, where the boisterous entry and greetings of her boys was bringing back the smile to Lady Seaforth's eyes, and a glow to the face that has looked pale and worn ever since that trying interview.

The boys were full of talk, chattering on about all they had been doing in London, and she saw no prospect of introducing the subject of which her mind was full. But Colin, the eldest, gave her an opening by dashing into the account of the stranger who had travelled with them—the most extraordinary likeness of Lord Seaforth, he declared, that could possibly be.

He did not notice how pale his mother turned as he spoke, nor what a pained expression came into her eyes, but continued to chatter on on the subject, and give further details, till Andrew grew provoked, and complained of the interest and excitement his brother had got up in "some cad, who had travelled with

them second-class from London; so that he had
talked of nothing else ever since."

"He didn't look like a cad, at any rate," exclaimed
Colin, hotly; "he was one of the handsomest fellows
I ever saw; and, as I say, the exact image of—— "
But here Lady Seaforth broke in. She *could* not hear
that unwelcome intelligence again. Far rather would
she that her younger son's report should be the true
one, and that the expected heir should prove indeed a
" cad," as he so tersely expressed it.

Her great hope now—almost all the hope, poor
woman, she had left—was that her husband's nephew
should prove such; that he would be ashamed of him,
and that her high-bred, good-looking boys should
shine in bright contrast by his side.

"I am sure Andrew is right," she said. "Lord
Seaforth is expecting his nephew, the son of his
outlawed brother, so you may imagine what kind of
youth he is likely to be. I imagine he has been
brought up entirely among blacklegs and card-
sharpers."

She spoke hurriedly and nervously.

" What's he want here ?" exclaimed Andrew, a
dim suspicion of the truth coming over him.

But Colin, more simple-minded, did not take it up
at all. " How long does he stay ?" he inquired.

"Lord Seaforth has adopted him," said his
mother, in a hard, dry voice, "and he is coming to
live here."

Andrew glanced at her, and understood the whole

thing at once; but Colin only said, "I dare say he isn't a bad fellow. I am sure he doesn't look the least like a cad, and he's not obliged to be good-for-nothing because his father is."

"Well, I forbid your having anything to do with him," said Lady Seaforth. "He may be a card-sharper himself, for anything we know; and not at all fit company for you. Moreover, Lord Seaforth does not wish any communication between you at present; and the boy is to be kept a kind of state prisoner till we see if he is fit to be trusted."

"Poor wretch!" said Colin. "Well, I must say, mother, I think that's rather hard. To take a fellow's character away without giving him a chance, just because his father was a rogue! I thought that in this free and justice-loving country we believed every man to be innocent until he was proved to be guilty."

"In this instance," she answered, sharply, "it will be safer to consider this boy guilty until he is proved to be innocent. You seem to be in a great hurry to make friends with and stand champion for him, Colin; but perhaps you won't be so ready when you find that his arrival here ousts you and Andrew from your positions, and perhaps blights all your prospects."

They both looked so blank that she felt sorry she had spoken so strongly. She only wished to sow the seeds of suspicion; and her own bitter feelings escaped her, almost before she was aware.

Colin was the first to recover himself. He

laughed, "Better be friends than enemies, then," he said lightly. "You should bow to the rising sun. Next to the king himself, a true courtier always keeps on good terms with the heir-apparent. So he is the heir-apparent, eh, mother?"

Lady Seaforth could not answer, but she made an affirmatory inclination of the head.

"It's quite a romance," said Colin. "Shrouded stranger in corner of second-class turning out to be heir-apparent. Usurpers swaggering in first-class, and—— Hallo! was the carriage sent for *him*, mother?"

"Yes," she said anxiously, "I believe so. I ordered a fly for you. Didn't you come in it?"

"No, hang me if we did!" said Colin; "and what's more, we ran off with the carriage. It was his lordship's own brougham. And as to the heir-apparent, I don't know what became of him. He must have followed with the luggage." And Colin laughed more than ever.

"Oh, Colin!" said his mother, now really alarmed, "how could you?"

"How were we to know?" he exclaimed. "We saw the brougham, and hopped in. I thought it was rather unusually condescending of his lordship to send his own brougham for us, but still——"

Lady Seaforth's only answer was to ring the bell sharply, and to ask the servant who answered the summons if any one else had arrived by the train besides Mr. Fraser and Mr. Andrew.

"Mr. Seaforth, my lady," was the reply; and Lady Seaforth started at the name, but controlled herself directly.

"Shrouded stranger!" muttered Colin to himself, laughing. "Where is Mr. Seaforth?" he asked; "and how did he get here?"

"Mr. Seaforth hired a trap and came on, sir," said the servant. "He arrived ten minutes after you, and went straight to his lordship's room."

"I never heard anything drive up!" exclaimed Lady Seaforth.

"Mr. Seaforth came the back way, my lady, and through the offices into the house."

Lady Seaforth and Colin both got scarlet; she with fear, and he with suppressed laughter, which broke out the moment the servant left the room.

"Heir-apparent smuggled in through the kitchen," he said. "The best thing I ever heard in my life!"

"Oh, hush, Colin!" exclaimed his mother in an agony, for she heard footsteps coming across the hall. "Please, *please* be quiet."

Before Colin had time to recover himself, the drawing-room door opened, and Lord Seaforth entered, followed by his nephew.

"Helen," he said, advancing to his wife, in a voice which slightly trembled, "this is my nephew, Godfrey Seaforth. Godfrey, this is Lady Seaforth; and these," he added, indicating the Frasers with a wave of the hand, "are Lady Seaforth's sons."

Lady Seaforth felt, rather than saw, that the figure

following her husband was quite as tall, and of the same noble bearing.

She knew, somehow, within herself, that this youth, in outward appearance, at any rate, was an heir of whom any man might be proud.

Such a pang of jealousy and vain regret shot through her that her very heart seemed frozen within her, and a demon of rebellion and resentment took possession of her.

She *could* not, she *would* not, hold out her hand. Without looking up, she bowed distantly and stiffly, without saying a word. Andrew followed suit, and Godfrey silently returned their salutations in the same formal manner.

But Colin came forward with outstretched hand, saying, "We were fellow-travellers. I wish I had known who you were; and I am so sorry about the carriage."

Lady Seaforth glanced at her husband as her son spoke, and took fright at the expression of his face.

"There was a mistake," she said, nervously; "it was the servant's fault."

"There was," he answered coldly; and there was that in both tone and manner, besides the icy coldness of his voice, which made her turn to Godfrey and make a few inquiries about his journey.

But when she met the grave look of his beautiful eyes, a sharper pang shot through her heart, and unwillingly she was obliged to corroborate Colin's assertion that he was her husband's very image ; he might have been his own son.

Admiration and a wistful longing struggled in her breast with the jealousy and impulsive dislike which was springing there.

Jealousy, not only as regarded the boy himself, but as regarded her husband.

There was a peculiar look in Lord Seaforth's eyes which she had never seen before ; a certain glow of feeling and interest which made him look so much handsomer than usual.

This jealousy culminated in astonishment when Lord Seaforth, with a scrupulous attention she had never seen him display to a guest before, led Godfrey away, and himself conducted him to his allotted apartments.

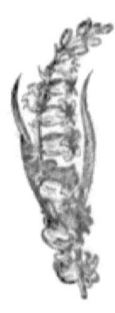

CHAPTER VI.

THE GHOST IN THE PICTURE-GALLERY.

VERY weary, both physically and mentally, was Godfrey that night when he found himself alone in his own room.

At once restless, and unable even to think of rest, he was in a feverish state of nervous exhaustion, arising partly from fatigue and partly from his over-strained feeling.

The events of the day, the finding himself at last in the presence of the *bête-noir* of his life, and the novelty of his position and surroundings, all this had so excited him that he could not compose his mind at all.

He sat down in a chair, and tried to think over the scenes in which he had that day been an actor.

But he could not think; he could not even sit still. A sense of oppression came over him. The tapestried walls of his room seemed to hem him in, and stifle him. He opened his door, and went out into the passage to get a little air.

All was dark; and, after groping about a few minutes, he returned, or rather tried to return, to his own room. In so doing he lost his way; and, all unknowingly, kept advancing further and further from the room he wished to find.

At last he came up against a door, and he pushed it open and advanced into a room, supposing it to be the one he had lately quitted.

He found himself in a lofty picture-gallery, which was flooded with moonlight from one end to the other.

By this faint and, as it seemed to him, unearthly light, every picture on the walls, every statue in every corner, stood out clear, but pale and ghost-like.

The scene was so unexpected, the whole force of it came upon him so suddenly, that for the moment he was startled. A strange, eerie feeling, born of much reading and little experience, came over him, and his heart beat high.

Just at this moment, too, the heavy oak door behind him swung to with a heavy crash, which went echoing through and through the empty place, till it died away into a stillness deeper and, as it seemed to him, more unearthly than before. A fantastic feeling cast its spell around him, a feeling he could neither understand nor overcome.

It came over him suddenly that he had been

through the whole scene before; that at some time
and somewhere he had groped his way along in darkness till he had come to an oaken door, and that,
pushing it open, he had come upon the moonlit and
unexpected scene by which he was now surrounded.

Nay, more; that on that other occasion he had
seen more and heard more, that something further
had followed, and that this was only the beginning of
a scene, the first act of a drama in which he himself
was to be an actor.   Had he dreamt it? heard of it?
read of it?

All of a sudden he remembered whence the feeling
came.   He was thinking of one of his boyhood's
heroes.   What he had in his mind was the Knight of
the Leopard and the scene in the Chapel of Engaddi.
Like him, Kenneth had groped his way in the darkness, had come to a closed door, had pushed it open,
and come suddenly upon a dazzling scene.   In Kenneth's case the entrance into the chapel had only
been the preliminary to what had followed.

There was more to come!

With this feeling strong upon him, Godfrey advanced into the gallery, his own tread alone breaking
the stillness which held him in thrall.

Even by moonlight the beauty of the old paintings
all around him made a strange impression upon him.

Suddenly the sound of approaching footsteps fell
upon his ear.   He withdrew himself behind one of the
statues, and waited to see what would follow.

A door at the other end of the gallery opened

very softly, and some one, or something, stole gently in.

It moved so lightly, and seemed to be so very small, that he could not conceive what it could be. So swiftly, too, that he could not distinguish it clearly, and it disappeared with rapid and stealthy steps in the opposite direction to that in which he stood concealed. What could it be? Every old house, he had read, had a haunted chamber. Was this one?

He could hear the light footsteps passing rapidly down the long passage that divided the gallery into two parts, and at the far end the footsteps seemed to stop. *What* was it? *What* could it be? What could it be doing? He was afraid to move lest he should disturb it, and reveal his own presence. Curiosity, however, at length overcame every other feeling; and, leaving his hiding-place, he crept cautiously along from statue to statue till he had neared by many yards the spot where the figure was stationary; and then he paused again, for he was getting near the window. The shadows had ceased, and he must step out into the moonlight if he went any further.

No sound broke the stillness for a minute, and he stood there hardly daring to breathe.

Suddenly every fibre in his body thrilled at the sound of his own name.

"Godfrey!" rang in a passionately appealing cry through the gallery, and then died away into a sob.

10

In his astonishment, Godfrey was about to cry out in answer, " Who calls me ? " when the plaintive voice rang out again.

" Could I help it ? " it wailed, in sobbing accents. " Oh, Godfrey, Earl of Seaforth ! Could I help it ? could I help it ? "

It was a child's voice, and a cry of such unutterable sadness that it went straight to Godfrey's heart. But it was evident it was not addressed to him. So he restrained his impulse to advance ; and, without moving from his hiding-place, he leant forward and strained his eye to the spot from whence the sounds proceeded.

Kneeling in the moonlight, like a worshipper at a shrine, with eyes and hands upraised to the picture above her, was a lovely little girl. Her fair hair, hanging over her shoulders, her clasped hands and kneeling figure, clothed in white, were all glorified by the same light.

Ere he had time to examine further, her plaintive voice broke out again, and he shrank back and listened.

And standing there, dazed and bewildered, he became the auditor of one of the saddest bursts of grief, the receiver of one of the most pathetic bursts of confidence he had ever in his life either heard or read of, and found himself face to face with a life sadder, a fate harder, a sorrow greater, than his own.

How shall we paint the feelings that passed

through him, as he stood, motionless, leaning against the pillar? How shall we follow the course of the new aspects of life and thought which broke in upon him as he listened, the rush of new grief, new regrets, new longings?

Oh! this pathetic revelation of the inner life of a child, young in years, but old in trouble; how it thrilled through and through him!

Here, then, was another victim of one man's pride and injustice.

Here, too, was another whom he himself, all unwittingly, interfered with, and stood in the way of.

Here, too, probably, was another who would hate and shrink from him.

Go where he would, do what he might, for ever and for ever must he be face to face with this bitter wrong and injustice, and the most unwilling, the most unhappy cause of it all? "Oh, my God!" cried the boy at last, almost aloud; and he moved unconsciously forward.

Was he going to pray for the child's forgiveness? Was he going to hold out his pitying hands and raise her from the attitude of despair in which she had thrown herself at the foot of the picture? Was he going mournfully to tell her the place she longed for was not such a happy and enviable one as she seemed to imagine?

If he had any such intentions he was too late; for she rose rather suddenly from her kneeling position, and retired as softly as she had come.

Godfrey then came out of his hiding-place, and, with a look on his face which told of the storm which had raged within him, he left the gallery and groped his way back to his own room.

BOOK IV.

CHAPTER I.

THE FIRST DAY AT SEAFORTH.

Lord Seaforth slept very little that night. Past and present were mingled together in his thoughts, and excitement kept him awake.

When he got a few fitful snatches of sleep his newly arrived nephew appeared to him in his dreams, and spoke to him in the voice and with the smile he had loved of old.

All through his hours of wakefulness his one feeling was longing to see him again. He kept wishing for the day, that he might have the face before him.

He rose in the morning with a sense of restored youth and interest in life, for which he could not account. As soon as he was dressed, he sent a message to his nephew to come and breakfast with him in his private room, and his disappointment was great when he was told Mr. Seaforth had had a cup of coffee at half-past seven and had gone out. Strange to say, there was no feeling but disappointment in

Lord Seaforth's mind, although the day before, the
very idea of such a proceeding would have filled him
with vague suspicions.

All feelings of suspicion had been allayed, far
more than he himself had any idea of, by Godfrey's
appearance. He did not, somehow, connect him with
his *vaut-rien* brother at all. Even in his dreams that
night it had never once been as the gambler's son
that the thought of the boy had presented itself to
him. After breakfast he went into the library, and
there awaited the return of his nephew from his walk
with feverish impatience. His heart quite beat when
he heard a step outside, and Godfrey entered the
room.

No! he had not been mistaken! He was quite as
handsome, quite as much every inch a Seaforth, as
he had thought him last night. Indeed, he was
handsomer. For his early morning walk had brought
a colour to his cheek, and a glow to his eye. He
looked very grave, and there was an almost stern
expression in his whole face, which made his uncle
wonder a little. It had not, he thought, been there, or
at any rate not to such a great extent, the night before.

He little guessed how the scene in the picture-
gallery had deepened in the boy's heart his already
antagonistic feelings towards him.

Godfrey did not return the smile of welcome with
which his uncle greeted him. He replied to his
morning salutation as shortly as possible, and then
stood without speaking.

Lord Seaforth found it difficult to begin. All the rules and regulations, the " state-prisonership," as Lady Seaforth had called it, which he had intended to impose upon his nephew appeared to him in quite a new light now. The setting them forth to the grave, noble-looking youth before him he felt to be an insuperable difficulty the first moment, growing into a sheer impossibility the next. He felt more as if he would have to ask him as a favour to give him his company in the library whenever he felt disposed.

And if he felt so powerless now, while Godfrey stood so grave and silent, he knew he should feel doubly so when the boy began to speak or smile, and by the mysterious power of association bring back the sweet though painful memory of days gone by.

But there was no fear of Godfrey's smiling this morning. Grave and stern he looked ; grave and stern he felt. The strain he was putting upon himself was quite painful to him. He was awaiting his dismissal with impatience. His one feeling was a desire to escape from a presence so distasteful to him.

Something of it must have communicated itself to Lord Seaforth ; for he coughed rather nervously, and seemed at a loss to know what to say. He then made a few commonplace observations and inquiries, to which Godfrey briefly replied.

Lord Seaforth could not get on ; so, noting the boy's quick glance towards the well-filled shelves of the library, he asked him if he was fond of reading. He was rewarded by the glow which shone in his dark eyes as he answered, for the first time with real interest, in the affirmative. Lord Seaforth then gave him ready permission to range over the books at will, and the conversation at once came to an end; for Godfrey advanced to the bookcase, chose his book, and, sitting down, became lost in it, and did not raise his head or speak again.

Lord Seaforth watched all this narrowly; noticed with pleasure the style of book he had chosen, watched with interest his absorption in it, and reflected on the power of concentration he displayed.

It argued well this; the boy was neither frivolous nor idle. His father had been both. It struck him certainly as rather extraordinary that he should be able to absorb himself like this on the first day of his arrival at a new place—and such a place! and a place which was to be his own some day—while all its glories were around him unseen and unexplored. But still what a thing this power of attention and concentration was! No one, he reflected, could ever be very miserable for long who possessed it. Oh, what a help it would have been to him! This power of losing *self* in something else, and being, for the time, entirely independent of present surroundings and existing circumstances—*what* it would have been to him! How many and many an hour of gloomy thought he might thus have been spared! How many a dreary day might thus have been cheered and enlivened!

Where did the boy get this love of reading? How

had he contrived to contract the habit? Who could have trained him in this way? Ah! his mother, of course. She was Edward Stanhope's sister, and he was a reading and studying man.

How curious, he said to himself, that he had never taken into account this element in his heir's possible education. He must question him further on this head when he came to know him better. But he soon began to wish he would stop reading and look up and speak.

He wanted to engage his interest and woo that lovely smile. He wanted to talk over plans and prospects, to make friends with him a little, and find out what he was like. He wanted to get at him, and to make him express his opinion on divers and various subjects. But still the handsome face was bent over the book, and still the leaves were turned at regular intervals.

"You seem interested in that work," he said at last, when he felt he could bear the silence no longer.

Godfrey started and looked up; his delight in what he was reading driving away for the moment every other thought.

"Yes," he answered, the longed-for smile shining in his eyes; "it is indeed a wonderful book, and the language is so beautiful, too."

Lord Seaforth shaded his eyes with his hand as he looked at him, and his heart beat quickly.

"But I beg your pardon, Lord Seaforth," added Godfrey, stiffly, the next moment, smile and glow

fading away and the grave look returning, as he
closed the book and rose from his seat; "I had not
intended reading so long."

"*Don't*," said Lord Seaforth, putting out his hand
imploringly—"don't call me Lord Seaforth; call me
Uncle Harold."

In those old days Edward Stanhope had called
him Harold, and he had never heard the name since.
Pained at the coldness that had again crept over his
nephew, he hastily referred to the book, and tried to
make him talk of it again, and by asking him to read
the passage that had so struck him he succeeded in
calling back the animation to his face. From that
he led him on to speak of his tastes and pursuits, and
so got him on the subject of his education. He was
able therefrom to tell him what his wishes were with
respect to his immediate future; and informed him
that he intended sending him to a private tutor to be
worked up for his matriculation at the University the
following year; but that, as he imagined he would be
deficient in many ways, he had engaged a tutor to
work with him for the next five or six months at
home.

Godfrey expressed himself agreeable to all these
arrangements, and the conversation ended by Lord
Seaforth proposing to take him out and introduce
him to those parts of the estate that were adjacent.

So the two started on their tour of inspection,
Lord Seaforth riding, and Godfrey walking by his
side. They pursued their course over the most

beautiful parts of the property. Lord Seaforth purposely chose these, as he wished to impress his nephew with a sense of his future position; and this, he thought, would be best done, or at any rate best begun, by unrolling before his eyes the beauties and glories of these precious belongings, and so laying the foundation of that family pride, and pride in possession, which was so strong a feeling in himself that he believed it inherent in every nature.

He had even sometimes allowed to himself that, had his brother even been in the position of heir, his whole character and career might have been different.

He watched Godfrey narrowly as they went along, but did not require of him any comment, any expression of astonishment or admiration. Admiration on such a theme, said Lord Seaforth to himself, would be idle! futile! It was well he expected no remark, for Godfrey made none.

Lord Seaforth's hope was that he was too much impressed to speak, too much overwhelmed by the thought of this princely inheritance to talk about it.

So Godfrey was allowed to pursue his walk in silence; though Lord Seaforth himself, after a time, discoursed at intervals—explained, dilated on, and pointed out different things, and then watched to see the effect.

He was convinced before the walk was over that his nephew was intelligent and observant. Also that there was nothing frivolous about him. He appeared to him to be both thoughtful and earnest, and altogether he was as favourably impressed by him on a further acquaintance as he had at first been by his general appearance.

On their return home he was equally pleased to see him at once resume the book he had been reading, and become as absorbed in it as if he had never left it.

For himself, he was content to sit and gaze at him, and speculate about him. But his original plans with regard to Godfrey seemed to him an insult now; and so, to the surprise and disgust of Lady Seaforth, he brought him in to dinner that very night.

After dinner he would fain have taken him back with him to the library to finish the evening there; but Godfrey was thoroughly worn out with the strain of this uncongenial companionship, which only his promise to his mother enabled him to bear. He therefore excused himself on the plea that he wanted to write home, and, wishing his uncle good night, he retired to his own room.

CHAPTER II.

THE GAMEKEEPER'S DILEMMA.

THE first of September dawned brightly, and the young Frasers descended to their mother's breakfast-room in high spirits, arrayed in gaiters and shooting-jackets, ready to start the moment breakfast should be over. Colin had given all the orders over night; the meeting-place for luncheon had been fixed upon, and Lady Seaforth was to come out and join them there at two o'clock.

"Look sharp, Andrew!" said the impatient and eager Colin; "don't be all day at your breakfast. It's nearly ten, and I told Cherryman to be ready to the minute. I'll go and see if he's anywhere to be seen."

So saying, Colin went off whistling, and Andrew went on eating and talking to his mother.

Ten o'clock struck, but Colin did not reappear.

"I like Colin's cheek," said Andrew, glancing at

the clock, which now said ten minutes past ten, "blowing me up, and then keeping me waiting."

As he spoke Colin came back. "I never knew Cherryman unpunctual before," he said, as he entered the room. "There's no sign of him yet, and it's getting on for a quarter past ten."

"Ring the bell," said Lady Seaforth.

Colin did so, and Lady Seaforth sent a rather sharp message to the keeper by the servant who answered it.

In a few minutes the man came back with the news that the keeper had gone out very early, and had not returned.

"Gone out!" exclaimed both boys together, swerving round, in their astonishment, to look at the speaker.

"Gone out!" repeated Lady Seaforth, angrily. "Where has he gone?"

"The keeper had orders to go out shooting with Mr. Seaforth this morning, my lady," was the reply.

If a bombshell had fallen in among the trio it could hardly have created more consternation than did this unexpected reply. All three, however, were obliged to control themselves before the servant, who perversely chose that moment for remaining in the room to put some coals on the fire, so that no conversation could take place.

"Send the keeper to me directly he comes in," said Lady Seaforth to the servant as he left the room.

"I told you so, Colin," she added, bitterly, directly the door was shut. "I told you the advent of this boy, that you took so coolly, would oust you and Andrew from your position here, and you wouldn't believe me. What do you say now?"

Colin did not answer; he looked utterly disconsolate, and stood with his hands in his pockets, gazing blankly out of window, where the September sun was shining, and the distant woods and corn-fields looked so fair.

Andrew's brow was dark and cloudy. "Hang the fellow!" he muttered, as he walked up and down the room.

Poor boys! they were speechless from many feelings, but the predominant one at the moment, to such keen sportsmen as they were, was, no doubt, bitter disappointment at the loss of their day's shooting. This, in Colin's eyes, far outweighed anything else; and Andrew shared the feeling, though he also took his mother's view of the dismal prospect of the future.

The mother could not bear to see their disappointment, and controlled her own bitter feelings to try and cheer them up.

"Why don't you start by yourselves?" she said, "or with one of the underkeepers?"

"The dogs, mother!" exclaimed Andrew, aghast at her display of ignorance.

"Very likely they have not taken any," she answered. "It is probably only a lesson in shooting.

11

This — this boy can't know how to handle a gun. At any rate, go and see."

The boys rushed off, and soon returned in high spirits to say they had found the underkeeper, and that their particular dogs had not been taken.

Then they started for their day's sport, the disagreeable *contretemps* already forgotten.

But Lady Seaforth sat on where they had left her, brooding bitterly over the occurrence.

Hitherto she had held uncontrolled sway over the shooting department. Lord Seaforth did not care for shooting, and it was kept up for the amusement of the guests. She herself always arranged all the shooting parties, and Lord Seaforth never interfered in the slightest degree. So that this was not a matter of mutual interest; herein she was paramount, and long habit had made her look upon the keeper as more her servant than her husband's.

She was determined to make an effort for the mastery still. Several hours sooner than she had expected him, the keeper appeared.

"How could you form another engagement on the first of September?" she indignantly asked him. "You must have known Mr. Fraser and Mr. Andrew would require you."

The man stood before her respectfully, hat in hand, with an expression of perplexity on his honest face.

"I'm in a dilemmy, my lady, and that's just about where it is," was his reply.

"A dilemma!" she exclaimed; "and why?"

"Just this," he answered; "his lordship's orders are one way, and your ladyship's the other. The Bible tells us no man can serve two masters, and I'm beginning to see the Bible says true. It comes to this—Am I his lordship's servant, or am I your ladyship's? That's just about where it is."

"Did his lordship give you the order to go out this morning himself, with his own lips?" she asked quickly.

"He did, my lady; and when I said I'd got my orders for this morning from Mr. Fraser, his lordship ups and he says——"

"Said what?" exclaimed Lady Seaforth, seeing the man hesitate. "Speak out!"

"Well then, my lady, I will; and your ladyship musn't take it ill of me, for it is his lordship's wishes, and not my own. He says, says his lordship, 'I know nothing about Mr. Fraser's orders, or anybody else's orders. Understand at once, and once for all, that Mr. Seaforth is your master for the future, and take your orders from him, and from nobody else.' Them's his lordship's own words, my lady, and you must see yourself as how I'm bound to obey them."

So saying, the keeper bowed respectfully and took his leave; and Lady Seaforth, in a storm of feeling, went up to put on her things to go and join her boys at luncheon.

CHAPTER III.

MUTUAL FIRST IMPRESSIONS.

AFTER this, there could, of course, be no doubt as to the relative positions of Lady Seaforth's sons and Lord Seaforth's nephew.

I leave the reader to imagine what kind of feeling Lady Seaforth bore towards Godfrey, as the first fortnight of his stay wore on, and she every day more fully realised it.

However, she saw but little of him. He was always with her husband; enjoying, as she said bitterly to herself, the companionship she so longed for, but to which she was never admitted.

And now, turning to Godfrey, let us see what impression his new life is making upon him—this sudden entry into English life and habits.

Supposing some hardy ancestor of ours suddenly brought into our highly civilised nineteenth-century life, with all its refinement of luxury, what sort of effect would it have upon him ?

For Godfrey, fresh from the simple, almost pastoral, life he had lived from his babyhood, and from a home where poverty and economy reigned supreme, was very much in the same case when he arrived upon the scenes of pampered ease and comfort, among which we all live without hardly being aware of them ; and he was daily and hourly astonished.

Used to the simplest fare, the fantastic pandering to appetite by the number and variety of wines and dishes appeared to him quite extraordinary. A great deal, in all ways, which we—so much is habit a second nature—consider absolute necessaries, and all-important, appeared to him mere luxuries.

The way in which "every corner of our life is cushioned," the luxurious comfort of the sitting and drawing rooms, the couches and the deep armchairs, were all to him matters as novel as they were surprising.

Then he was so independent, so helpful, so used to shift for himself, that he could not understand why everything in England was always to be done by the servants.

Even Lady Seaforth noticed this, and unwillingly owned to herself how helpless and dependent her boys were in comparison. Their bells were always ringing. They could not do the simplest thing without assistance ; must have their things packed, and their parcels corded, and their letters stamped for them.

They could not even carve a chicken or open a bottle of seltzer-water, or lace their own shooting-boots. They could not take the trouble to put a bit of wood on the fire, or to carry a bag from the carriage to the hall door; all and everything must be done by the servants.

Another peculiarity which struck him very much was the constant talk and grumble about the weather, the perpetual consultation of the glass, the fresh lamentations at each change in the atmosphere, and the universal discontent and impatience if there was a wet day.

He could not help sometimes comparing Seaforth with all its advantages to the tiny châlet where, during the rainy season, he and his were all cooped up for weeks, without any newspapers or new books of any kind.

And here, the tables were daily covered with every sort of newspaper, pamphlet, and new periodical; and there was the whole vast library to choose from, as well as all the lighter literature of the day.

Here, too, there was every sort of luxury to make people independent of outdoor exercise and amusement; a tennis-court and a racket-court, a billiard-room, a music-room, and a picture-gallery; to say nothing of the size of the house itself, which alone afforded scope for any amount of exercise. And yet, with all this, a single wet day set the Frasers and everybody else grumbling.

But such impressions were, of course, only those made by the outside and superficial part of English life; its undercurrent interested him more and more.

Beneath all this, was deep, deep interest and enjoyment in his surroundings. It could not but be so to a thoughtful and cultured mind like his.

Brought so suddenly into contact with art and civilisation, into a house fraught with historical interest, and replete with memories of the past, he stood as it were on spots " dignified by some association ; hallowed by some great name."

Then he was also deeply interested by the varied individual life around him ; and by the different kinds of men and women with whom he was brought in contact.

But his most fervid impression was that meeting with little Joan.

He had never seen her since that night, but his heart went out to the lonely child, and her forlorn cry often sounded in his ear.

He longed to meet her again.

He fancied he could perhaps do something to comfort her. At any rate he could remove from her mind the idea that to be the boy-heir she longed to be was such a very happy position ; and perhaps a comparison of their mutual trials might bring her some consolation.

He was determined to try and meet her.

Once or twice he had been to the picture-gallery at that same hour, but had found all silence and darkness. He had caught sight of a child at the end of the long family pew in church, but had lost her in coming out.

One morning he distinctly saw a little figure in a straw hat, with long flowing hair, standing on the grass-plot by the fish-ponds, but before he could get up to it, it was gone.

It was like pursuing a phantom or a shadow, and he began at last to have an eerie feeling about the little creature, almost believing she was a creation of his own fancy and imagination.

Lord Seaforth himself, all this time, was happier than he had even been before.

He continued to lead the life that habit had made second nature to him, but now a new and absorbing interest had come into it. Still every hour brought its allotted task and its fixed occupation, but bright, fresh, and happy thoughts underlay the routine of his day.

Those long, solitary rides, looking into the concerns of the property, were no more.

His daily progress was now made with his heir by his side, and it was to him a new and most pleasurable sensation to unfold to another, and that other as nearly concerned as himself, all that had been done, and all that was doing, to enhance the value of this idolised possession.

His leisure hours, too, were filled with new and pleasant musings.

The pain of the past and its affections were beginning to be merged in the pleasure and affections of the present, with which they were all so curiously linked. It became his delight to sit and watch Godfrey as he read, and to let all the dreamy past float over him at will.

Every day convinced him more and more of the worth and stability of his nephew's character; and what details of his life he could elicit from him showed him what a careful training he had received.

He began even to be ambitious for him, and to speculate upon his future. "The boy is a born student," he would often say to himself. Sometimes, when Godfrey's interest in what he was reading had held him silent for hours, the longing to hear him speak would make Lord Seaforth desire him to read aloud what was striking him. And then the beauty of his intonation, and the additional meaning he gave to the words by his own deep interest and delight in what he read, would quite carry Lord Seaforth away.

The flaw in his happiness was the cold reserve which his nephew maintained towards him. He never talked more than was absolutely necessary, never gave him any details of his home life; and if, by any chance, Lord Seaforth in any way approached the subject of his father, Godfrey always turned the conversation immediately.

The first fortnight of his stay now drew to a close.

The Frasers returned to Eton without Godfrey coming across them, except just at dinner. Of Lady Seaforth he saw little, and knew less. She never took any notice of him when he was in her presence, nor did she ever address him directly.

A new experience was now to be his. He was to be introduced into society.

CHAPTER IV.

A SHOOTING-PARTY was imminent, and a few days before it assembled arrived on the scenes a certain Lady Alicia Fullerton, a single lady of about five and forty, without whose presence and assistance no Seaforth party could be expected to go off well.

She was a "talking woman," shrewd, sarcastic, and worldly; not very good-natured, but clever and agreeable, and a great friend of Lady Seaforth's. This lady took a violent fancy to Godfrey. She was not slow to perceive how often Lord Seaforth's eye strayed to the part of the table where his nephew was sitting, nor how immediately she was able to awaken his interest whenever she made Godfrey the subject of her conversation.

Having been a guest at Seaforth, on and off, for many years, she was well accustomed to the sight of her host sitting grave and silent at the head of his table, taking but little interest in the remarks she from time to time addressed to him. Her curiosity was roused concerning the object of so much attention, and she determined to try and see what he was like; and whether she should be able to get him to talk, which she observed the lady he had taken in to dinner had quite failed to do.

So she had herself formally introduced to Godfrey directly the men came into the drawing-room after dinner, and she kept him at her side all the evening.

He was thus, perforce, obliged to remain on in the drawing-room after his uncle had retired.

"And so, Mr. Seaforth," began Lady Alicia, "this is your first introduction to English life?"

"Yes," he answered; "I have lived abroad all my life, between Nice and Monaco."

"Is there good society at Nice, now?" was the next question.

"I beg your pardon?" he said inquiringly.

"I asked if you had good society at Nice?" she repeated.

Godfrey looked puzzled. "The society I have chiefly had all my life is my own, or my mother's. I can answer for hers being the best anywhere," he said, with a blush and a smile.

Lady Alicia looked at him with interest.

"This is your first introduction to *society*, then, as well as to English life?"

"Yes," he answered doubtfully, "I suppose so; but, really, I have heard that word 'society' used in such different senses since I have been here that I have got quite puzzled as to what it really means. Perhaps you could explain it to me."

"How shall I define it!" began Lady Alicia.

"Johnson says——" interrupted Godfrey, but he stopped confused at the smile he saw on Lady Alicia's face.

"Have you really looked it out in the dictionary?" she said, "or are you laughing at me?"

"Yes, really," answered Godfrey; "because it seems to me there is some double meaning in the word, from the way they use it here."

"Dear! dear! I think I rather envy you, Mr. Seaforth. Fancy having so much that is untrodden ground before you! And did Johnson's definition help you?"

"Not much," answered Godfrey; "at any rate, not in all the meanings it seems to have. For instance, when Lady Seaforth spoke to-night of some one being in 'society,' and the next moment of some one else as being 'not in society,' what did she mean? And when you ask me if there is 'good society' abroad, what do you mean exactly? I should be very much obliged to you if you would explain it all to me."

Lady Alicia smiled.

"Freshness and simplicity truly Arcadian," she said to herself. "I will try," she said aloud; and he cleared her throat to begin. "Society," she said, "good society——"; but she got no further.

Godfrey's earnest eyes fixed so intently upon her disconcerted her, and she could not get on with her explanation.

"These things are so difficult to explain," she said. "One understands them oneself, and a season in London would teach you better than any words of mine what ' good society ' is, and what it is to be ' in ' or ' not in ' society. I suppose, to put it in plain words, to be ' in society ' means to be in *fashionable* society. But I have never tried to put these things into words before, and I really find it very difficult. How to define good society or fashionable society accurately, I don't know! Well, now, for instance, in good society you would be sure to meet only people everybody knows, or wishes to know. They would be all worth knowing, if you understand."

"I see," put in Godfrey; "all clever, or famous, or distinguished for something. It must be very pleasant."

"Well, no; not exactly that," said Lady Alicia, moving rather restlessly in her chair. "It's no use, Mr. Seaforth; I *cannot* explain it to you. When one comes to put it into words, everything one says sounds foolish and even a little vulgar. It makes me feel rather ashamed of all our little distinctions and lines of demarcation. But still, as they exist, I ought to be able to explain them to you. You'll learn soon enough," she added, with a little laugh, "when you have mixed in society a little, and been toadied and spoilt, as all *partis* are, sooner or later. For you are a *parti*, you know, Mr. Seaforth!"

"A *parti!*" he repeated. "What is that?"

"It is a thousand pities you should ever know,"

she exclaimed impetuously, "and I really think I will not tell you. But I'll tell you what I'll do for you, if you like. I'll give you a sketch of what you may expect in the shooting party which is going to assemble here next week, and you shall tell me after it has dispersed whether my sketch has been a true one or not."

"Oh, do!" said Godfrey; "it will be very kind of you."

"We will suppose," began Lady Alicia, "that you have arrived first, and have been with your host and hostess a day or two; or, in short, that you are living in the house, as in your own case.

"Well! the day comes, and the guests arrive. You are all sitting in the drawing-room awaiting them, and tea is ready on a much larger table than usual.

"Wheels are heard on the approach, and then little more till the butler throws open the doors and announces divers names in a string. All come into the room in their dark-looking dresses, travelling costumes of all kinds. Some smart, some shabby; in ulsters, over-cloaks, waterproofs, wraps of every description.

"But one you pick out at once as the good dresser of the party.

"She is attired in a dark-green travelling dress, fitting like a glove, and a hat and feather to match. Keep your eye on her, and meanwhile, if you will look into the hall, you will pick out some enormous black boxes, with which you may at once credit her, and which will give you some idea of what you have to expect. What do those boxes not contain?

"She is the one who night by night and day by day is to regale your eyes with one *toilette* after another, each more *ravissante* than the last, till she culminates on the last evening with something which is to leave a final impression on your bewildered and admiring mind.

"Well! all these shrouded forms come into the room in a flutter of greeting, and a good deal of talk and a good deal of tea ensues.

"These ladies have mostly arrived in the carriages sent down to meet them at the station.

"Now the door is thrown open again, and enter the men, who have walked up to stretch their legs after the journey.

"Husbands mostly, young unmarried men some, elderly good shots one or two.

"More greetings, and discovery of friends, who, in the darkness of the station, had not perceived or recognised each other.

"And now the divers kinds of people begin to exhibit themselves in more distinct colours.

"There is the warm-mannered man who grasps his hostess's hand with fervour, assures her how delighted he is to find himself in her house at last; and in the same breath asks for a 'Bradshaw' to see how soon he can get away. Then there is the man who begins to fuss at once for his letters and telegrams, and gets immersed in them directly. Under this head, too, come the ladies, who do the same, and who call their husbands to their sides and enter at once into the domestic concerns suggested by their correspondence.

" Then there is the lady who admires the house, and the lady who asks for the children ; the lady who is tired after her journey and would like to go and rest before dinner.

" This leads to a general move, and the ladies all follow their hostess out of the room, leaving the men in possession. Each lady is conducted to her own apartment, told the dinner-hour, the room in which they assemble before dinner, and the shortest way to get at it.

" By-and-by the host is heard bringing up the men. He generally takes them all to the wrong rooms at first, and a good deal of tramping up and down the passages and shouting ensues.

" And now silence falls for a time over the mansion, broken by the loud booming of the dressing-gong and the ringing of all the ladies'-maids' bells (futile in many cases, as the bell seldom rings into the proper maid's room).

"In about half an hour more comes the soft rustle of silk on the staircase, as the ladies stream down, dressed for dinner. And at each corner appears a maid peeping after them.

" We will suppose the ladies now assembled in the drawing-room, and all the men.

" The lady who arrived in the dark-green travelling dress enters the room last. She is always careful to do this; to make sure her audience is assembled before she appears on the scene. Her entry is followed by a slight silence, by the admiring glances of the men, the critical glances of the ladies, and by the quick, dissatisfied glance of each husband at his own wife.

"Dinner is announced immediately, and all troop in.

"The conversation at dinner will vary so much that I can give you no idea of it. It will depend upon so many circumstances.

"But there will very probably be one lady very full of the last party she was at, which, it is evident, has been so much gayer and so much pleasanter than this is likely to be, that the heart of the hostess sinks within her, and she feels how flat this must appear in comparison.

"And here I must confess to you, Mr. Seaforth, that the rudeness of good society is beyond belief. Accustomed to it, as I am, I still observe it very much and with great regret. Rudeness, I mean, of that kind which springs from want of consideration of the feelings of others—a wilful want of tact, if I may so express it. I may call it bad manners, but it has its root in something worse.

"Well! the dinner ends, and the evening begins by the ladies chatting in the drawing-room by themselves; but, as that is a part with which you will have nothing to do, I need not enter upon it.

12

"When the men come in, different things are proposed, but, as a rule, the first evening is a little dull. Every one has been travelling, and is more or less tired, and the different elements of which the party is composed have not, as yet, assimilated comfortably together. Nobody is particularly inclined for music, or for whist, or for a round game; and it usually ends in nothing but talk, and every one is ready to go pretty early to bed.

"Next morning at breakfast one of the features will be the inevitable nursery letters that somebody or other will be sure to receive. First the child's letter: 'Nurse's duty, and the children are quite well and very happy. Master Charles is riding on a stick, and Miss Molly was so pleased to get dear mamma's letter; and they both send their love and many kisses to dear mamma, and Master Charles wishes to know when mamma is coming home again.' This letter, of course, ends with the inevitable row of kisses; sometimes expressed by * * * * *, and sometimes by o o o o o o, according to the taste of the young scribbler. Also the inevitable blot or smear, with 'Master Charles made that blot,' written underneath it.

"Then the baby letter :—

"'Dear baby is very well and his tooth is through, and as it seems so bright we are going out for a walk. Please to excuse this writing, as dear baby is in my lap, and has got hold of the pen. I tell him I am writing to dear mamma, and he looks as if he quite understood, bless his little heart!' This also is followed by blots and scribbling, though of a less advanced kind.

"After a long delay, and a great deal of hanging about, and aimless walking in and out of the drawing-room, the men at last start for their day's shooting. The ladies spend the morning in working and talking. Some write letters, one or two go out for a walk.

"A certain number go out in the middle of the day to join the men at luncheon.

"Towards dusk the men, muddy and tired, return. At five o'clock everybody reassembles in the drawing-room for tea; and shortly afterwards there is a general disappearance.

"One thing, however, I must not omit to tell you of, though you will not experience it here. It is a very prominent feature in most country houses, and to my mind an unnecessary one. I allude to the 'children's hour.' Now, I am not fond of children myself, and I consider they are most unduly brought forward in these days; so I generally gather my things together and go to my room when the hour approaches.

"But still I have experienced it, or rather endured it, often enough to be able to give you some slight account of it.

"It will be heralded by the chatter outside in the passage, and the hasty exit of those who do not wish to take part in it, of whom, as I tell you, I am one.

"The door will then be thrown open, as if a Pope

or an Emperor were about to enter, and the 'curled darlings' will appear.

"At first every sound will be lost in the burst of admiration with which their entry will be greeted; and they themselves hidden in the embraces with which they will be received.

"But when the enthusiasm has a little subsided, you will find yourself in the Land of Twaddledum at once.

"There will soon be a general barking and mewing from that corner of the room. The Noah's Ark has been got out; and now one person is lowing like a cow, another bleating like a sheep, and a third roaring like a lion; one man is crawling about on the floor, growling, with a brick in his mouth.

"I have often been distressed to see some good-natured man, or benevolent lady, making elaborate preparations for a child's amusement; for I know by experience how very brief will be the notice bestowed upon them by the volatile being for whom they are being made.

"I know how a child's 'Don't do that,' 'I don't like that,' 'I don't want to come in your lap,' has made some sensitive woman, unused to children, or some shy girl, uncomfortable for some minutes after the small and ruthless creature has stalked away, leaving the open picture-book unlooked at, and the watch waiting to be blown upon.

"I have seen a man hide under the table to play 'Peep-bo' with a very young child. He at first appears from beneath and says 'Peep.' The child is delighted; and pleased with the success of his attempt, the man retires again under the table to make the finish-off of the sentence more effective by reappearing from beneath in quite another direction. But by the time he emerges flushed and dishevelled with the 'bo!' the child is no longer there. It has got tired of the game, and has walked off to another part of the room in search of a fresh diversion.

"I have noticed, too, the anguish endured by the young mother on this and similar occasions; more especially when the entertainment has been provided by some one she herself knows is being most especially condescending, and acting in a most unusual manner; perhaps even putting a strain upon himself for her sake.

"And I have caught the whispered entreaty to the remorseless child: 'Do, darling, go and look behind the curtain. There's poor grandpapa been roaring away for such a long time!'

"The children's hour comes to an end just before the sounding of the dressing-gong; and guests and children alike disappear.

"The dinner the second night will be very likely varied by such incidents as the non-arrival of the fish from London, a calamity every one feels much less than the hostess herself; and the advent of some neighbours; when the agreeable man, and general favourite of the party, will very probably take it into his head to devote himself entirely to a shy little bride of the locality, to the great disgust of the lady who arrived in dark green.

"The evenings I need not enter upon. Their amusements depend so entirely on the fashion of the house.

" The morning of departure comes, and once more you see the wrapped-up forms with which you first made acquaintance.

" The good dresser subsides again into 'the dark-green travelling dress in which she came,' and goes off to another country house to exhibit her treasures to fresh eyes and another admiring audience. There is a general flutter of leave-taking and pretty parting speeches, and then they all drive off.

" You feel rather flat after they are all gone. The long dinner-table dwindles down to a small round one, the joint is carved on the table, you are reduced once more to a trio, and every one is well talked over.

"You now gather from the conversation how much more disagreeable and how far fuller of faults and failings every one was than you had any idea of; how very much both host and hostess have been bored; how glad they are their guests are all gone; how infamously So-and-so shot; how very nearly there was a row between So-and-so and Such-and-such; and how ill-natured this person was about the other.

" You feel rather ashamed of having liked somebody who you now hear is the 'greatest bore in the world,' and are nervously conscious of having been amused by his 'tiresome old stories' and 'more tiresome and older jokes.'

"You retire to bed with the feeling that either there are very few nice people in the world, or else that very few people have true friends, or really care very much for one another. And here I must stop, Mr. Seaforth," said Lady Alicia, rising from her seat, "for I see Lady Seaforth is taking the ladies to bed, so I will wish you good night."

CHAPTER V.

MOORE'S MELODIES.

LADY SEAFORTH had a good deal to bear during the week of the shooting party.

First there was the care with which her husband made his nephew's position in the house apparent, and the pointed way in which he introduced him to each guest.

Then she was irritated beyond measure to see the attention and interest Godfrey excited among the guests themselves.

They seemed to take their cue from their host, and one and all made much of him, and did their best to spoil him. This was especially the case with the ladies.

What was, perhaps, more provoking to her than anything was to see how well he stood the fire of spoiling to which he was exposed. He did not seem conscious of it. It all fell harmlessly upon him. Very grave, very silent, but perfectly gentlemanlike and courteous, his bearing, she could not but own, was just what it ought to be; and his quiet, distant manner, while it provoked his admirers, only rendered him more attractive.

Lord Seaforth encouraged Godfrey to go into the drawing-room in the evening after dinner instead of retiring with him. This was a great self-denial; he was surprised himself to find how much he missed his company, and often longed for the boy to follow him, in spite of his own given permission.

The second night, Mrs. Mildmay, one of the pretty young women of the party, was asked to sing.

She rose and went to the piano, followed by several of the men.

Godfrey, who was sitting talking to, or rather being talked to by Lady Alicia Fullerton, rose eagerly and went and stood by the piano.

"Are you fond of music, Mr. Seaforth?" asked Mrs. Mildmay; and he answered warmly in the affirmative.

When she had finished her song, he, contrary to his wont, entered into conversation with her of his own accord, and asked her if she knew a certain German song he mentioned. She answered that she knew it well, but that it was a little too low for her, adding, "Have you ever heard Madame Sainton sing it?"

"No," he answered. "My mother sings it, but I have never heard any one else."

"Perhaps you sing it yourself," she said; "or, if not that, something else."

"I sing a little," he answered, "but I have never sung to any one except my mother and sisters."

"Oh, do try!" she exclaimed; "I will accompany you." And turning to the rest of the company she exclaimed, "Mr. Seaforth sings."

There was a general demand from all the ladies. Godfrey fell back from the piano, and a deep blush mounted to his brow.

"I had rather not, really," he said in a low voice.

But Mrs. Mildmay would not hear of a refusal, and appealed to Lady Seaforth to assist her in persuading "her nephew" to sing.

Lady Seaforth felt herself stiffening all over. She would rather have done anything else, but, determined not to betray her feelings, she turned to Godfrey, and said formally, "Pray give us the pleasure of hearing you sing."

It was the first time she had addressed him since the evening of his arrival, and he instantly obeyed.

He returned to the piano, and asked Mrs. Mildmay if she knew any of Moore's Melodies, "for I know no modern songs," he said apologetically; "only the old ones my mother used to sing when she was young."

"Nothing in the world so pretty as Moore's Melodies," declared Mrs. Mildmay; "and I know all the accompaniments by heart. Which will you sing?"

Godfrey chose his song. She struck a few chords, and he began :

"I saw from the beach when the morning was shining,
  A barque o'er the waters move gloriously on ;
I came when the sun o'er that beach was declining,
  The barque was still there, but the waters were gone.

"And such is the fate of our youth's early promise,
  Thus fleeting the springtime of joys we have known ;
Each wave that we danced on at morning ebbs from us,
  And leaves us at eve on the bleak shore alone."

As the melting tones of the boy's clear voice sounded on the ear, a deep silence fell upon the company. Every one was more or less moved.

Each note and each word of the song was distinctly heard in every part of the room.

Lady Seaforth, sitting at some distance from the piano, with her eyes resting on the ground, was determined neither to listen nor to be moved.

But presently, all involuntarily, a choking sensation came into her throat, and as the song went on, sad yearning thoughts filled her mind.

Her imagination, she knew not wherefore, *would* carry her to a room not far distant, and her fancy *would* conjure up a silent, solitary form, sitting brooding over the fire ; a face grand and handsome indeed, but with a stern, cold expression stamped upon it, and a loveless look in its eye. A sob came before she could stop it, and the tears rushed to her eyes.

Hastily dashing them away, in her proud fear that

they might have been observed, she gave a hasty
glance round the room to assure herself no one was
looking at her.

As her eyes swept round they were suddenly
arrested by something at the door. They travelled
no further.

What she saw there caused her such astonishment that she started as if a serpent had stung her,
and nearly cried out.

There in the doorway stood her husband! Her
husband, who never for years had appeared in her
drawing-room—there he was!

He was standing, as in a dream, with his eyes
fixed on the piano, drinking in every word of the
song.

There was a far-away look in them, as if he saw
and heard something beyond. He appeared quite unconscious of his surroundings; a marvellous softness
had come over his own countenance, and she could
almost fancy she saw tears in his eyes.

The melting tones of the voice went on:

" Ne'er tell me of glories serenely adorning
   The calm close of our day, the calm eve of our night;
  Give me back, give me back the wild freshness of morning,
   For its tears and its smiles were worth evening's calm light. "

As the wild beauty of the music and the words of
the refrain rang through the room, an expression of
yearning passed over the face she was so fixedly
watching; she almost fancied he stretched out his

hands to the blank distance ; to some far recollection in the past, as if echoing the passionate cry—

"Give me back, give me back the wild freshness of morning."

Never in her life had she seen his face look like this !

Beautiful now in its tenderness, as it was always beautiful in its power.

She gazed upon it as if to photograph in her memory this new expression, which so enhanced his beauty ; but even as she gazed it faded, and when the song ceased it was gone !

*　　*　　*　　*　　*　　*

The music came to an end, and the room rang with applause. Lady Seaforth shook herself free from the feelings which had overpowered her, and hastily glancing round the room, saw, to her relief, that the doorway was empty, and that no one but herself had noticed the occurrence.

But she was determined there should be no more of this kind of thing ; and she effectually put an end to Godfrey's acquiescing in the general demand that he should sing again, by carrying everybody off to the billiard-room to play " Pool."

CHAPTER VI.

THE MEETING UNDER THE GAINSBRO'.

GODFREY meanwhile, overcome by associations with his home and his mother evoked by the song, slipped away from the applause which followed his singing, and sought the silence of the picture-gallery that he might give vent to his sad feelings undisturbed.

As he entered, he became aware that *this* time, all unwittingly, he was to succeed in his hitherto unsuccessful endeavour.

This time he was not to be disappointed.

The little ghost was laid at last!

Yes! there she was!

A small, fairy-like little creature, with a queenly little head, on which the rippling hair grew low. She held in her hand a little lamp. Her dark eyes were full of tears, and her voice sadder than on the former occasion, as she began talking to the picture at the foot of which she stood.

And a deeper pang strikes Godfrey as he hears

her say how much more unhappy she has been since
the new cousin has come; and how she knows her
mother hates the sight of her more than ever since
the wicked brother's son has been in the house.

"Could I help it? Could I help it?" she sobs as
she appeals to the picture.

Her rapt gaze is on it; she seems to look at it
through and through.

But there was something in her grief to-night
that was not soothed so soon as usual, for after gazing
fixedly for some moments she turned sobbing away.
Godfrey at this moment came forward, and very
softly called her by her name.

She started like a frightened fawn. "Who calls
me?" she said fearfully; "who said, 'Little Joan'?"

Godfrey advanced a little nearer, but as soon as
she caught sight of him she turned in terror and
tried to run away. But he followed her, and detain-
ing her gently, took her little cold hands in his, and
begged her to have no fear.

She trembled, however, so violently that he let
them go, and, stooping down, soothed her as if she
had been one of his own little sisters.

"Don't be afraid, Little Joan," he said softly.

"But who are you?" she cried, still trembling,
and standing before him, without daring to look up.
"What is your name?"

"I am your cousin, Godfrey Seaforth," he answered, "and I want to be your friend."

"Oh!" she cried, in alarm still greater, and wring-ing her hands as she spoke, "what have I said? What have you heard? What have I told you?"

"Nothing, dear child, but what is as safe with me as if I were indeed the inanimate picture to whom you thought you were speaking."

She was trembling still, trembling with astonishment and mystification, as much as with fear; but she tried no longer to run away. She timidly raised her eyes to his face.

But when she met the dark eyes that were looking down so sorrowfully and pityingly upon her, the sense of familiarity with their expression came over her with such force that she exclaimed, "Oh! but I have seen you before! You are not a stranger to me!"

Her eyes strayed on to the picture above him, and came back again to his face. "Why, you are the picture come to life!" she exclaimed. "Look! look!" she pointed to it excitedly.

Godfrey raised his eyes, and saw the likeness himself.

"Godfrey!" cried the child, turning to the picture, "do you see him? do you see him?"

The picture gazed down as usual, but the eyes had lost their power. She turned quickly back to the living eyes, and to the expression shining there, to the sorrow and the pity pervading every line of the living face, and her starved heart went out to the living, breathing Godfrey at her side.

"*Godfrey!*" she cried, holding out her hands to him in mute and pitiful entreaty for something, she knew not what, but it was something which the picture could not give her.

"Poor little thing!" was his answer.

"Say it again," cried the child; "call me 'poor little thing' again."

"Poor little thing!" repeated Godfrey, tenderly. "I am so sorry for you."

"No one was ever sorry for me before," she cried, bursting into tears, and clinging to him; "no one ever called me poor little thing before."

Godfrey's overcharged heart almost overcame him. His very soul was stirred within him by pity and sorrow, and, bending over the child, he poured forth such a flood of feeling, rendered intenser by long suppression, that

> "Her very sorrow was silent,
> And her heart stood still to hear."

She listened, spell-bound, to his passionate protest against the tyranny which held them both in thrall, against the injustice which had marred her life and his. He vowed himself from that moment to do all that in him lay to make up for the sorrow of which he was the unwilling cause, and for the added suffering his presence in the house had heaped upon her.

And, as if to soothe her sufferings by painting and unfolding his own, he told more of his own life and feelings than he had ever told to earthly ear before. He laid bare all his long-concealed griefs, to atone, if by ever so little, for the burden he had been

13

the means of laying upon her. All unheeding on what childish ears it was falling, he poured out his life-story to the wondering child.

But she understood him. The sad language of sorrow, of longing, and vain regret, was to her, alas! a familiar language, and every word that he uttered found a responsive chord in her heart. Instinctively, her eyes sought the picture, as if asking its sympathy in this new experience of her life. But again she seemed to read no response in its eyes.

For the first time in her life it struck her that their expression was cold and lifeless! It was but painted canvas after all!

Yet, in spite of this new conviction, she felt no chill of disappointment. She only turned to Godfrey, and hid her face in his hands.

Ah! little Joan. Your idol is demolished; its altars are thrown down. Never will you offer it your heart-whole worship, or kneel at its shrine, again!

"Has it been so very sad and lonely for you all this time?" he said tenderly, as he bent down over her.

"So lonely!" she answered. "No one cares for me! No one loves me! No one wants me!"

"But it will never be so any more," he whispered gently. "All that is past and over. You shall be my little sister, and I will love you and care for you as I do for my own."

Standing at the foot of the picture, with her hands

in his, and her eyes raised in wonder and gratitude to his face, she realises that what he says is true.

Lonely and uncared for no longer! Neglected and unwanted never more!

"Godfrey, Earl of Seaforth," looks down upon them as they stand, their hands clasped together, their eyes meeting in full and mutual understanding.

"*He* was my elder brother all these years," she whispers, "but you will be my elder brother now!"

Yes! the power of the picture is gone for ever; the idol of her childhood brought low; for the light of *living* sympathy has dawned upon its darkness, and a new era has begun in the life of little Joan!

CHAPTER VII.

LADY ALICIA FULLERTON REPROVED.

"WELL! Mr. Seaforth," said Lady Alicia, the even
ing of the day on which the party had dispersed
"was my sketch well drawn?"

"Indeed it was," answered Godfrey; "man
things happened almost exactly as you predicted
The breaking-up, though, has not been so literall
fulfilled as the rest, for we did not at dinner to-nigh
talk everybody over, and find fault with them all, a
you said we should."

"This is not Tittle-tattle Hall," she answered
"your uncle's presence alone is enough to put an en
to anything of that sort. But if you had been at te
this afternoon you would have heard Lady Seafort
and me going at it tooth and nail. I am glad yo
were not. But I should like to hear your Arcadia
views of society after your introduction to it."

"Oh, it interested me very much," said Godfrey
"It was like reading a new book every hour."

" But I think," he added, at first hesitatingly and then more boldly, "I think there was a great deal more in it, and everybody was much more pleasant and amiable, than I expected from your account. After what you prepared me for I quite thought I should dislike it all very much. The impression your sketch left upon my mind was that country-house society, and the world in general, was composed of very ill-natured and disagreeable people, full of faults and failings, with few redeeming points, some vain, some selfish, and all more or less insincere and un-interesting. Now, I found it quite the contrary."

"You cannot deny," said Lady Alicia, "that we had some of the people I described to you. That vain little Lady St. Aubyn, for instance, wasn't she exactly the dark-green lady I told you of?"

"Yes," answered Godfrey, " there were, of course, some of the people and characters you prepared me for. But there were many others much pleasanter and more interesting."

" I described the world as it appears to me," she answered lightly. " I have a very poor opinion of human nature. I content myself with a superficial view. Life is not long enough to dig deeper. But come! Tell me what you saw in it. I should like to hear. You are so fresh to it all that I dare say you saw a good deal that was hidden to my *blasé* vision."

Godfrey at first seemed disinclined to comply with her request; but, on her renewed entreaty, he gave some account of the impressions he had received from the divers scenes and characters which had lately passed before him. He had noticed a hundred little traits of character and pathetic incidents which had been hidden to Lady Alicia; and his deeper insight into the feelings of others, and the moving springs of their words and actions, made her feel that she was both superficial and unsympathetic, if not positively unfeeling.

The shy little bride of the neighbourhood had confided to him what her feelings had been when the "good dresser" had come into the room, and her husband's look of dissatisfaction had been cast at her; the first look of disapproval she had seen in his eyes since their lives had been linked together. The young mother had told him of the joy that nursery letter at breakfast had been to her; how she had not slept all night for thinking of her baby boy, from whom she had never before been separated.

And as he talked she felt rather ashamed.

Words she had somewhere read flashed across her:—" But insipid as Life is to one who comes close up to it, and meddles with its trivial passages, there is in all, even in its humblest forms, an undersong of poetry which makes itself heard to those who listen for it. . . . . The deep undertone of this world is sadness, a solemn bass occurring at measured intervals, and heard through all other tones. Ultimately, all the strains of this world's music resolve themselves into that tone. . . . ."

"Ah, well!" she said at last, "it is a great thing

to be so fresh and full of feeling. I don't think I
have a heart at all. I don't envy you, though, for if
you take every one's troubles on your own shoulders
like that, you will soon be weighed down, and be twice
as old as me in ten years' time. And yet," she added
rather wistfully, and half to herself, " and yet——"

But the sentence was never finished, for Lady
Seaforth, irritated by the attention her friend was
paying to Godfrey, called her away on some trifling
pretext, and he did not come across her again all the
evening.

That was their last conversation, as Lady Alicia
went away a few days after.

Godfrey's tutor arrived the following week, which
was the signal for his commencing a life of study, in
which he soon became completely absorbed. So that,
except just at dinner, he saw nothing more of society.

This tutor formed a very high opinion of Godfrey's
abilities, which, coupled with his power of concentration and wonderful industry, made him predict a
great future for him.

Lord Seaforth would talk to this man by the hour,
and listen for any length of time to the history of
Godfrey's attainments, and to these gratifying pro-
phesies. His affection for his nephew was increasing
in intensity every day.

The very sound of his footstep would make his eye
glisten, and a glow come into his face ; and he would
turn eagerly round to catch the first glimpse of him
as he came into the room.

He would fain have had him there always during his leisure hours, but he would not force it. He wanted him to come of his own free will, and left him to choose, in order to see how much time Godfrey would, of his own accord, spend with him in the library.

He craved so for the boy's love, and he could not but own to himself that he was making no progress in gaining his affection.

Do what he would there was no change in Godfrey's demeanour to him. Cold and distant he had been from the very first; cold and distant he remained.

CHAPTER VIII.

GODFREY AND LITTLE JOAN.

GODFREY himself, meanwhile, had an outlet both for his interest and his affections, and while Lord Seaforth was chafing at his absence, and wondering where he spent so much of his leisure time, he was sitting in the picture-gallery with little Joan. Quaint, fantastic conversations they held at the foot of the picture; curious comparisons of each other's lives and circumstanceses. At any rate, with hands clasped together, they agreed that *they* bore each other no grudge; enemies they ought to be, dear friends they were.

"Could *we* help it?" laughing Joan would say, and the change in the little pronoun took away all the sting of the cry.

Happy little Joan we may call her now, for passionate resentment has fled away, rebellion is felt no longer.

A deep well of love and gratitude has risen in her

heart, and she is rejoicing in the power of a new affection, and the dawn of a brighter life.

He has averted the coldness that was creeping over her, and his love has smoothed all the hard lines of her life away.

"Oh, Godfrey," she would say sometimes, " I should have been so wicked if it had not been for you ! "

" And I," he would answer, " should be so lonely but for you ! "

Little Joan's heart responded so quickly to any longing after affection. She would have done anything in the world to save him from a moment's pain.

It was such a new feeling to her to find herself necessary to some one, and a part of anybody's happiness.

It was not always in the picture-gallery that they met. They had trysting-places out of doors, or he would come upon her suddenly sometimes as he walked about with his book.

*   *   *   *   *   *

Finding her one day on the grass-plot by the fish-ponds, with some daisies in her hand, happy memories of his own little sisters came over him, and, sitting down by her side, he told her stories of their merry games, and twined daisies in her hat, while he talked of Hester, and Olive, and Venetia.

And as he told her of them his brow grew sad, and he sighed as he wondered when he should see them all again.

Little Joan, who watched every change in his face, who was learning to read his every expression, looked wistfully at him, and put her little hand in his.

Seeing her face overshadowed by the shadow passing over his, he smiled, and to divert her thoughts, began telling her of that sunny morning when he had found little Venetia so puzzled with the perversity of her daisies, who would not give her the answer she desired.

And he made Joan laugh, as he repeated his little sister's plaintive words: "I think the daisies *must* have made a mistake, Godfrey, for I know I *do* love you, and three times they have told me that I don't. *Do* daisies make mistakes, I wonder?"

"What do *you* think?" he said, smiling down upon the child. "Do you think daisies make mistakes, little Joan?"

"The Seaforth daisies never do," she answered, softly; "for whenever I ask them, 'Does Joan love Godfrey?' they always give me the right answer."

"What do they say?" asked Godfrey. "Je t'aime un peu?"

"No," said the child; "they would not be true daisies if they did."

"What do they say?" again questioned Godfrey.

"Passionnément," she answered in a low voice. "And that's true," she added, looking up at him with all her gratitude and adoring affection in her dark eyes.

"As much as that, little Joan?" he said rather

sadly. " I don't think I deserve as much as that ! "

"Now, I am going to ask them, ' How much does Godfrey love me ? ' " she said, picking a daisy and beginning to pull off the petals.

" M'aimes-tu ?

" Un peu ?

" Beaucoup ?

" Passionnément ?

" Point du tout ? "

It came to " un peu."

" Try again," said Godfrey.

" You do it," she said, handing him another.　He took it, and she watched him eagerly as he pulled off the first one, saying, as he did so,

> " Godfrey Seaforth, tell me true,
>   Do you love Joan ?　Does she love you ? "

It came again to " un peu."

Joan looked disappointed and threw the daisy away.

"A daisy's mistake, little Joan," he said soothingly, noticing the shadow that passed over her face. " The Seaforth daisies are no more to be trusted, you see, than those that grow in the orange grove at home."　He said the last words softly, and his eyes wandered to the blue sky above.　An overpowering recollection of his home and his little sisters had again come over him, and his thoughts had flown to the sunny vineyards and oliveyards and beloved ones far away.

"Are you longing to be there?" Joan said wistfully.

The tone of her voice roused him from his dreams and recalled him to himself. He looked at her, and reading the plaintive feeling expressed in her mournful eyes, overcome by the recollection of her forlorn position, he had not the heart to tell her the thoughts of which his mind was full.

And the innate chivalry of his nature did really, for the moment, prevent his wishing to leave her to the loneliness of her life.

"If I could take you with me, little Joan, I do not care how soon I go."

"But as you can't?" she said, leaning forward, and looking as if she would read his very thoughts.

"As I can't," he said quietly, "we will both stay here."

She drew a long breath, and there was silence on the grass-plot for some time.

"I couldn't live without you, Godfrey," she cried suddenly. "I think I should die."

"Don't," he said hastily, "don't talk like that, little Joan."

There were times when he could not bear it. The sense of his own share in her misfortunes at such moments overpowered him.

* * * * * *

Their conversations were not always as sad as this. Sometimes he would paint bright pictures of happy days to come, when she should learn to know and love her "Aunt Hester," as he taught her to call her; and should have bright companions in her merry little cousins.

How, or when, or where, he had no notion; but he liked to carry little Joan's thoughts away into visions of hope and dreams of future joy.

At other times he would talk of his own future, and of all he wished and hoped to be; all he felt capable of becoming; all he meant some day to accomplish.

He was getting immersed in the pleasures of study, and the faint movements of personal ambition were beginning to stir within him.

*   *   *   *   *   *

All this, and more, was poured into the ear of little Joan day after day, as the autumn glided away. They would sit for hours talking, he charmed out of his reserve by her sympathy, she drinking in his words with eyes sparkling with pride and joy.

Happy, happy hours! Golden days of light and love; subjects for future harvests of happy memories, which both will treasure in the time to come!

But at present there is a difference. The boy, intent on pity and kindness, has no other thought as yet; but the girl, whose long pent-up stores of affection have found a vent at last, has already got a spark of the divine fire in her breast.

Growing with her growth, and strengthening with her strength, daily and hourly it is becoming a part of her very being.

She is only a child as yet, loving with the tender trust and boundless confidence which belongs to a child's affection.

But her nature is deep, and passionate, and un-changing.

By-and-by, with her dawning womanhood, the love and trust of childhood will be merged in a deeper feeling.

Joined together, they will fan that spark into a flame which neither time, nor slander, nor separation shall lessen, nor death itself be able to extinguish!

CHAPTER IX.

LADY SEAFORTH'S PROCEEDINGS.

ALL this time Lady Seaforth's hatred of Godfrey had been deepening day by day. She had watched her husband closely ever since that night of the song, and, to her mind, he was a changed man. She saw how absorbed he was in his nephew, how his eyes were always straying to Godfrey's face, how eagerly he listened to every word that fell from the boy's lips; and how his attention wandered at once from what any one else was saying directly that quiet, earnest voice made itself heard.

How she hated that voice! She observed, too, the pride Lord Seaforth took in him: the look of gratification and delight that came into his face whenever what Godfrey was saying attracted attention, and the quick glance he shot round the table to enjoy the effect produced.

There was no mistaking, and he seemed to her to take no pains to disguise, his interest and affection.

She became conscious that the deep feelings, whose existence she had always suspected, were roused at last.

This boy, then, possessed the power for which she had always in vain striven. He held the reins she had never for a moment contrived to grasp.

She felt now as if she would rather think her husband *had* no feelings, than know that it was she who had not the power of drawing them out; than see another succeed so fully where she had so completely failed.

She began to long to lower Godfrey in her husband's eyes. She would have given anything to catch him tripping, or to see him act in such a manner that his uncle might be disenchanted.

It was something of the same feeling that Godfrey's father had had towards him, and, like him, she never could succeed in dragging Godfrey down.

She never could catch hold of anything he did or said out of which she could make any capital, or turn to account against him.

Her hatred of him was growing so strong that she was constantly laying traps for him; but it was no use. He never fell into them.

Moreover, she had now discovered that he was the son of her husband's early love; and with that knowledge her feelings towards him had become more bitter than ever.

With the quickness of a jealous woman, she had, from the moment she had watched his face during

Godfrey's singing, felt sure there was some memory in the past, and that Godfrey was somehow or other connected with it. She determined to find it out.

She had abandoned all hope of gaining her husband's affections, and so she had no longer that feeling she had formerly had towards him, which had prevented her ever doing anything she thought he would not like, or trying to make discoveries on subjects he chose to conceal from her. "Why should she care to please him?" she asked herself bitterly. "What did she get by it? Nothing. She had borne a great deal from him. What good did she get by her endurance? None!"

So she gave free vent to her curiosity, and set to work to discover anything she could which would throw any light on his early life. It was not very difficult. A few words with one of the old women in the village, and all was clear to her. She would probably have heard the story long before, but she was considered a "very haughty lady" by the people about, and they were afraid of her, and ill at ease in her presence. Moreover, she seldom went into their cottages.

On this occasion, having come with a fixed purpose, she condescended to assume a more easy and talkative manner than usual, and the tongue of the garrulous old lady she was visiting was unlocked at once.

But with the return of her boys for the Christmas holidays other thoughts began to fill her mind. Their opening lives, and the fulfilment of her plans for them, brought now so near by Colin's Eton life being over, occupied her mind, and Godfrey came before her more in the light of a possible stumbling-block in their paths than in the painful one of which we have been speaking. She made up her mind, however, that he was not likely to be in their way. Neither the seat for the county nor the family living would be required for him.

She felt quite sure that Lord Seaforth was not going to put his nephew into Parliament. None of the Seaforths had ever been in the House of Commons. They were a race of landlords and agriculturists, not politicians, and from what she saw of the training her husband was giving his nephew she felt sure he intended him to follow in their lead.

Did she not day after day meet them inspecting and overlooking every part of the estate? And she felt sure that deep drainage and the rotation of crops formed the staple interest of their conversation.

No. She had no fear about that. She felt, however, that it would be well to mention her plans to her husband soon, and also to sound her boys, so as to be quite sure of their minds being made up before she made her requests on their behalf.

CHAPTER X.

THE DEEP SEAT IN THE WEST WINDOW.

A FEW days after Colin and Andrew arrived, therefore, she told them at breakfast that she wished to have a serious conversation with them both on the subject of their future, and desired them to come in early in the afternoon, and to meet her in the west drawing-room, where she would be waiting for them.

Four o'clock found her sitting there by the fire, rehearsing in her own mind, as she gazed thoughtfully at the blazing logs, all that she was going to say to her sons in the coming interview.

Now it so happened that that afternoon Godfrey had been to the picture-gallery to speak to little Joan, but had not found her there. After waiting a few minutes, he gave her up, and came downstairs with the intention of going into the library. But, as he passed the west drawing-room, he was attracted by the beauty of the sunset, which caught his eye through the open door. He came in, and walking straight across the room, sat himself down in the deep seat of the middle window, to watch it.

Sunsets always carried him back to his home and the Mediterranean, and he remained there, lost in thought, and quite unaware that the room was occupied.

Lady Seaforth, gazing into the fire, also lost in thought, had not observed his entrance; so there the two sat, each unconscious of the other's presence.

Andrew was the first of the boys to make his appearance. He came in by another door.

"Where is Colin?" said his mother.

"He's coming," answered Andrew; "but he's not quite finished a match he is having with the marker."

Lady Seaforth gave a movement of impatience.

"I wish he would take things a little more seriously," she said. "I told him I wanted to talk to him on a subject of great importance, and he can stay playing at tennis instead of coming to hear what I have to say."

Andrew looked uneasy. "It's about our prospects, mother, I suppose?" he said anxiously.

"Yes," she answered, "it is; and you, Andrew, I know, have the sense to see what an important matter it is, and can understand how anxious I am to get things settled while there is still time."

"While there is still time?" he repeated.

"Yes," she said. "I mean while the things I have in view for you are still unappropriated."

"You mean," said Andrew quickly, "that you are afraid they may be wanted for other people."

"Exactly," said Lady Seaforth. "It is everything to be first in the field. You still wish to go into the Church, do you not?"

"To be sure I do," answered Andrew. "I am to be curate to Uncle William Cartwright first, and then rector of Seaforth."

"We must not be too sure," she said.

"Why not?" he exclaimed. "Godfrey Seaforth can't interfere with me. *He* can't want the family living."

"Well, no," she answered. "Of course he can't want it for himself; but how do we know what friends he may have, or what friends he may make, to whom he may ask Lord Seaforth to give it? He is going to college; he will find plenty there who may try to get him to promise it. It is worth 1200*l.* a year."

"If it were worth 600*l.*," said Andrew vehemently, "I would rather have it than any living in the world."

"You don't know much about the value of money," she said, "or you would not talk so lightly of it. But why do you say this?"

"Because I love the place and all the people," he answered. "I should like to spend my life among them and in their service. I would rather live at Seaforth in a cottage than at any other place in a palace! It's come over me lately, too, that after all

Colin and I have no real business here, and that we shall be kicked out some day. So that if I can look forward to being rector of Seaforth it won't seem so hard. I can still hope to live and die in the dear old place."

"Are you so *very* devoted to Seaforth?" she said.

"Why, of course I am, mother; what other home have I ever had?"

"What do you remember before you came here?" she asked.

"Oh! kicking about in little houses in London, in dull, poky streets," he answered. "I don't feel as if I had had a home at all till we came to Seaforth."

"Don't you remember the Glen at *all?*" she asked, in surprise; "nor the little burn where you and Colin, two babies, used to paddle about with your bare feet?"

"No," he answered. "I don't remember it, really. I feel as if I did, sometimes, because Colin has always talked about it so much, but I know I don't myself."

"How strange it seems!" she said, half to herself. "I had no idea all recollection of Scotland had so entirely disappeared. It is not the case with Colin, I am sure."

"Oh no!" laughed Andrew; "Colin is an out-and-out Highlander. His great hope and day-dream is to be rich enough some day to go back to the Glen, and live there. Then, too, he remembers further back than I do. He's always talking about it, and he remembers the people about, and how devoted they were to us."

Colin's entrance here interrupted the conversation, and, catching the last words, he began to whistle, first, "Should auld acquaintance be forgot?" and finished up with, "Far away in bonnie Scotland."

A few minutes before Lady Seaforth would have been provoked at what she would have considered his want of consideration of the importance of the matter under discussion. But the realisation of the total disappearance of her younger son's nationality had given her rather a shock, and so Colin's burst of Highland enthusiasm did not displease her.

"Well! now that you *have* come, Colin," she said, "be steady, and listen to what I have to say."

As she spoke, the door opened a little way, and little Joan peeped in. She looked straight at the west window, where Godfrey was concealed, and was going to spring towards him when she suddenly perceived the other occupants of the room. In an instant she was gone, before any one but Colin noticed her, and he was too much interested in what his mother was saying to make any remark on the little girl's unwonted appearance in the drawing-room.

Lady Seaforth then recapitulated what she had said to Andrew, and asked Colin whether he had also quite made up his mind as to his future, and whether the prospects held out to him were really what he desired. "For there must be no changing," she said, "after I have once spoken to Lord Seaforth."

Colin expressed himself perfectly satisfied. He had always wished, he said, to go into Parliament, and he wished it still.

"Very well," said Lady Seaforth, well pleased with the result of the interview; "then I think I clearly understand that your minds are made up, and I shall speak to Lord Seaforth at once. It would have been a great disappointment to me if either of you had taken any other idea into your heads, and I am delighted to think that your wishes and mine should coincide so exactly."

There was a lull in the conversation after this, and in the silence, the sound as of some one moving in the window was distinctly heard.

All three looked round in that direction.

There was a moment's pause, and then, to their undisguised dismay and astonishment, Godfrey suddenly emerged out of the deep recess, and, without looking to the right or to the left, walked out of the room.

CHAPTER XI.

THE CLASHING OF INTERESTS.

LADY SEAFORTH started to her feet and threw up her hands in dismay. She was speechless, but the boys were loud in their exclamations of horror and astonishment. "Well!" exclaimed Colin. "I never knew anything so shabby in my life! I would not have believed it of Godfrey Seaforth! I can hardly believe it now!"

"Sneak!" cried Andrew; "eavesdropper!"

"Can he have been there the whole time!" exclaimed Lady Seaforth, when she at last found her voice. "What *is* to be done?"

"He must have been," said Andrew. "He did not come in since I have been here, that I'll declare. He must have heard every word we said."

Lady Seaforth began walking up and down the room in an agitated manner, going over in her own mind every word of the recent conversation. "Will he repeat it? Will he repeat it?" was the question that kept forcing itself upon her. Judging him from her own standard, measuring his feelings towards her by her feelings towards him, imputing to him the motives by which, in such a case, she would herself have been actuated, she most undoubtedly would! And, in great alarm, she quickly left the room and took her way to her husband's private apartments.

The door of the library was partly open. Voices were heard from within, and she stood still and listened.

"And you really would like to go into Parliament?" were the words which fell upon her ear. "I am willing—indeed, I am anxious—that you should. I was not in the House of Commons myself, nor were my father and grandfather. But, then, our tastes did not lie that way. With you the case is different. Have you ever tried your hand at speaking? I suppose not."

"Only by myself," came in quiet tones, the voice she hated so bitterly. "I have sometimes, when alone on the hills at home, made imaginary speeches on different subjects."

"You shall try at a tenants' dinner some day. There will be one before you go. Let me see, how old are you?"

"I shall be eighteen on January the 26th."

"Well, then, you will be twenty-two just at the time of the next general election, and that would be the time, too, when you are leaving Oxford. "So it all fits in admirably. You are, of course, the proper person to represent the county, and—— "

But Lady Seaforth waited to hear no more. She rushed back to her sons in a tumult of indignation.

"He has been listening the whole time," she exclaimed; "he has heard every word we said, and then rushed off to his uncle to foil all our plans."

She then repeated what she heard, adding comments of her own.

The boys were at first dumb with dismay and astonishment.

"Never mind, mother," said Colin at last, soothingly; "there are plenty of other seats to be had. And, to tell you the truth, I would far rather represent my own county, or some Scotch borough. It is much more natural I should."

"Your own county! a Scotch borough!" she exclaimed bitterly. "You talk as if you had a large fortune at your command. Who is to pay for your election? When will you understand that you and Andrew are paupers, absolute paupers?"

"Well! I declare, mother," exclaimed Colin, rather warmly, "this is the first time you have ever enlightened us! I always thought——"

"Thought what?" she said, with increasing bitterness. "That Lord Seaforth was going to leave you each a large fortune, I suppose?"

"Well! don't let us quarrel over it, mother," said Colin, lightly.

His own temper was quite imperturbable, and he always changed the subject when his mother lost hers.

"And so you actually spotted the eavesdropper in the room?" he went on. "How *did* he look when he saw you?"

"He didn't see me. No one saw me," said Lady Seaforth, without perceiving the admission she was making. "I didn't go in when I found he was there."

"Then how do you know what he said?" inquired Colin, innocently.

"I listened at the——," began Lady Seaforth, but suddenly stopped herself; "I mean the door was a little open, and I couldn't help hearing what was being said."

"I am sorry for that," said Colin, quietly.

"Why?" she said sharply.

"Because," he answered gravely, "we can't make out a case against him for listening if we came by our proofs the same way."

The implied reproof stung Lady Seaforth.

She answered at random. "We shan't want proofs, as you call it. The proofs of his meanness will be that, when I ask Lord Seaforth for the seat and the living, he will tell me he has promised both."

"But why the living?" broke from Andrew.

"I don't know," she answered desperately. "I feel as if it would slip from us too. Everything is against us. Our luck is quite gone."

Colin here slipped away, annoyed at the turn the conversation was taking; but Andrew came nearer, and sat down by his mother on the sofa.

"If you can convince Lord Seaforth," he said, "that his nephew is a sneak—which he *is*, which he must be—he will not perhaps be so ready to do what he asks him."

Lady Seaforth looked at her son, and felt how little he understood the matter, and how impossible it was to explain it to him.

"I hate him, Andrew!" she cried, her self-control leaving her entirely.

"I know you do, mother," he answered; "and, as far as I can see, he deserves it."

Now this, though Andrew did not know it, was the very balm his mother needed. It was, as we know, one of her sorest grievances that she could never catch Godfrey tripping, nor drag him down.

But now she really had a handle against him, and if she only used it properly she might succeed in lowering him in her husband's eyes. At any rate, he was in her power.

This thought restored to her her equanimity, and raised her drooping spirits once more.

"It's an ill wind that blows no one any good," she said to herself, as she rose from the sofa, and followed by Andrew, went into her own boudoir to tea.

CHAPTER XII.

A RIDDLE AND ITS ANSWER.

THIS was only the beginning; for when Lady Seaforth formally announced to her husband that she was sending her younger son to the University, with a view to Holy Orders, and asked him to put his name down for the next presentation to the living, he informed her that he had, that very day, by his nephew's desire, promised it to the tutor now resident in the house.

From that day she lost no opportunity of trying to make Godfrey feel that he was in her power. There was not an innuendo, not an allusion of any kind, that she did not turn to account at dinner before every one. She would make meaning remarks, and then try to abash him by looking fixedly at him.

But, strange to say, Godfrey neither blushed, nor avoided her eye, nor did any of those things a guilty person is supposed to do.

"Hardened effrontery," Lady Seaforth called it; but her eldest son had a different opinion.

It was a most disagreeable atmosphere to live in, and Colin wanted his mother to put an end to it by taxing Godfrey with his conduct to his face, and giving him a chance of speaking in his own defence.

But this Lady Seaforth would not do at present. She enjoyed too much the feeling that she had at last caught her enemy in a trap, and she wanted to harass him as long as possible before dealing him his death-blow.

What this death-blow was to be she had not as yet made up her mind.

There was a certain awkwardness in making her husband acquainted with the facts of the case and the details of the conversation. She did not know how much Godfrey might have repeated and how much he might have left unsaid; and she did not wish Lord Seaforth to know more about it than could possibly be helped.

She wanted very much to lower Godfrey in his uncle's eyes, but then it was difficult to do it without revealing much concerning herself and her sons which she would rather keep concealed.

For her pride with respect to her boys had risen very much since she had found how hopeless it was to expect any help for them in their future from Lord Seaforth.

In the course of her interview with her husband she had gathered very clearly that, even had the things she wanted for her sons not been already appropriated, he would not have given them to Colin and Andrew.

She saw more clearly than ever his consistent determination to have nothing personally to do with them, and to ignore altogether his connection with them.

So she was determined he should not see how very much she had counted upon him in her plans for their provision in life.

He should not, at any rate, have a chance of exulting over her discomfiture. All this necessitated a very careful consideration of her dealings with Godfrey, and she determined to do nothing in a hurry.

Her feelings of disgust may, therefore, be very easily imagined when one day, as she was sitting in her boudoir, revolving the crisis in her mind, and wondering how her husband could with safety be brought into it, Colin suddenly burst in, exclaiming, "Acquitted! acquitted! Honourably acquitted!"

"What do you mean?" she said hastily, "and who are you talking about?"

"Who?" he repeated. "Why, Godfrey Seaforth, of course. Mother! after all, he never heard a single word we said!"

"Nonsense!" she said quickly. "How do you know? How *can* you know?"

"From the best possible authority," he answered. "He has just told me so himself. I have been having a long conversation with him. I——"

15

"I don't believe a word of his story," she interrupted.

"But you haven't heard it yet!" exclaimed Colin.

"Well! what is it?" she said unwillingly; "be quick and tell it. Don't keep me on tenter-hooks like this."

Colin went on to say that Godfrey not only utterly denied having heard a word of the conversation, but that he could hardly get him to believe that any one had been in the room at all. He seemed quite puzzled at the idea, having imagined the room to be perfectly empty. It had been empty, he declared, when he came in and when he went out; and there had not been a sound in the room during the whole time he had been there.

Lady Seaforth interrupted the narrative several times with such exclamations as, "Nonsense! And you believe this!" etc.; but Colin went quietly on. He seemed determined to tell the story his own way. He was evidently working up to some point, which he kept in the background, for there was a twinkle in his eye the whole time, more particularly when his mother broke in with her impatient exclamations. "The proof," he said, "is that he cannot tell me one word we said."

"Really, Colin," she said at last, "you are very simple for your age. How can you submit to have dust thrown in your eyes in this way! How can you believe such nonsense, or call such a cock-and-bull story a proof!"

"I am expounding a riddle, mother dear," answered Colin. "You are a clever woman, and must guess the answer. The answer to a riddle, you know, always seems impossible till you know it. Now here it is:

"He *was* in the room, *we* were in the room. We talked, and yet he never heard a word of our conversation! *Je vous le donne en cinq, je vous le donne en dix.* Do you give it up? Well, then, here is the answer. *He was asleep the whole time!* There, now, mother, what do you think of that?"

"I don't believe a word of it," she said, walking up and down the room with ill-concealed fury. "I wish you hadn't interfered. Why were you so officious?"

"Mother," he said gravely, "this condemning a man unheard was more than I could stand. It went against me; I couldn't bear it any longer. The evidence of his having listened was too strong for me to dispute it, but I did always doubt his having made use of his information. I felt sure it was a mere coincidence. I couldn't believe Godfrey Seaforth capable of such meanness. You have only to look at his face."

"You are like a romantic school-girl!" she exclaimed contemptuously. "What is there in his face to make such a fuss about? I don't believe in him one bit, and I tell you he has trumped up this story for fear of getting into trouble with his uncle."

"Mother dear!" said Colin, reproachfully. He

was horrified to see how his mother's hatred of Godfrey was triumphing over truth, justice, and every
other noble feeling. He could hardly believe his
ears.

But Lady Seaforth had quite passed the bounds of
reason now.

"Who is to say whether he was asleep or not?"
she exclaimed. "We have only his own word to go
upon, and that is not worth much. If you could say
you saw him asleep yourself, I would believe his
story; but you can't. No; nor any one else. There
is no one to corroborate his assertion; no witness to
the truth of his tale. And I tell you I don't believe
it, and I won't!"

Colin looked disconcerted for a moment, and then
a sudden thought seemed to strike him.

"Stop a minute, mother," he said eagerly. "You
say you will believe his assertion of being asleep if I
can find a witness?"

"Certainly," she answered, a smile of triumph
coming into her face. "I will believe it then, but
not till then."

"Very well," said Colin; "I also will consent to
abide by the testimony of a witness. Mind, mother,
I hold you to your word. Now I want your leave to
summon a witness at once, and your promise that my
witness, whoever it may be, shall be allowed instantly
to appear in this very room."

"Certainly," said Lady Seaforth again. "I grant

both requests. So summon your witness, O learned judge, and arbitrator in other people's matters!"

"Then," said Colin, whose spirit was now thoroughly roused, "then, in the name of truth and justice, I summon my sister Joan!"

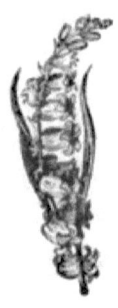

CHAPTER XIII.

THE VULNERABLE PART.

The entrance of Andrew here interrupted the conversation, and gave Lady Seaforth time to recover from the astonishment into which her son's unexpected words had thrown her. By her desire, Colin made his brother acquainted with the facts of the case; and when he had finished, she turned to him, and said, "And now, Colin, explain yourself. What do you mean? Why do you bring the child's name into this affair? What on earth can she have to do with it?"

"This," answered Colin. "You may not have observed it, as you were speaking at the time, but that afternoon she came into the west drawing-room for a moment, looked straight at the window where Godfrey was sitting, and then ran away. Now, both you and I, mother, will consent to abide by the testimony of a little child."

He laid his hand on the bell as he spoke.

Lady Seaforth's face assumed a most disagreeable expression.

She almost put out her hand as if to prevent her son carrying out his intention, but she checked herself, and sat down upon the sofa, pale and agitated.

She shrank from the thought of the coming interview. She would have given anything to cancel her promise, and to forbid the appearing of her neglected and unloved child. But she did not dare.

Her son's sudden assumption of authority and determination surprised and overawed her; and, besides, if she withdrew from her word, it would look as if she were afraid of being defeated.

When the servant appeared she had partially recovered, and herself sent the message up to the schoolroom.

The trembling form of little Joan presently appeared in the doorway.

Colin was advancing towards her, but Lady Seaforth imperiously called him back.

"Leave it to me," she said.

"Come right in," she continued to the child. "Answer the questions I am going to ask you, and then you can go upstairs again."

"Do you remember, about a fortnight ago, coming into the west drawing-room, at about half-past four in the afternoon, when it was getting dusk?"

Little Joan thought for a moment, and then answered in the affirmative.

"Who did you see in the room ?"

The child thought again, and then, indicating her half-brothers, she said,—

"They were there, and you, mamma."

"Anybody else ?"

"No, nobody else."

A faint smile of triumph overspread Lady Seaforth's face, and Colin breathed quickly.

"You are sure," resumed Lady Seaforth, "that there was no one else in any part of the room ?"

"No, — oh, except Godfrey. He was in the window seat."

"Oh ! he was in the window seat ! You are quite sure of that ?"

"Yes ! quite sure."

"What was he doing ?"

"Nothing. He was sitting there ; or at least——"

"At least what ?"

"I mean he was half sitting, half leaning, with his head—— "

"With his head bent forward," interrupted Lady Seaforth eagerly, "as if he was listening to something ?"

"No," answered Joan, "with his head against the window. He was fast asleep."

"That will do," said Lady Seaforth ; "you may go."

Colin went away also.

He had no wish to exult over his mother's defeat.

Justice was done, and with that he was satisfied.

Lady Seaforth gave way to a burst of agitation directly the door was closed.

"He foils me everywhere," she cried, as she threw herself down upon the sofa. "He thwarts me every way, baulks me of my revenge, and lowers me in the eyes of every one. What am I to do!"

In her despair, she felt Godfrey to be like the man in the ancient fable, who, dipped by his mother in the river, was rendered invulnerable in every part.

Worse! That man, at least, was vulnerable in the heel by which his mother held him; but this boy! he had no weak point, no vulnerable part; she could neither wound his feelings nor catch him tripping.

Unscathed he had come out of the trial, his honour unsullied, his name unblackened still.

"If only that child had not come into the room at that particular moment," she went on passionately, "all might still have been well. Why—oh, why should such a thing have happened! Why, except that she should be my bane, as she has been from the moment of her birth! What spirit of evil omen could have brought her there just then?"

She was moaning all this to herself, but Andrew caught the last words, and, anxious to soothe his mother, and in the hope of distracting her a little, he answered—

"She came to look for Godfrey Seaforth, I dare say. They are great friends."

"*What!*" she cried, turning upon him so sharply that he was quite startled.

Andrew repeated what he had said, and took the opportunity of saying he thought it was rather hard that he and Colin should never have been allowed to see anything of their little sister, nor to have any communication with her; and that this comparative stranger should make her his companion, and be so much with her.

"But who allows it!" exclaimed Lady Seaforth. "What do you mean?"

"I'm sure I don't know," answered Andrew; "but they are a great deal together upstairs."

"Upstairs!" said his mother; "in the school-room! What can the governess be thinking of!"

"No!" answered Andrew, "I don't mean in the schoolroom, but I have seen them once or twice sitting in the picture-gallery since I have been home these holidays. She seems quite at home with *him*, but Colin and I never can get her to speak, even when we do see her. She seems too shy and frightened to answer."

Lady Seaforth paid no attention to what her son was saying. She made some hasty excuse and left the room.

She went straight up to the picture-gallery, pushed open the heavy oak door, and looked in.

By the light of the silver lamp Godfrey and little Joan were to be seen in deep and earnest conversation.

The child, with her hair thrown back from her flushed face, was looking up at him, evidently giving him an account of the recent interview.

He was listening with deep interest, and when the tale was finished, he bent down, and took her hands in his, saying, "Thank you, little Joan. You have, all unknowingly, cleared me from a most unpleasant suspicion."

* * * * * *

On the dark face watching, was painted many and various expressions, and she moved away stealthily, muttering to herself, "At last! at last!"

Down the passage to her own apartment she went, still muttering the same words over and over again.

Yes, at last! At last she has discovered his vulnerable part! At last she has found the weak spot in his armour! And at last she can take her revenge!

She has at last a weapon in her own hands, which she can wield as she pleases, and with which she has full power.

"But not to-night," she said to herself wearily, as she gained the door of her own bedroom. "I am too worn and weary with the strain and excitement of the day. Wait till to-morrow!"

CHAPTER XIV.

THE SPEECH IN THE BANQUETING-HALL.

WHAT will to-morrow be?

Who can tell?

The "to-morrow," for which Lady Seaforth waited to execute her scheme of revenge, was Godfrey's birthday.

The day dawned brightly, and she was roused at an early hour by the ringing of the joy-bells, and the boom of the guns, which had never been fired since the day she had arrived at Seaforth a bride.

She soon discovered that the day was not to pass unobserved.

A tenants' dinner was to take place in the banqueting-hall, in honour of the occasion, and both Lord Seaforth and his nephew were to be present at it.

Godfrey all day had a sense, whenever he was in his aunt's presence, of there being thunder in the air.

There was something in her manner that made

him feel a storm was impending; but his mind was taken up with many matters, and more especially with thinking over the speech he was to make to the farmers; so he did not trouble himself much about her.

The dinner was to take place at four o'clock, and his speech was to follow his uncle's at the close of the repast.

In the passage which overlooked from a height the great hall where the tenants' dinner was to take place, there was a wide slit in the thick wall, which formed a kind of peep-hole, from which all that was going on below could be seen and heard.

Originally designed for purposes of safety in troublous times, it had in more modern days been used for overlooking balls or banquets; and the guests would often be conveyed up there to look down upon the gay and festive scene below, which made such a pretty *coup d'œil.* At this niche it was settled by Joan and Godfrey that she was to establish herself at the hour when the speeches were to begin, and here she would see without being seen, and hear all that was said below.

She was to put her little white handkerchief up for a minute as a signal, so that he should know when she had arrived.

Matters being thus arranged between them, he came to wish her good-bye before descending to the dinner, and told her he would come straight to the picture-gallery from the banqueting-hall to meet her directly the speeches were over and he could get away.

"You will see from the niche," he said, as he left her, "when I leave the hall, and then we shall arrive at the picture-gallery at the same time."

At four o'clock precisely Godfrey and his uncle entered the hall and took their seats at the head of the table.

The dinner was long, and would have been tedious had Godfrey not been interested by the novelty of the proceedings.

It was over at last, and the tables cleared.

Lord Seaforth then rose and said a few words, which were warmly received; and then Godfrey's turn came. He rose directly, but ere he opened his lips, he cast one upward glance at the niche far above him. Yes. The little white handkerchief was visible; the signal was there. Little Joan had arrived.

Secure of at least one sympathetic listener, Godfrey felt more confidence, and he began.

All present turned towards him with interest, and the deepest silence reigned in the hall, as his clear, quiet voice made itself heard.

The beauty of his intonation, the force of the words he chose, the fervid language in which he clothed the thoughts of his mind, fascinated his audience at once, and, as he warmed with his subject, completely carried them away. Every one, his uncle included, was taken by surprise, and all listened eagerly.

He spoke with that utter freedom from self-con-
sciousness which is such a charm.

His earnest manner, its intensity and its quiet,
the entire absence of any tricks of delivery, or of any
affectation in his choice and arrangement of words,
all added to the effect of his speech.

The speech itself, too, was of that kind which, so
to speak, seems only to scratch the surface of the
speaker's knowledge.

He seemed to have so much beneath it, to hold so
much in check; never in any degree to exhaust his
subject. The impression he left on the minds of his
hearers was more how much he *could* say than how
much he was saying.

His was the eloquence that comes from the heart's
fire acting on a cultured mind, and coloured by deep
feeling and a brilliant imagination.

There was in it the living germ of oratory, and it
brought him to a close which, all unrealised by himself, was a peroration of a very rare kind.

He sat down when he had finished, as quietly as if
he had been speaking to himself; as if, having said
what he had to say, he considered that that was all
that was expected of him; and not as if he thought
he had done anything out of the common way.

And when cheer upon cheer rose, and hands were
eagerly held out in congratulation, a flush of surprise
mounted to his brow, succeeded by an emotion of shyness at finding himself suddenly the object of so much
attention and adulation.

For one and all were delighted, and "Bravo! Mr. Seaforth!" "Three cheers for Mr. Seaforth!" rang from lip to lip.

His dark eyes glowed as he turned from one to the other, as he met the grasp of his uncle's hand, and saw that stern face working with emotion.

He was astonished at the effect his words had produced, at the general demonstration they had called forth.

It seemed to him he had gained the applause too easily; as if what he had done was unworthy of so much; for he knew in himself that this was nothing as compared to what he felt he might do; as compared with the standard at which he aimed.

It seemed hardly right that words which came to him so easily as the expression of his thoughts and opinions should be made so much of.

As soon as he could escape, he left the crowded hall, and went up to the picture-gallery to keep his appointment with little Joan.

She was already there when he entered, and came running to meet him with glowing eyes, and cheeks flushed with excitement.

"Oh, Godfrey! it was so beautiful; and it made me feel so proud and happy!"

"And did you hear it well?" he said, smiling down upon her.

"Every word," she answered. "And how they did all cheer!"

"But you must have left," said Godfrey, "before it was all over. Why did you do that?"

"Ah, yes!" said the child. "I was so disappointed, for I wanted to see the excitement, and I liked feeling all the cheering was for your sake; but just as it was getting so loud, and all the handshaking beginning, who should come to the niche but mamma!"

"Lady Seaforth!" exclaimed Godfrey in surprise.

"Yes," said Joan; "so, of course, I came away directly. But now tell me, Godfrey," she went on, throwing back her hair, and gazing eagerly up into his face, "tell me all about it."

Just at this moment hasty footsteps were heard approaching; one of the doors was thrown rather violently open, and Lady Seaforth and her sons entered the picture-gallery.

CHAPTER XV.

LADY SEAFORTH's face was flushed and angry, and she looked like one possessed of an evil spirit.

In truth she was. For she had been a witness of all little Joan had been so sorry to miss, of all that would have made her "so proud and happy;" and I leave the reader to imagine what kind of spirit the sight had roused within her.

Yes; she had seen the eager hands held out to congratulate her triumphant adversary; she had heard the shouts which had made the rafters ring with his hated name. She had seen him in the very position she had always hoped for for Colin; and, above all, she had seen her husband's eyes glowing with love and pride, his face working with the tenderest emotion.

Both as a mother and as a wife her feelings had been outraged.

They had been those of Haman when he heard

the shouts accorded to Mordecai: "Thus shall it be done to the man whom the king delighteth to honour."

Little Joan shrank back on her mother's entrance, and kept close to Godfrey, as if for protection.

"I told you so, Colin," said Lady Seaforth, turning with a sort of impatient triumph to her eldest son, whose pleasant face was clouded, and who looked as if he wished himself hundreds of miles away. "I told you so, and you would not believe me. Joan," she continued, suddenly turning upon the child, "what are you doing here? What is the meaning of your being in the picture-gallery? Go back to the school-room directly."

Joan obeyed at once, and walked quietly away.

She merely looked upon the accident of her mother's arrival as a disagreeable interruption, and fully intended returning later for her interview with Godfrey.

But Godfrey, who, as we know, had all day long had an uneasy feeling with regard to Lady Seaforth, felt that there was more in all this than met the eye. Something in her whole air and manner told him that this was no accidental interruption, but that the whole scene had been premeditated and predetermined.

He felt that if he did not speak at once, the fast-disappearing little figure in the distance would be the last he should see of little Joan.

"I am leaving Seaforth in a few days for many

months," he said; "may I not go after my little
cousin and wish her good-bye ?"

Here Colin looked up, and seemed about to speak,
but changed his mind, and suddenly left the picture-
gallery.

"You can say good-bye now," said Lady Seaforth,
coldly.   "Joan!"

The child heard the call, and came back.

"Your cousin wishes to take leave of you.   He is
going away very soon, and you will not see him again
before he goes; for I forbid your coming into the
picture-gallery any more."

She stood utterly unmoved by the look of despair
that came into little Joan's face, by the quick in-
voluntary clasping of her two little hands together.

The child looked round with her great dark eyes
like a hunted stag which is trying to escape from its
tormentors, and sees no way open.

First at her mother, standing stern and relentless;
then at Andrew, whose head was turned away; till
she rested them on Godfrey, who was waiting to meet
them.

And then their expression changed.

Whether Godfrey had at first had any intention
of resisting the decree may be doubted, but at any
rate a look he had intercepted of Lady Seaforth's
directed at her daughter had caused him to change
his mind.

For it was a look he knew well, and he knew, too,
the feelings it denoted.   It was the selfsame look his
father had been wont to cast at him.

Alarmed for Joan's sake, he settled in his own mind that resistance would be a fatal course to pursue, and that her greatest safety lay in complete submission.

The child would only otherwise suffer hereafter, and he would no longer be at hand to help.

So, when Joan's imploring eyes sought his, he was ready.

She read in them what he would have her do.

Long and earnestly she gazed, as if learning her lesson, as if gathering every moment strength, and calm, and counsel, from their rapt and speaking expression.

And, acting under their guidance, yielding herself to their power, she came nearer, and held out both her little hands.

" Good-bye, Godfrey," she whispered.

He bent over her gravely, almost solemnly, holding her trembling hands in his. " God bless you, little Joan ! "

They stood thus for a moment, he looking down tenderly upon her, she with her eyes still fixed upon his face.

" You can go now," said Lady Seaforth.

Joan's hands dropped listlessly at her side, and she turned away; while Godfrey stood motionless, watching her.

There—where they had met—they parted; with " Godfrey, Earl of Seaforth," looking down upon them, and the groups of smiling children around.

Slowly she began to recede down the long, long gallery towards the door at the further end.

She had the noble spirit of a martyr, this young child; for though her heart was bleeding within her, she would not let him see what it cost her to part like this. She turned round as she went, and tried to reassure him by a faint smile.

God help her! that smile was sadder than any burst of tears could have been.

He stands erect and silent, watching the little figure disappear, marking with yearning love and pity the light childish step that tries so *hard* not to falter, the queenly little head which strives to hold itself so firm.

He sees the sweet little face turn and turn again to take another look at him, till the door at the further end is reached; and then he begins to move too, and walks with a firm step back to the door by which he entered.

He pauses on the threshold for a moment, and strains his gaze to the far distance. She is standing still now, waiting, with her arms wreathed about the oaken door, which she holds partly open.

Brave she stands, and smiling; all the courage of a noble and unselfish spirit coming to her aid in this the supreme moment of her young existence.

Is she not bearing up for his sake, and acting at his unspoken command?

Bright and firm, as long as she can see him; ready to sacrifice herself as long as her eyes can still discern the form she loves so dearly, her only thought to spare him pain who has glorified her lonely existence, and showered upon her the love and the sympathy of which she stood so sorely in need. " Bright and firm! Brave and smiling! . . .

But, as the old oak door closed upon him, the light went out in the life of little Joan!

BOOK V.

CHAPTER I.

GODFREY AT COLLEGE.

GODFREY remained with his tutor till October, and then matriculated at Oxford.

Many who are reading this will remember, and those who have had no opportunity of knowing can imagine, what that hour must be to a young man when, leaving home and school behind him, he comes to the University. I have heard the sensations of the first few days described, by a man verging on forty, as some of the happiest of his existence; like nothing that goes before, nor that comes after.

Now at last the boy is a man. Now at last, drawing up his own armchair to his own fireside, he feels himself a householder, a gentleman at large, independent and free. This in the case of any ordinary individual. But when it is the case of a youth of mind and culture, there are added many other feelings to enhance the charm of the new position. How deeply must such a one be stirred by the associa-

tions of the place and their power. The seat of
learning is alive with the dead, with the memory of
all those men who went out from it to the world
beyond, and left great names behind them.

The possibility of being even as they is before
him, since what man hath done man may do. Everything is before him as it was before them. Life and
its possibilities, success, fame, and distinction.

Such feelings were all in turn experienced by our
hero in his new life.

In his case, too, were added to the leisure, liberty,
and sense of independence, the relief of having
escaped from an atmosphere of dislike and suspicion,
and the strain of an uncongenial companionship.

Here he was far removed from all depressing
influences and surroundings, from the shadow of
jealousy, and the sense of being in the way.

Here he found free scope for his own thirst for
knowledge and love of study.

Here, buried in his books, he could live in the
past, or, holding converse with all sorts of men, could
hear opinions discussed, debated, and looked at from
all points of view. He enjoyed thoroughly the contact with cultivated minds and intellects; and began
to realise "the vastness of the sea of knowledge,"
and the "diversity of all shades of human opinion."

"A born student," had been his uncle's exclamation soon after he made his acquaintance.

"A born orator, and a close reasoner," the de-
bating societies he joined soon declared.

Two years passed away. Godfrey had spent many vacations at Seaforth; but all communication between him and little Joan was still ruthlessly cut off. In all that time, he had never been more than ten minutes with her alone; and even these brief meetings had been purely accidental.

All resuming of their former state of pleasant intercourse and companionship was out of the question.

Joan was too closely watched to make it possible. Nurse and governess were alike under Lady Seaforth's orders, and tools in her hands. It was useless to try and break through them, worse than useless—cruel.

Any such infringements would only have brought down upon the head of little Joan a swift retribution. So of these brief meetings they made the very most, and lived on the hope of them from day to day.

Faint glimpses they gave him of her dawning mind, and filled him more and more with admiration of her noble and unselfish character.

She was hardly a child now; her natural thoughtfulness was deepened by the solitary life she led, and both in thoughtfulness and intelligence she was far beyond her years.

Dawning upon him faintly was a dream of days to come.

Softly at evening it came floating over him that a time might come when he might take her happiness into his own safe keeping, into the shelter of his own love and care; shield her for ever from all pain and persecution, and make her young life glad!

His career at college was thoroughly satisfactory to his uncle. A great career was confidently predicted for him. Lord Seaforth's heart swelled with joy and pride at the thought.

There were no bounds to his dreams, or to his ambition for his darling. A second William Pitt; perhaps Prime Minister at an early age. Who should say?

Godfrey would be twenty-two about the time the next general election was expected; and as soon as he was twenty-one his uncle bought him a house in London near Westminster, and gave him an allowance of two thousand a year. His own private intention was to come up to London and live a good deal with him. He saw himself sitting, in fancy, in the peers' gallery, listening to Godfrey's oratory, and hearing whispers of his growing fame.

There now, therefore, remained about a year of Godfrey's university life, and then he was to stand for the county, and by entering the House of Commons plant his foot on the first rung of the ladder of fame and distinction, which his proud and happy uncle felt sure he was destined to climb.

CHAPTER II.

THE GATHERING OF THE CLOUD.

It was at about this time that a great and mysterious change came over Godfrey.

His uncle, watching him as usual as he read, observed how often his book dropped upon his knee, and he sat gazing into the fire in disturbed and gloomy thought.

It was not study or meditation, such as he had been wont to see him indulge in. It was more like the abstraction of some one who had something on his mind, and the fit of moody thought would often end in an abrupt return to his book, as if he were forcing himself to resume it, in order to banish uneasy thoughts and to drive the gloom away.

Often he sat with his book before him, and did not turn over the leaves for half an hour.

Lord Seaforth noticed all this with ever-increasing anxiety. A feeling of alarm, and a dread of impending trouble, took possession of him, and he longed to question his nephew, and to beg him to take him into his confidence. But he felt it would be useless, unless Godfrey chose to do so of his own accord.

From day to day he hoped he might speak, and give him some clue to his disturbed state of mind.

But he hoped in vain.

Godfrey remained silent, and Lord Seaforth saw him depart at the end of the vacation with a feeling of vague uneasiness.

All this time the husband and wife were drifting further and further apart.

Ever since she fully realised that he still continued to resent her early deception, and was determined to punish her for it, she had felt her boys' cause to be hopeless.

Ever since she had discovered his early history she had felt equally hopeless about her own.

She at once realised the intensity and the tenacity of his affections; and the intensity and the tenacity of his resentment.

She was frightened at the nature that could silently bear malice so long, and so consistently carry out a scheme of premeditated revenge. A reaction took place in her feelings towards him. In a violent and passionate nature like hers, love and hate lie very close together. And the one now changed places with the other.

She began to hate her husband; to hate his stern, cold face, his set, formal speeches, and his courtly and distant manner.

She began to long to get out of his silent presence, and to feel how much happier she should be in London with her boys.

For they never came to Seaforth now. Their future having so entirely changed in its aspect, made it necessary for them to be a great deal in London; and also her way of punishing her husband for his treatment of them was to keep them away from him altogether. She was determined they should not sleep under the same roof. Colin was now in the Foreign Office, as a first step in a diplomatic career. He had come of age some time; but there was no prospect of his ever being rich enough to live at his little place in Nairnshire, of which she had once spoken so confidently to Lord Seaforth, and it had been re-let for another term of years.

Andrew was at the University. In spite of his mother's wish that he should, under the altered circumstances, abandon the idea of going into the Church, he had been firm to his original intention.

So that she had an excuse for being a great deal in London if she chose; and she began to make use of it, more especially at vacation times, when Andrew was in want of a home.

The punishment, as regarded Lord Seaforth, fell quite flat.

He did not appear to notice the absence of his step-sons from Seaforth, and never made any inquiries about them.

And not only so, but he seemed callous and un-

17

observant as regarded his wife's frequent and pro-
tracted visits from home.

He made no objections to her comings and goings,
accepted with courtly readiness her somewhat bitterly
expressed reasons for being occupied with her sons,
and answered her with his usual set and formal
sentences: "Pray do as you please; pray make
what arrangements you like."

The fact was, he was glad to be quite alone. His
mind was full of troubled thoughts.

For, growing ever in his breast, was that uneasy
feeling about his nephew, and dark fears and forebodings were stealing over him.

Was his confidence misplaced after all?

Had Godfrey got into some trouble of which he
dared not tell him?

He awaited his return for the next vacation with
deep anxiety, though not without a hope that he
should find the cloud had passed away, and his
darling his old self again.

But, to his alarm and disappointment, when Godfrey returned he was just the same. If anything, he
was worse; more abstracted, more silent. There was
a look of settled despondency on his face that was
painful to see, and he seemed with the greatest
difficulty to force himself to do anything, or to take
any pleasure in his usual pursuits.

That he had something on his mind there could
be no doubt.

At last some light was thrown upon the matter.

It came to Lord Seaforth's knowledge that Godfrey was overdrawn at his banker's for £1500.

He at once sent for his nephew, and taxed him with his extravagance. He had been, he reminded him, in receipt of £2000 a year, and that for not longer than seven or eight months, and he was already overdrawn to such a large amount. What had he done with the money?

Godfrey was evidently not only unwilling, but determined to give no explanation of the manner in which it had been spent; and on Lord Seaforth's pressing the question, he answered, with an impatience which was quite foreign to him, and which sat most unnaturally upon him, that he found his allowance wholly inadequate to meet his expenses. It was the very expression his father had used years and years ago, and a cold feeling of dread struck upon Lord Seaforth's heart as the words fell upon his ear. Was history going to be repeated after all?

There flashed across his mind the proverb, "What is bred in the bone will come out in the flesh."

But he was determined not to be hard.

He merely pointed out to his nephew that he could not be speaking the truth when he made such an assertion; and urged him to own he had got into some trouble, and been obliged to spend that large sum in consequence.

But Godfrey would make no such admission.

It was in vain that Lord Seaforth, in a most

tender appeal to his feelings, prayed him to confide in him. Godfrey only repeated what he had at first said, that the allowance was wholly inadequate.

Lord Seaforth was terribly upset, but he would not be harsh. He said, after a few moments' thought, that he would make it £2500 if Godfrey would promise, on his word of honour, to live within that sum; but even this Godfrey would not do.

Lord Seaforth now grew suspicious, and changed his tone.

"I do not want to be hard on you, Godfrey," he said, "but there is something here which I must not treat with leniency. I should not be doing my duty by you if I did. Many fathers would, in my case, at once deprive their sons of their allowance, and trust them no more. But I believe in you, as you know, and trust you most thoroughly. So I overlook what has passed, and without asking you any questions, trust you for the future. Only, remember, it must not happen again. You are on trial now."

Godfrey thanked him coldly, but did not seem the least relieved, nor touched by his forbearance and generosity. He left his uncle's presence with the same heavy step and clouded brow.

Perhaps the bitterest part to Lord Seaforth in all the bitterness of that interview was that the appeal to his nephew's feelings had been without the slightest effect, and that he had realised more than ever that Godfrey had not a spark of affection for him in his breast.

He loved the boy so dearly, and, alas! he loved him not.

He could have taken him in his arms, and wept over him like David of old, with the old passionate cry, "Oh, my son! my son! Would God I might suffer for thee!"

And in return, there was in Godfrey's demeanour not only an entire absence of affection, but throughout the conversation there had been a kind of impatient shrinking from his uncle's demonstration of feeling and affection towards him, even a sort of unexpressed antagonism.

CHAPTER III.

THE CLOUD BURSTS.

ANOTHER six months passed away, but there was no change in Godfrey.

In spite of the increased allowance he was more and more heavily overdrawn, and on the subject of the disposal of these large sums he remained obstinately silent. Lord Seaforth waited till his university career was over before he took the matter thoroughly in hand. But as soon as Godfrey returned to Seaforth for good he was determined, if he could not extract a confession from him, that he would deprive him of his allowance altogether, and deal with him with the utmost severity.

He summoned him to his presence the day after his arrival, and entered again upon the subject. He began by urging Godfrey to confide in him, and not "to drive him to extremities, from which he shrank quite as much as his nephew himself could do."

But Godfrey answered that it was quite impossible.

Struck with a sudden idea, Lord Seaforth suddenly turned upon him and said, "You are supplying your father."

It was a wild hope, and his disappointment was great when the young man replied, with a decision which there was no mistaking, "I have never sent my father a five-pound note, and I never will."

"Godfrey," implored Lord Seaforth, "make a free confession. You have been gambling, racing; but only confess, only take me into your confidence, and I freely forgive you. I will overlook all and everything. Speak, I implore you!"

Godfrey remained silent.

"Then!" said Lord Seaforth, "listen to me. You have been taken from poverty and expatriation, and raised to a position all might envy. *I* have done this for you, but I solemnly declare that if you persist in this course I will deprive you of all the advantages I am ready to shower upon you. No spendthrift shall be taken by the hand by me. And remember you can do nothing without my help. Remember, too, that, old as I look, I am only forty-nine. You may be kept out of your inheritance till you are an elderly man. And in the mean time I will do nothing for you—nothing!"

Godfrey received all this in the same apathetic manner.

He would make no promises, pledge himself to nothing.

"But don't you care for yourself?" burst out his
uncle. "Have you no family pride, no pride in possession, no feeling for this princely estate, nor for the
grand old name that has been handed down to you
through countless generations?"

"None," answered Godfrey. "Why should I? I
was born and bred abroad. I and my sisters are
foreigners. You made us so; it was not our doing.
But the fact remains. I care nothing for name or
property. They are nothing to me."

It was a fearful thrust, and it cut Lord Seaforth
to the heart. If he had been harsh to his brother in
those old days to which that brother's son was now
alluding, he was heavily punished. At that moment
Godfrey Seaforth the outlaw was amply avenged.

"Uncle Harold!" exclaimed Godfrey suddenly,
"let us agree, you and I, to cut off this entail. Dis-
inherit me altogether, and leave everything to your
own legal heir."

"*My* legal heir!" exclaimed Lord Seaforth.

"Yes," said Godfrey, eagerly; "your daughter!
Only in her hands can it be safe, I do assure you."

Lord Seaforth rose from his chair in the surprise
of the moment, and then sitting down again, he said
scornfully, "I see what you mean. You want the
money *now*. You want to bribe me to give you a
larger income to make ducks-and-drakes with, by
consenting to cut off the entail. True gambler that
you are, imbued so truly with a gambler's spirit, you
are ready to sacrifice the future for the sake of the

present, and to barter your inheritance for a mess of pottage!"

"Not so," answered Godfrey; "you mistake me. I neither ask nor will I accept one shilling from you. I resign my pretensions unconditionally. All I ask is that you will leave everything to your daughter, and let me go my own way."

Lord Seaforth gazed at him in bewilderment.

"You do not care for your family or your inheritance," he said bitterly; "but what has become of the ambition of which I believed you to be so full? Richly endowed as you are, are all your talents, all your abilities, to come to nothing? Your powers of oratory, and all your many gifts? Are you going to shut yourself out from a career of brilliancy and usefulness? from that political life the thoughts of which you held so dear? You can do nothing without money, nor can you stand without my influence. Nor will any constituency take a representative with a brand on his name. And I will denounce you at any hustings. I will hold you up as a gambler and a villain; I swear I will do it, though my heart should break as I said the words."

He had hit the right nail on the head now. At the thought of the crumbling away of that bright dream of distinction and success the young man writhed in his chair. But he made no answer.

Lord Seaforth now dropped the upbraiding, even threatening, tone he had adopted, and made a last mournful and passionate appeal to his nephew's feelings.

"Must I," he concluded, in faltering accents, "must I give up all hope of your confession?"

"*All*," answered Godfrey.

"Very well," said his uncle, in a voice choked with emotion; "*I* can make no impression. To honour, duty, gratitude, and affection you are deaf and blind; but one thing remains." His voice faltered more. "You love your mother. That I *know*, and where *I* fail *she* may succeed. I shall send for her."

"Oh no!" cried Godfrey, springing to his feet with a cry. "Spare her! spare her! Uncle Harold, you do not *know* what you are doing. Spare her the terrible sorrow, the unutterable shame. Oh, spare her! spare her!"

Both were powerfully agitated. But Lord Seaforth saw the advantage he had gained, and would not budge an inch from his position.

"My mind is made up," he said firmly: "nothing that you can say will turn me from my determination."

CHAPTER IV.

AT LENGTH WE MEET AGAIN, LOVE.

AND so it came to pass that, a few days after this interview, in the room where, four years before, Lord Seaforth had sat waiting for Godfrey, he now sits waiting for Hester.

The carriage has gone to fetch her at the station, and he is expecting her every moment. It is early morning, for she is coming by the night train. She can only be spared from home for two days, and must return to Monaco with all possible speed.

He has not seen her for four and twenty years, and those years have, of course, wrought a change in his feelings towards her.

She is not so much to him now the idol of his youth, as the mother of the idol of his later years; and the thought of her coming does not so much rouse in him the memory of past joys and sorrows concerning himself, as hope that she may be able to throw some light on his present troubles and perplexities.

And yet he trembles when the door opens and the love of his life stands before him. The rush of old memories would come over him all the same, as his eyes rest once more on the beautiful face which has haunted the chambers of his soul for so long.

It almost seems to him as if she must be transported back to the old days too ; that she will let the years roll back, and will speak of that time again.

But there is no answering memory in her look.

All the mother is in those lovely eyes of hers as, after the first hasty glance at Lord Seaforth, they look beyond him and all round the room, as though searching for something on which they had long been yearning to dwell.

That other connection of her life with his is so far away in the past, it forms so completely a part of her early girlhood, that it is to her only like a tale she had once read and well-nigh forgotten.

And Lord Seaforth felt that it was so. If there was any disappointment in his heart, he concealed it successfully ; and his manner was a mixture of gentleness and deep respect as he advanced to meet her, and then led her to a seat by the fire.

He thanked her earnestly for coming, and for coming so promptly ; and then asked her if she would not like some rest and some refreshment before they entered on the painful business which had brought them together. But Hester would have nothing. She could think of nothing but her boy ; and she begged him at once to tell her the story from be-

ginning to end. "For I know so little," she said
sadly, "so little!"

"But, Lord Seaforth," she added quickly, drawing
herself up proudly, "I am full of hope and confidence.
I trust my son so fully. My faith in him is so complete."

Lord Seaforth, pained that she should for a
moment think it necessary to defend one he loved so
deeply, prefaced his narrative by an earnest and
pathetic entreaty that she would not think he had
been harsh to her boy; and as he did so, his love for
Godfrey showed itself so plainly, that the mother's
heart was won at once.

"I have no son of my own, as you know," he said
in a faltering voice, "but, before God, I assure you
that I do not believe a son of my own could be dearer
to me than your boy."

Hester could hardly restrain her tears of gratitude
at the thought that her boy was so loved and appre-
ciated. "God bless you, Harold!" she exclaimed;
"God bless you for words like these!"

The relief it was to speak out, and talk of him to
another who loved him so!

Their individual lives and histories were merged
at last—merged in one object of mutual love and
adoration.

He then gave the whole account of the affair from
the beginning as the reader knows it, and detailed
all the different conversations he had had with his
nephew. When he had finished Hester rose from her
seat.

"Now take me to him," she said. "I feel that if I may only speak to him face to face, all will yet be well."

Lord Seaforth led the way, and she followed him with a beating heart.

"Tell me, Harold," she said as they went along, "is he tall? Is he handsome as when I sent him to you?"

"He is beautiful as the day," he answered in a trembling voice, "and taller than I am myself."

As they turned down the passage that led to Godfrey's rooms, and stood outside his door, her step suddenly faltered. A great fear came into her heart at the thought of the coming interview. It was a man past twenty-one she was now going to see, and not the boy of seventeen with whom she had parted.

"Nearly four years," she said to herself. "Will he be quite what I remember? Is he not almost a stranger to me? How will he meet me under these new and unhappy circumstances?"

She must have him to herself. No other human eye must see the meeting between them.

"Leave us, Harold," she said beseechingly, turning to Lord Seaforth; "leave me and my boy together. I must meet him alone."

Lord Seaforth opened the door with a trembling hand, and remained, as she desired, in the passage.

"Godfrey, my darling!" he hears her cry as she enters. "My precious boy, come to me."

He hears no answer, no sound; and in an agitated

voice he calls out to her to go through the study into the bedroom beyond, for that perhaps he is not yet dressed. And unable to bear the suspense, he follows her, and they stand together in the doorway, as in a dream.

A dead silence follows, broken by a low cry of pain.

For the rooms are both empty; the bed is unslept on; and it is clear that Godfrey has fled!

CHAPTER V.

HUSBAND AND WIFE.

LADY SEAFORTH had been spending some weeks with her sons in London, but as they had now both gone on a visit to Lady Margaret Cartwright, she prepared to go back to Seaforth. She had not heard anything from home for a long period, and she felt it was time to return.

She wrote to her husband to announce her advent; and she arrived on the evening of the day after that on which the events recorded in the last chapter had occurred.

She was greeted with the astounding news that Lord Seaforth was away from home, and, on advancing into the hall, she saw her own letter to him lying unopened upon the table.

This was just the sort of thing which Lady Seaforth could not stand.

She could not bear that the servants should see how completely her husband kept her in ignorance of his movements, and how little communication there was by letter between them.

She would gladly have asked nothing more and pretended she knew all about it; but bewilderment and curiosity impelled her to put a few questions.

The answers nearly took her breath away.

Lord Seaforth had left very early that morning, and had gone to Folkestone with Mrs. Seaforth, who was to cross that night. Mrs. Seaforth had been staying at the house since the morning before. She had arrived from abroad on Tuesday, and was obliged to return immediately.

A few more short sharp questions from Lady Seaforth and she was in possession of the news with which the butler was bursting, with which the whole place was ringing. Mr. Seaforth had got into trouble and had gone, no one knew where. He had taken flight in the middle of the night, and no clue to his whereabouts could be discovered.

" His lordship," added the butler, feelingly, " was terribly cut up. He seemed quite knocked over; and as to Mr. Seaforth's mother, she had looked more dead than alive when she left."

Lady Seaforth felt quite stunned with all these startling pieces of information. Godfrey disgraced and flown !

That was the first feeling, and a feeling of wild exultation it was. But above the triumph of the fall of her enemy was a burning resentment against her husband for the way in which he had treated her, and

18

the humiliating state of ignorance in which he had kept her. He must have known for some time past that *something* was impending; it could not have been a new or sudden thing to him, since he had had time to summon his sister-in-law to his help.

And he had never told her a word ! Never written her a line ! Had kept her completely in the dark !

Hastily escaping from the inquisitive eye of the butler and men-servants, she made her way to her own boudoir, breathless with the rush of wild anger and rebellion which swept over her.

She could not sit still. She walked up and down the room panting. She persuaded herself she had seen the servants laughing and exchanging meaning glances with each other. It maddened her.

She sat down positively trembling with rage, fiercely biting her lips almost through, while passionate and incoherent exclamations every now and then escaped from her.

At length a rattle of wheels in the courtyard below announced the return of her husband, and, looking out, she saw him getting out of the carriage.

At the sight of him her passion broke out with renewed strength. She would have it out with him at once. He should hear the truth at last! Many, many years she had restrained herself, and kept it all down, but he should hear it now.

If it came to a quarrel and a breach between them, what then ?

Could anything be worse than the present state of affairs?

She was determined to return to London that very night. Nothing will make her stay! But he shall hear the truth first!

She rang the bell, and desired that the carriage should remain at the door till further orders.

Then she went across the hall, up the corridor that led to the library, and knocked imperiously and impatiently at the door.

*   *   *   *   *   *

Lord Seaforth entered the house weary and heart-broken, despairing, and sore and sick in spirit.

There was no doubt about Godfrey's guilt now. He would not meet his mother; all views of the subject met and ended in that. There was the proof of his guilt. All hope was over. There remained nothing now but to harden his heart, and cast him off for ever, and it should be done. But he did not look much like a Nemesis as he sat there, cowering over the fire, holding his shaking hands to the blaze, his lips quivering, and the proud tears rising to his sunken and weary eyes. It is the bitterest moment of his life; more bitter even than when the love of his life had fled with his vagabond brother.

Hester had been the idol of months, but Godfrey was the idol of years.

Oh, how lonely and how crushed he felt!

Ah! Lady Seaforth, this would have been your moment. Your rival gone, and lowered in his eyes;

cast off for ever; his heart aching and sad. Could you have stolen in now gently, just as his heart is so sore, and craved his pardon for that old deception, and begged him to condone it as an offence of youth— begged him to gauge your love for your boys by his own love for his nephew, and to look upon you as one who had erred for the sake of her children—you might have won him still!

But, instead! there bursts into his presence a woman mad with fury, a woman who stands over him and glories in his grief; who taunts him with the way he has been taken in, and tells him she always knew his nephew was bad and worthless, and had said so from the very first; who triumphs over his misery, and then heaps upon him the bitterest reproaches; who reviews all her married life, and recapitulates every grievance and every injury which she says she has had to suffer at his hands; who accuses him of every sort of cruelty and neglect; who tells him she will remain with him no longer, to be treated in such a way as this, to be shut out alike from his joys and his sorrows, to be humiliated before the whole household, and kept in such ignorance of his affairs that every servant in the house is better informed than she; who lets loose, in short, all the pent-up torrent of years, and, regardless alike of his feelings or his displeasure, allows that torrent to have its full vent, and to burst as it will the bounds of truth, respect, and decorum. Self-control is no more; habitual awe and fear have fled. Alike violent and intemperate in speech, manner, and tone, she gives way freely to her feelings and her temper, and—is degraded in his eyes for ever!

Exhausted at last by her own passion, she comes to an end of her vocabulary of vituperation; and she rushes out of his presence, dashing the hot tears of fury from her eyes, and she goes away and away through the passages, across the hall, to the entrance where the carriage is still standing at the door.

The presence of the men-servants restore to her for a moment some sense of what is due to appearances, and she enters the carriage with something of dignity, and controls her voice to give the necessary orders before she drives out into the cold, foggy night.

Then she throws herself back among the cushions, and the carriage rattles out of the courtyard.

But, as she drove rapidly away in the darkness, she sat up suddenly, and let down the window to take one last look at the home she felt she was leaving for ever.

The stately old house looked grim and phantom-like in the fog which was beginning to encircle it. No lights gleamed from the windows. The state rooms were closed, the guests' rooms untenanted, her boys' rooms dark and empty.

She gazed at it with a beating heart, hastily reviewing her life in it, with all its hopes, dreams, mortifications, and disappointments.

The contrast between this day and those early ones, when she had been so gay and happy, so pleased

with her new position, and so secure of her boys'
prosperous future, forced itself upon her.

The contrast, too, between the gaunt, deserted look
of the mansion now, and its aspect in those days,
when it was made so bright for feasting and hospitality. Where once each window had been a blaze of
light, now all was darkness.

One more hasty glance before she disappears in
the fog, never to return.

Something causes her to throw herself hastily
back in the carriage, and a sudden sharp pang of
bitter remorse strikes through her heart, penetrating
even the hard cold wall with which that heart was
encircled, and melting for a moment the ice of her
proud rebellion and resentment against her life, her
fate, and her husband.

Her eye had fallen for a moment on a tiny
glimmer, shining faint and small in the darkness.

Far away in one of the upper storys of the house,
a little light in the schoolroom window had spoken to
her pathetically of her neglected and deserted child!

CHAPTER VI.

"NOT WANTED."

SHORT work did Lord Seaforth make of his wife's concerns; short work indeed.

The very thought of her for days and days after that scene in the library was enough to make his lip curl with the most ineffable contempt and disdain.

She shall never return to Seaforth. She shall be banished evermore.

There shall be no formal separation, no publicity of any kind. It shall just be settled that for the future she shall make her home in London.

Did she not herself propose it? So far as he could follow the course of the intemperate language used on that occasion, he had gathered that that was her meaning.

Thus, then, for the future it shall be.

So that matter was promptly and finally settled, and then he turned his back upon that part of his life, and entered on a new stage of his existence.

Yes, he has cast off all the past—wife, step-sons, nephew, all the associations of the last sixteen years— and a new future is opening out before him. A new programme is shaping itself in his mind.

What can this new programme be?

He is going, as Godfrey himself had suggested, to cut off the entail, and to settle everything on his daughter. She will then be one of the greatest heiresses in England; and her second son shall inherit the property and take the family name.

He has even got a son-in-law in his eye; the eldest son of his neighbour and acquaintance Lord Ainsbro', whose estates join his own.

But for all this he must wait. These plans cannot be carried out yet. He must wait till Godfrey is five and twenty, by which time Joan will be past eighteen.

His life will now be waiting, waiting—and then! this new future and this fresh programme of life.

So, still unsubdued, from the ashes of another past, his will, phœnix-like, springs with a new force.

Again, no thought of submission, no bowing to the hand of God.

As determined as ever to carve out his own life; to make it what he deems it should be. The tide of time has taught him no lessons; he has learnt nothing from its flow. The waves of life have but borne him on a little further, and carried him up a little higher on the shore.

Yet in this matter, wherein his love, his pride, his

trust, and his ambition have all alike suffered, he does not come out quite unscathed from the fight. The hard lines on the face, the bent figure, and the snow-white hair, a certain nervous trembling of the hands, and an occasional uncertainty of gait, all testify to a partial defeat.

And thus we leave him for the present, to wait till those three years shall have passed away.

Alone, all alone, in his empty house, his deserted rooms, his silent, echoless halls, the proud man passes into another phase of his curious life of self-will and failures.

All alone did I say?

Yes. Save but for the silent presence in the rooms above of his neglected and unloved daughter, living out her young life all alone too.

And yet, after all, all his hopes are now centred upon her.

His new programme of life, with all its dreams and projects, hangs now entirely on that fair young girl; the child who has borne from her birth the brand "not wanted" on her brow.

BOOK VI.

CHAPTER I.

THE ENCHANTED ORANGE GROVE.

Not quite three years after the events recounted in the last chapter, a young Englishman might have been seen strolling along the country which lies between Nice and Monaco.

Tall and fair, with an open countenance and bright, laughing eyes, the reader will have no difficulty in recognising Colin Fraser, now a fine-looking young man of six or seven-and-twenty.

He had been wandering somewhat lazily along, for the heat was very overpowering, and he was hoping every moment to find some shade, when his ear was suddenly caught by the sound of voices not far distant, and he stopped short and listened.

What he heard evidently excited his surprise and his interest, for he at once left the dusty road, and turned off to the right upon a mule track, which seemed to him to lead to the spot from whence the sounds proceeded. Following this little path, he found himself being led further down into the valley, till it entered a grove of olives, and there it stopped. Colin stopped too, and looked about him. He saw rising above the trees, close at hand, the roof of a little châlet, and it was from between the olives and the châlet that the sounds which had attracted him seemed to come.

He listened again. No, he had not been mistaken; they were laughing girls' voices he had heard —English voices; he could hear them more plainly now.

After a moment's thought he pushed his way through the olives, and parting the branches of two which grew rather close together, and emerging from their shade, he came suddenly upon a scene which he never afterwards forgot. Three lovely English girls, wearing the picturesque hats of the country, which protected while they did not hide their pretty features and bright complexions, were sitting in an orange grove.

One was working, one reading, and the third making garlands of the wild flowers which were lying all round her.

Colin was so taken by surprise, and so struck with the beauty of the scene, the beauty of the young girls, and the beauty of the shade and coolness of their retreat, upon which he had come so suddenly, that he stood gazing fixedly without attempting to move.

Startled at the sudden appearance of a stranger,

the young girls sprang to their feet and looked at Colin in astonishment.

He recovered himself at the sight of their alarm, and stepping forward with a slight blush, he took off his hat, and apologised for his intrusion.

"I beg ten thousand pardons, ladies," he said, as he bowed respectfully, " but I had no idea what I was coming upon. You must excuse me if the surprise of suddenly coming on such a scene as this, where I expected to find only washerwomen, should for the moment have overpowered me. The sight of English ladies at home in these solitudes made a boor of me at once, and I could only stare as the boors do."

He laughed as he spoke, but he was still so confused and astonished, that he was more nearly feeling shy than he had ever done in his life before.

The young girls' high-bred appearance, and a sense of something like familiarity with their appearance ; a kind of dream-like feeling of having seen them somewhere before ; all this bewildered and, as he said himself, overpowered him.

The three sisters were looking at him all this time with interest. His gentlemanlike demeanour reassured them at once, and his frank courtesy prepossessed them in his favour.

Olive was the first to speak. "Who are you?" she said, "and where do you come from?"

"I am an Englishman," he answered, "and I come from Monaco."

"What brings you here?" was the next question; "and how *did* you find the secret path to our châlet?"

Colin felt very much as if he were in fairyland. It seemed to him he was like some of the wandering princes he had read of, who, following some unknown path through a labyrinth, had come upon an enchanted region, peopled by fairer beings than the rough outer world contained.

"It was the soft sound of English voices," he answered, "which attracted my attention, and guided me here!"

"Why, you said you thought we were chattering washerwomen," she said, with a pretty little toss of her pretty head. "Paysannes have the most hideous voices in the world, just like a lot of magpies. Besides, I don't think we were talking at that moment; Hester was reading out loud. It was a poor compliment to her reading, wasn't it?"

Colin felt rather embarrassed, and to hide it he said, "What were you reading? The Pastorals, I am sure. I feel as if I had stepped into a bit of Pastoral poetry myself. Perhaps Miss Hester will kindly go on."

"Why, how did you know her name?" said Olive, astonished. "Do you know mine, too?"

"You called your sister by that name just now," he answered. "I have not yet had the pleasure of hearing yours; but I can assure you that if you will tell it to me I shall never forget it!"

"My name is Olive," she said, "and I am called after the dear old trees."

As she spoke, she twined her arms round the branches of the one under which she was standing, and looked more picturesque than ever. "And the little one is Venetia," she added, "or, as she is generally called, Venice."

"Olive and Venice!" repeated Colin. "What lovely and romantic names!"

"Well, you have not told us your name yet," continued Olive, who was now getting quite at her ease, and talking as she would have talked to her father, who was almost the only gentleman she had ever seen. "And you know all ours now. Neither have you told us what you are doing here."

"I am making what we call in England a 'walking tour,'" he answered. "I wanted to see what all this country was like."

"But it's very hot for walking," she said; "we should never think of walking this time of the day."

"So I found it," he said, with a little laugh. "I was walking at the rate of five miles an hour up there on the dusty road, and I was beginning to long for a little shade."

"Oh, now I guess who you are!" she exclaimed; "you must be Mr. Waukenphast, the original of the picture in Bradshaw. You needn't tell me your name now. I shall call you Mr. Waukenphast."

"That will do very well," he answered, laughing; "but I am ready to tell you anything you wish to know, and to answer any question you may please to put to me."

"Won't you sit down," said Hester's soft voice, "before Olive begins her questions? You must be tired after this long, hot walk you speak of."

He thanked her, and they all sat down.

"Well, now," said Olive, "let us begin. Where do you come from?"

"From Monaco," he answered.

"Ah, yes, I know; but I mean before you came to Monaco."

"Before that I came from Berlin, at which court I hold the proud and lucrative position of an unpaid attaché!"

"Don't they pay you anything at all?" she exclaimed.

"Not a sou," was the reply. "*Tant pis pour moi!*"

"Then I wouldn't be an attaché, I am sure."

"Beggars cannot be choosers," he answered lightly; "and in these days we poor Englishmen are glad to get anything we can, which *may* lead to something better, some day?"

"Oh, then it will lead to something, some day?"

"*Some* day, perhaps, it *may* lead to envoy extraordinary, but it will be very extraordinary if it does."

"And in the mean time—?"

"In the mean time, I come to Monaco, and lose my money at *rouge-et-noir*, like a fool as I am."

"But I thought you said you *had* no money, and were a very poor man."

"Ah! well, I *am* a very poor man; but, then, I have always been brought up as if I were a rich one, and so I make mistakes sometimes. The lessons taught us in our youth, Miss Olive, are very difficult to unlearn, and I am going through that process with difficulty and great pain."

"Before you came to Berlin, you lived in England, I suppose, did you not?" asked Hester.

"Yes," he replied, "I did. But Scotland is my real home, my native land, as they say."

"And what brought you from Berlin to Monaco?" asked Olive.

"The ambassador is at Nice for a little while, and I came with him," he answered.

"And what do you think of Monaco?"

"It's the loveliest place in all the world," he answered, "and the wickedest. But have you not been there?"

"No, never. Mamma never will allow us to go."

"I think she is right. I intend to get away from it myself as fast as I can. I ought not to have come, or rather, I ought not to have played. However, I was soon cured of it. But, as I tell you, I always forget I am a poor man, and having always been accustomed to think I could go in for everything, why, in I go! And, of course, I ought to remember that I oughtn't even to buy a new boot-lace till I'm quite sure the old one is really worn out."

"No, of course not," laughed Olive. "We should

never think of such a thing. Why, we haven't had new gowns for I don't know how long; and as to our hats—— ! "

" She took off her broad paysanne hat, and showed it to Colin. " Do you see, it is quite sunburnt," she said. " Now, guess how many years I have worn it."

" It couldn't be prettier if it was brand-new," said Colin. " It's the prettiest hat I have ever seen."

" And I am sure," put in little Venetia, " it's better the hat should be sunburnt than Olive; isn't it ? "

" Yes, that it is, indeed," said Colin, warmly. " I can't think how you ladies shield yourselves from the effects of the sun so successfully. The paysannes are all quite burnt brown."

" Mamma is very particular about our complexions," said Olive, simply.

" By the way," said Colin, " will you not introduce me to your mother ? "

" She has gone to Nice," exclaimed Olive. " Isn't it extraordinary ? She has not done such a thing as long as I can remember. She won't be back till late. So we are taking care of ourselves to-day."

" And," said Colin, " if you will not think me inquisitive, have you a father also ? "

" Yes," she said shortly; " but he's always more or less away."

Colin felt as if he ought not to ask any more questions, though he longed to know why these lovely girls were hidden away in these wilds, and what the history of the family might be.

"Well, ladies," he said regretfully, looking at his watch, "I must be going. It is sad to leave such a Paradise, but it must be. I must return to Paradise Lost, as they call Monaco."

"Oh! but the train does not start for at least an hour," exclaimed Olive. "You really must not go yet!"

"Won't you have something to eat in the mean while?" said Hester; "you must be hungry and thirsty. And you will be glad to wash your face and hands, after your long dusty walk."

He looked at them all for a moment, and hesitated. "I don't know if I ought," he said.

"Why not?" asked Olive.

"There's no chaperon, you see," he said.

"No *what?*" exclaimed Olive.

Colin did not seem to be inclined to explain himself, and, after a moment's thought, he accepted the invitation.

They all walked towards the châlet, and the girls took him into their father's room, which was deliciously cool, all paved with white tiles. All three hovered about, getting it ready, on hospitable thoughts intent.

Olive came in with a large classically shaped pitcher on her head, which she had herself filled with water in the little kitchen, and set it down before him. Colin hastened to relieve her of it, exclaiming with horror at her having given herself so much trouble.

"There is not enough water," she said; "I must go and get some more." As she spoke, she heaved up the pitcher again.

"Oh, don't you do it!" exclaimed Colin; "please let me ring!"

She stood before him, with her arm round the pitcher on her shoulder, laughing merrily.

"Ring!" she exclaimed. "Who for?"

"For one of the servants," he answered. "I cannot let you wait upon me like this."

"*Servants!*" she repeated, laughing more than ever. "Why, we've only got one, and of course she's getting your dinner ready."

"You might be Rebecca at the well," he said in answer. "I almost expect to hear you say, 'Drink, my lord!'" But Olive was already out of hearing of these observations.

The meal was very simple, but tastefully set upon the table. Colin found he was expected to eat alone, as the girls declared their intention of awaiting their mother's return from Nice.

They hovered round him, providing for his wants, and would not allow him to get a single thing for himself, in spite of his protestations.

"No!" said Olive, decidedly, "when we come to see you, you shall wait upon us; but now you are eating of *our* salt, and we must wait upon you."

Colin was indeed sorry when at last it was decided

he must start if he wished to be in time for the train.

"But you'll come and see us again," said Olive, imploringly, as she said 'Good-bye,' "and very soon?"

"That I will," he answered, "and you must introduce me to your mother."

The three girls came out on the balcony to see him go, and leant over the railings, waving their hands to him till he was almost out of sight.

Olive remained there the longest, shading her eyes with her hands, as she strained her gaze after his departing figure.

When she could no longer see him, she sighed. Everything, somehow, seemed different to what it had been in the morning, and she had lost all interest in the book Hester was reading.

Meanwhile Colin, after taking one last look at the figure on the balcony, sighed also.

And as he pursued his way back to Paradise Lost, he felt as if he were turning his back on Paradise Regained.

CHAPTER II.

LORD SEAFORTH AND HIS DAUGHTER.

The rolling of the wheels of Time had done but little to better Joan's position.

Little as she had ever seen of her mother and half-brothers, their total disappearance from the scene, and the disappearance with them of all life and society and movement from the house and place, rendered everything more dull and dreary than ever. The only change, as regarded herself, was the fact of being brought more in contact with her father. For Lord Seaforth, urged by his rigid sense of duty, had, very soon after his wife's departure, sent up a message to the schoolroom, that for the future his daughter and her governess would dine with him.

But that is some time ago. Joan is now past eighteen. Her governess has been gone a long while. Unable to bear the dulness of the life, she had returned to her friends abroad; and her place had not been filled up.

Joan is now a good deal with her father—that is to say, in his presence; otherwise they were miles apart, and very little conversation ever passed between them.

Still, Lord Seaforth's feelings towards his daughter are very much warmer than they used to be. The very fact of her being his heir at once created in his breast an interest in her which he had never felt before.

He gives her a good deal of power in the place, and as much money as she wishes for; and is ready to further any schemes for good that she may wish to promote. She has made herself a home in the hearts of the poor; and whenever there is trouble there is Joan ever at hand to help, more especially if a little invalid or a lonely child be in question.

But it is a lonely, lonely life for a young girl; her own heart is void and empty, and it has no one on whom its treasures of affection may be poured.

Hers are golden memories, but no present joys. She lives still on the memory of those sunny days when love and sympathy were showered upon her; and, except them, all is blank in her life, and succeeding events shrouded in a deep and impenetrable mystery.

Let us look in upon the father and daughter, sitting in the library to-night. It wants just about three months to the day for which Lord Seaforth has been waiting so long; three months to the 26th of January, Godfrey's twenty-fifth birthday.

Lord Seaforth is sitting in his usual chair, gazing into the fire. His daughter is bending over her book, under the soft light of a reading-lamp, which shines on her small, well-shaped head, with its fair rippling hair. A very lovely girl has the lonely child become. Even her father's eyes are not closed to his daughter's beauty, and there is not a man or a boy about the place who is not in love with little Joan.

The usual silence is reigning in the room.

It was broken by the sound of a little cough from Lord Seaforth. He spoke so seldom that his voice got husky, and no sound would come unless he first prepared the way.

The little cough was a sign that he was going to speak, and at the sound his daughter raised her eyes from her book, and waited to hear what he was going to say.

"Joan."

"Yes, father."

"How old are you now?"

"I was eighteen last month."

"I thought you must be nearly that age. You are growing up now, Joan."

"Yes, father."

"You ought to be seeing something of society, like others of your age. This is a gloomy house, and a gloomy life for a young girl; but that cannot be altered. You must seek change and society elsewhere."

Here he paused, and took a letter out of his pocket.

"I have an invitation for you here from my friends Lord and Lady Ainsbro', inviting you to pass a few days with them next week. Lady Ainsbro' says she has no particular inducements to offer you in the shape of amusements, but she thinks you will not perhaps mind that. She has at present with her one of her married daughters, her eldest son, and some of her younger children. I have a great opinion of Lady Ainsbro'. She has brought up her sons and daughters well; and her eldest son is a particularly worthy and promising young man."

Another pause.

"I have accepted the invitation, and it only remains for you to make the necessary arrangements. The distance is five and twenty miles, across country. The railway will not assist you. I shall, therefore, send you and your maid in the carriage the whole way."

Lord Seaforth then returned the letter to his pocket, and said nothing further.

Joan did not resume her book. Her thoughts turned with pleasure to the change.

The idea of a house with young people and little children in it was very pleasant, and she dimly remembered having once met Lady Ainsbro' on the stairs when she had been staying at Seaforth, and that she had stopped her and spoken to her very kindly.

CHAPTER III.

LADY AINSBRO'S family consisted of some married daughters, a grown-up son, and some younger children.

She had originally intended Godfrey for one of those daughters, but events having put that out of the question, they had married elsewhere; and now her favourite plan was that her son should marry Lord Seaforth's daughter, and unite the two properties. She had found that she and Lord Seaforth were fully agreed as to the wisdom of such an arrangement, and Joan's visit to Ainsbro' was the preliminary step to its accomplishment.

She had asked no one to meet her. She knew what a solitary life the girl led, and thought she would be more at ease in a home circle than with a regular party. She was a kind, motherly woman, and had always felt much for the forlorn child; but the great distance between the two houses, unconnected as they were by any railway, had prevented her being able to do anything for her.

At about five o'clock in the afternoon, after a long drive of twenty-five miles, Joan arrived at the gates of Ainsbro' Park.

She felt rather nervous, and very uncertain how she should comport herself under such new circumstances.

She was reassured directly by Lady Ainsbro's kind, motherly greeting. She received her alone in the drawing-room, made her sit down by the fire to warm herself after her cold drive, and gave her some tea, talking kindly to her all the time.

Lord Ainsbro' and her son, she said, were out shooting, but would be back ere long, and the children would be down directly. She hoped Joan would not mind a family party. Her daughter, who had been with her, she was sorry to say, had been obliged to return home on account of the illness of her baby.

As Joan sat there drinking her tea, listening to the kind voice, and receiving all the motherly attention to which she was so unaccustomed, a feeling of warmth and comfort stole into her heart, and she felt she would be very happy at Ainsbro'.

"Are the children quite little?" she inquired, looking up eagerly.

"Yes, two of them are nursery children still, a boy and a girl, Marion and Bertie. They are just at the right age," she added, smiling—"independent of the nursery, and not yet in the schoolroom; so I have

them with me nearly all day, and a most amusing
little pair they are. Will you come up to your room
before they come down? They will never let you go
after. They are so fond of society!"

Joan followed Lady Ainsbro' to her bedroom, and
took off her things.

When she returned to the drawing-room the children were already there, and they ran forward and
greeted Joan with great pleasure.

Joan sat down and took the little boy in her lap.
Her love for children was a passion which as yet had
been confined to the children of the poor. No one
could guess what it was to the poor forlorn child to
wind her arms round the little fellow, and to bury her
face in his soft hair.

The attraction was mutual. Bertie was evidently
greatly smitten. He took a prolonged look at her,
and then settled himself comfortably astride on her
knee, and asked her to tell him a story or to show
him some pictures.

"You mustn't tell Bertie anything sad," whispered
little Marion, "because it makes him so unhappy.
You mustn't let anybody die, or be cruel, or else he'll
begin to cry. And nobody must be unkind, or ill, or
unhappy."

As there seemed so many rocks ahead in the
matter of story-telling, Joan sheltered herself from
possible dangers by saying she thought she would
rather show them some pictures. Marion, therefore,
fetched a large volume of *Punch*, and placed it on her

knee. "But don't let Bertie see any wild beasts," she whispered; "no lions, or wolves, or bears, because he talks about them at night, and thinks they're under his bed, or peeping at him from behind the curtain."

Punch appeared to Joan to be a volume likely to be free from all terrors, and the entertainment began.

But they came at once upon the "British Lion" in one of the big political cartoons; and the peace of the evening seemed seriously threatened.

Joan hastily turned over several pages, and fell foul of a skeleton, wrapped in a sheet, rowing a boat.

This being at present an unknown danger, Bertie was at first considerably interested, and it led to a conversation on bones; but on a closer inspection of the illustration, he suddenly shuddered, and covering it up with his hands, said, "Better not look at it any more."

"Do you know," said Marion to Joan, in an awe-struck whisper, "I once heard somebody say there was a skeleton in the cupboard. I wonder," she added, looking rather fearfully round the room, "I wonder which cupboard it's in!"

"Oh dear!" cried Bertie, his blue eyes dilating with fright, "I hope it's not in the nursery cupboard!"

"No, no, darlings," said Joan, soothingly; "I am quite sure there is no skeleton in *this* house."

"Is there one in your's?" asked Marion.

Joan blushed deeply. She saw Lady Ainsbro'

was listening with some curiosity, and her relief was
great when the entrance of Lord Ainsbro' and his son
interrupted the conversation, and diverted the chil
dren's attention.

Lord Ainsbro' received her very kindly ; and after
a few words of inquiry after her father, etc., he sat
down by the fire and took up the newspaper.

Edward Manners was a tall, nice-looking young
man of about six and twenty.

Lady Ainsbro' came forward and introduced him
and he sat down by Joan's side, and entered into
conversation with her.

"The Mayor of York is dead," said Lord Ainsbro'
to his wife, presently.

Lady Ainsbro' expressed surprise and regret, and
a little conversation followed on the manner of his
death, and his probable successor.

Joan suddenly discovered that Bertie was weeping.

"Oh! what is the matter with him?" she exclaimed to Mr. Manners. "Poor little fellow! He is
crying."

"What's the matter, old fellow?" inquired Mr.
Manners, raising his little brother in his arms.

"I wish the Mayor of York hadn't died, poor
thing!" sobbed Bertie. "I don't want him to be
dead at all."

His brother hastily explained to him that the late
mayor had gone to heaven, where he would be so
much happier than he could be at York.

Bertie allowed himself to be consoled by this reflection, observing mournfully, "So should *I* be much happier in heaven than I am here."

" Come and play at cheeses," said Marion.

It was a new game, and for the present, while the novelty lasted, it was in her eyes the panacea for all ills.

Berti entered at once into the spirit of the game, and twisted round till he got giddy and nearly fell over.

"Don't!" he called out to Joan, who was sitting very quiet in her big armchair, " don't you go round when I do this! "

Lady Ainsbro' now stopped the game, and took the children off to bed.

The dinner passed off pleasantly. They were all so kind that Joan could not but feel at her ease.

In the evening Edward Manners played the violin to his mother's accompaniment, and Joan listened, while Lord Ainsbro' slumbered peacefully in his chair.

It was all very homelike and comfortable, and she went to bed feeling very much more what is called " at home " at Ainsbro' than ever she had felt at Seaforth.

The next day was Sunday. In the morning they all went to church, and in the afternoon they took a long walk.

Lord and Lady Ainsbro' and the children went on in front, and Joan and Edward Manners walked be-hind.

" The young people are getting on famously," said

20

Lady Ainsbro', with a smile, to her husband, in the course of the walk. "What a lovely little thing she is!"

"Wonderful eyes," he observed. "I never saw any with so deep and so varying an expression. She looks very sad, poor child. I fancy there is a great deal of character hidden under a very gentle exterior."

"I don't believe she knows the least how pretty she is," added Lady Ainsbro'; "she seems so unconscious, and so free from any sort of vanity. Altogether, I think, she is charming."

When, about an hour later, they reached the house in time for the children's tea, Lady Ainsbro' noticed, with great satisfaction, that her son and his companion were still far behind.

When the children came down at six o'clock Lady Ainsbro' read them "Mamma's Bible Stories."

Joan was sitting near, with her book in her lap, and she did not hear much at first; but when Lady Ainsbro' put down the book, and began to ask a few questions, she could not help listening to the children's answers.

"Once upon a time," said Lady Ainsbro', "there was no world. All was dark and empty. There was no such little boy or girl as you, nor——"

"No," set off Marion, "nor no such a woman as you, nor no such a nurse as Nana, nor no such a footman as Charles, nor no——"

"That will do," said Lady Ainsbro'. "No, there

was no one in the world, and nothing. Now, what was the first thing God made? Marion, you must let Bertie answer this."

"Adam and Eve," said Bertie, promptly.

"Oh no, Bertie," whispered Marion; "they'd have been all in the dark, you know."

"Well," said Lady Ainsbro', "you tell me."

"Light," said Marion; "sun, moon——"

"Let Bertie go on. What other kind of light, Bertie?"

"Gas," said Bertie.

"Oh no, Bertie," said his sister. "God doesn't make the gas. Smith makes the gas."

"Tell him," said Lady Ainsbro'.

"Stars," they both said together.

"God *could* make the gas, if He liked," argued Bertie, "for He can do everything, you know."

"Yes," said Marion; "He can write with his fingers, like when He wrote the commandments on the tables of stone."

"I wish *I* could write with my fingers," said Bertie, mournfully: adding, after a moment's deep and interested thought, "Of course, God's got plenty of pens, only He likes better writing with his fingers."

Lady Ainsbro' now dropped the questioning form, and read aloud to them a little till the gong sounded, and Bertie dissolved in tears and complained the day was so short.

His brother picked him up to carry him upstairs,

saying, "Well! *I* can't make the day longer, you know."

"But God can," urged Bertie.

"I want *you* to carry me up," he said, wriggling out of his brother's arms, and throwing himself on Joan.

"Oh no!" said Edward; "you're much too big and heavy."

"Oh, do let me," said Joan.

The touch of Bertie's caressing arms was such joy to her. She could not explain the happiness the fancy he had taken to her seemed to give her.

So she wound her arms lovingly round him, and carried him up, the little fellow giving her a quiet kiss every now and then, and patting her face with his fat little hands.

"I believe you think I'm a little girl," she said, smiling down upon him.

"So you are—a kind of big little girl," he answered. "You're not quite a lady."

"Not quite a lady!" repeated Joan.

"No, not quite. You're a sort of 'playing lady,' you know. Have you got a mamma?"

"No," said Joan, softly.

"No mamma!" he exclaimed. "Did you *never* have one?"

A look of great pain passed over the girl's face, and her forlorn heart answered, "Never!"

"Is she quite dead?" said Bertie, in an awe-struck whisper.

Joan bowed her head.

"I wish she hadn't died, poor thing!" said the tender-hearted child, half crying.

Joan, remembering his grief of yesterday, and the way he had then been consoled, whispered that every one was much happier in heaven.

Bertie seemed comforted, but thoughtful.

"It was a long way to go," he said, looking up to the skylight over the staircase, "all the way to the sky. Did she go by the wailwoad?"

"How silly you are, Bertie!" said the superior Marion, who was following close behind. "Don't you know that angels come and carry us to heaven?"

"Puppose they should drop us!" said Bertie; but Marion treated the remark with the contempt she considered it deserved.

"If *I* were in heaven," said the little boy, addressing himself again to Joan, "I would like *sometimes* to come down and see mamma. Do you think God would let me? I could, you know," he went on meditatively, "give God the direction: Ainsbro' Park, —Langdale,—Yorkshire."

"You'd be too happy to want to come," said Joan, softly.

"Would God read me 'Mamma's Bible Stories'?" was the next question. "Does He read them to hisself of a Sunday evening, do you think?"

And as Joan hesitated, he added eagerly, "He does *everything*, you know!"

Happily for Joan, the arrival at the nursery door took away the necessity of providing an answer.

She deposited her little burden on the floor, and kissing him fondly, wished him good night.

"Well, Edward," said Lady Ainsbro' to her son that evening, "and how are you getting on with Lady Joan?"

Edward Manners smiled, and slightly shook his head.

"She is much more in love with little Bertie than ever she will be with me!" he answered.

"My dear boy!" exclaimed his mother, "you cannot expect everything to come in a day. Why, how long have you known her? You really mustn't be so downhearted. Faint heart never won fair lady."

"I am not downhearted, mother," answered the young man. "Lady Joan and I are great friends I only mean that she will never care for me in that way. I am quite sure of that."

"Tell me why," said Lady Ainsbro'."

"Because," he answered,—"but this is quite between you and I, and must not go any further,— because I have a shrewd suspicion that she is in love with somebody else."

"Impossible!" exclaimed his mother. "The girl has been immured all her life at Seaforth, like a nun in a convent. She has never seen any one since she grew up. Who *could* she be in love with?"

"Ah! well," said Edward Manners, "I may be mistaken, and I can't undertake to mention names But you mark my words, mother; Lady Joan will never be in love with *me!*"

CHAPTER IV.

THE ASSIZES.

"We can offer you something in the shape of dissipation to-day," said Lord Ainsbro' to Joan, at breakfast. "The assizes are going on at York, and if you would care to go, Lady Ainsbro' and my son will be delighted to take you. I wish I could go myself, but it is one of my busy days at home."

Joan expressed her readiness; and Lord Ainsbro' added, "It is very interesting sometimes, and I believe there are one or two important cases to be tried this year."

Soon after breakfast, therefore, the party started, and reached York in about an hour.

They were given some seats not far from the judge, and Joan was placed with Edward Manners on one side, and Lady Ainsbro' on the other.

A case was going on when they entered; and soon after they had settled themselves, the counsel for the defence rose, and addressed the jury on behalf

of his client. But he had not proceeded far, before
a strange and bewildering feeling came over little
Joan.

As music, without our actually listening to it, note
for note, brings over us a rush of thoughts and associations, so did the voice and the words which now
fell upon her ear affect her. Something they recalled
to her—some memory, she knew not what.

Colourless she sat, with her lips apart, wondering
what it could be. Somewhere, surely, sometime, she
had looked down upon some such scene, and been
swayed by the rush of words like these. Some time
or other, sitting entranced and excited, she had been
carried away on the wings of like intense and forcible
language, while her ear had been charmed by the
like beauty of intonation !

In vain she strove to catch that faint memory,
that something lying in the past, of which she was
being now reminded. She strained after it with all
her might, without knowing what it was she was
trying to remember ; but with a strong conviction
that, could it only become clear to her, it would bring
some great joy in its train. Sometimes she thought
she had caught hold of it ; but it seemed always to
slip away again, and to elude her grasp.

Gazing down upon the upturned faces, and seeing
in their expressions how the speaker swayed them at
his will, came the memory of other upturned faces,
swayed in like manner too.

Something told her that, with the applause which

would follow the close of the speech, all would become clear in her mind.

The speaker was drawing to an end of his defence in a forcible peroration; and she forced herself to listen to the grand though simple language which was falling on her ear.

He ceased rather suddenly; but his words, powerful and pleading, rang in her ear still.

An irrepressible murmur of admiration sounded through the court.

That was not the murmur she had expected. What was it she had thought to hear?

Echoing back from the years that were gone, it came suddenly to her that what she had expected was, "Bravo, Mr. Seaforth!" "Three cheers for Mr. Seaforth!" and in an instant all was clear to her.

Yes! It was Godfrey!

It was Godfrey himself who, in the disguising wig and gown, was down there in front of her.

As in a dream she heard the voices round her commenting on the speaking, and asking the young barrister's name. And as in a dream, when Lady Ainsbro' leant across her to beg her son to go and find out who he was, Joan turned to her very quietly, and said, "There is no need to ask; I can tell you. It is Godfrey—Godfrey Seaforth!"

* * * * * *

The crowd at the doors was very great at the end of the day, when every one dispersed.

The Ainsbro' carriage was got up with some diffi
culty. Joan was hardly conscious of the crowd
hardly conscious of anything as she passed along
on the arm of Edward Manners, and got into the
carriage.

But as she drove away, she suddenly sat up with
a start, and leaning forward eagerly, gazed out of the
carriage window, at the same moment almost in
voluntarily putting up her little white handkerchief.

The young barrister, who, still wearing his wig
and gown, was leaning against the door, watching the
crowds disperse, started violently also. He threw up
his hands, and started forward, but restrained him
self, with an evident effort, from the impulse to follow
the carriage.

Instead, he went up to one of the *employés*, and
pointing to it made some inquiries.

Then, hastily stepping out into the street, he
strained his longing gaze after it, until it was quite
out of sight.

CHAPTER V.

THE DAISIES' MISTAKE.

JOAN woke the morning after the assizes to the vague feeling that something joyful had occurred, and that something disagreeable was pending. The first recollection soon returned in a tumult of tremulous excitement, quickly followed by the second; by the cold, blank feeling that her visit to Ainsbro' was concluded, and that she was to return to Seaforth to-day.

On descending to breakfast, she was greeted with the news that her father's horses had met with a slight accident on the way, and that they could not possibly do the long drive till they had had a day and a night's rest. One of them was a little lame. Joan must, therefore, positively remain at Ainsbro' till to-morrow, and a telegram to that effect was to be despatched to Lord Seaforth at once.

To Joan the respite was like the answer to a prayer.

To remain in Godfrey's near vicinity another twenty-four hours—to have the wild hope still that somehow or other he may try to see her! It was almost too good to be true.

"It was most unfortunate," said Lady Ainsbro', regretfully, "that she and her husband and son should be engaged to a shooting party which could not be postponed; but Joan should be put under the charge of the children, who would prevent her feeling dull."

Lord and Lady Ainsbro' and Mr. Manners took a very kind leave of Joan, and Lady Ainsbro' said she hoped she would make what use she liked of the children as companions. She might keep them to sit with her at dinner, and do just as she liked with them.

Joan felt very thankful for this permission as the hours wore on. She was so restless and excited that she could not bear to be alone, and she could not read, or occupy herself in any way. The children's unconscious conversation was the greatest relief to her, and helped her to get through the day.

She found herself starting at every sound: at the ringing of every bell, the opening or shutting of every door, the sound in the road of any passing vehicle, or the footstep of any one in the garden.

Towards evening these excited feelings settled down into deep, blank disappointment.

Hope ebbed away, and when the sound of the dressing-gong told her night had really come, it left

her altogether. She felt now the only thing was to
put these thoughts away entirely, and resolutely to
turn her mind to something else.

She therefore told the children they might sit up
to dinner with her. She could not bear to let them
go out of her sight for an instant.

Marion and Bertie were delighted with this
arrangement, and hurried into the dining-room to
make sure places had been laid for them. Joan soon
found her attention was likely to be directed from her
own affairs. They sat at dinner, one on each side of
her, discoursing on various subjects connected with
the nurses and household, in the presence of three
men-servants. The first piece of news was that
Nana was soon going for a holiday to see her mother.
Joan, whose ideas of nurses were a great deal formed
by the mention of one in " Home they brought her
warrior dead," asked if Nana's mother was not a very
old woman.

But here she found she was quite mistaken.
Nana's mother, she discovered from Bertie's answer,
was not at all old; in fact, she was not as old as
Nana; or, at most, there was only a difference of two
years between them.

The conversation next turned upon hair-dressing.
Bertie patted and smoothed Joan's hair, and said
how soft and curly it was; while Marion made a
minute examination of the thick plaits at the back.
Then she came round to Joan's side, just as the

butler was in the act of pouring out some claret, and
said earnestly, gazing up into her face, "When you
take down your hair at night, does it come *right* off,
like mamma's, or does it stick to your head, like
mine?"

There was a few minutes' pause after this question
had been answered, and then Marion asked Joan if
she was tired.

"No, darling," answered Joan.   "Why?"

"Oh, only because mamma said you were like
Mrs. Jones, our new housekeeper; so I thought you
might be," was the inconsequent answer.

"Am I like the housekeeper?" asked Joan, rather
puzzled.

"Only not near so fat," put in Bertie, who was
busy patting the salt.

"No, of course not," answered Marion.   "I mean
you are like her because you are not used to children,
mamma said, and might get tired of us, so that we
were not to bother you *too* much.   So you are like
Mrs. Jones, ain't you?"

"Is she not used to children?" said Joan, for the
sake of saying something.

"No," answered Marion.   "And when we wanted
to go and cook, she said she couldn't be bothered.
We thought she was cross, but mamma said it was
only because she was not used to children.   Of
course, if she'd been born with children," added
Marion, "it would have been different."

After this, other subjects were introduced of more or less interest.

"Papa and mamma," said Bertie, "were talking such funny things about you before you came down to breakfast. If I could remember the words I would tell you all about it. They stopped directly you came in."

The children were now fetched to bed, and Joan, at their earnest request, attended their *couché.*

The following quarrel took place between them as they undressed :—

"Marion! Marion! you have upset my shoes and socks off the chair!"

"No, I didn't, Bertie."

"But you *did,* Marion; I saw you."

"I wish you wouldn't tell stories, Bertie."

"But I *saw* you; Marion."

"Well, never mind, Bertie."

"But it *does* mind!"

A slight pause, and then Bertie said, "Marion's telling a lie."

"Well, you're not my mistress," Marion finished off pompously.

To divert their thoughts, Joan began to sing to them. She sang the old-fashioned ditties her nurse had years and years ago sung to her; and six times over, at least, was she called upon for the prime favourite, which they had never heard before.

La - ven- der's blue, lit-tle fin-ger, Rose-ma-ry's green;

When I am king, lit-tle fin-ger, You shall be queen.

Who told you so, thum-by, thum-by? Who told you so?

'Twas mine own heart, lit-tle fin-ger, That told me so,

'Twas mine own heart, lit-tle fin-ger, That told me so.

II.

When you are dead, little finger,
　　As it may hap,
You shall be buried, little finger,
　　Under the tap.
For why ? For why, thumby?
　　Thumby, for why ?
That you may drink, little finger,
　　When you are dry.

"May we say our prayers to you, to-night?" asked Marion, when the entertainment was over, and the nurse said it was time for the children to be in bed.

And before Joan could assent or dissent, her breath was almost taken away by the promptitude with which first one and then the other knelt down and plunged into, " Pray, God, bless papa and mamma, brothers and sisters, and all kind friends. Amen."

"*You're* kind friends, you know," said Bertie, coaxingly, "and nurse says you'll perhaps be our sister some day. Do you think you will ? "

" I hope so," said Marion. " Don't you ? " And without waiting for an answer they both scampered away into the bedroom nursery.

Joan felt rather startled, and when she got to her own room, she sat thinking over the children's words. And her vague thoughts resolved themselves into two of some distinctness. First, that she must never come to Ainsbro' Park again ; and secondly, that if ever she had children of her own, she should like just such another little pair as Marion and Bertie.

The next morning, as the carriage was not ordered till one, Joan yielded to the children's entreaties that she would take one last walk with them, and come into the fields to get blackberries.

It was a lovely autumn day, the children were in high spirits, and for a time Joan joined in their occupation, and helped to reach the blackberries which were too high for them.

But a feeling of heart-sickness and weariness came over her, and she sat down under a tree to rest.

21

The children brought her hedge daisies and other treasures, and then returned to the blackberries once more.

Her sad thoughts returned upon her, and she had no power to drive them away.

And so it was too true! She was forgotten.

Other interests had come into his life, and she was nothing to him any more.

It was all very natural, *most* natural. It had been only compassion, such compassion as any noble-minded man would have felt for a lonely and neg-lected child.

It was all very different now. She was a woman now, and he a man with other aims and objects, and a new and different life.

But child or woman, he is the one idol of Joan's life, and as she sits there musing, she knows it all too well. Oh, why had she put up her handkerchief as a signal! A burning blush rose to her cheek at the recollection, and, dying away, left her paler than before, while blank desolation settled down upon her lonely, empty heart.

Lonely, lonely, more lonely than ever!

en's voices grew faint in the distance a
'her and further away; the quie
'nd her seemed to reflect th

"May we   There was a step on th
asked Marion, ,   nd Godfrey was standing a
the nurse said it
bed.   s hands to her with the old

" At last ! " he said ; " at last, little Joan ! "

A sense of overpowering shyness came over her. She felt as if he must read her very thoughts, and she turned away her head and did not answer.

" Am I quite forgotten ? " he said sadly.

She could not resist the yearning in his voice. Slowly she turned her dark eyes upon him, but they dropped beneath his gaze. She was afraid to let him see them lest he should read in their depths all that she was trying to conceal.

He stooped down and picked up some of the big hedge daisies the children had left lying at her feet.

Pulling off their petals one by one, he repeated to himself the old childish rhyme :

" M'aimes-tu ?

" Un peu ?

" Beaucoup ?

" Passionnément ?

" Point du tout ? "

It came in two cases to " Point du tout."

Godfrey threw the daisies down again, saying, as he did so, " Lie there, faithless daisies. As untrue to your old answers as Joan is untrue to hers. It is all so long ago that I am quite forgotten, and Joan does not love her elder brother any more ! "

Joan watched him as he did all this, and the old scenes of her childhood rose before her. The meadows disappeared, and she was standing again on the grass-plot by the fish-ponds.

It seemed easier now to connect the rising lawyer

with the Godfrey of her childhood— girlish dreams.

The old answer rose to her lips as words fell upon her ear.

Almost unconsciously, she turned whispered, " I think the daisies mus mistake, Godfrey, for I know I *do!* "

CHAPTER VI.

DIVIDED.

"AND you are still little Joan," he said softly, looking at her intently after the first burst of questions and answers had passed between them; "very little changed. Still the little Joan I found in the picture-gallery nearly eight years ago. But," he added anxiously, "a happier little Joan, I hope. Not quite the sad and lonely child I found there then?"

"Just the same," she answered; "no happier. Just as sad, and much more lonely."

A look of great pain passed over his face.

"I had so hoped," he said, "that changes in circumstances might have wrought a change, and brought you and your father closer together."

She shook her head.

"Is it his fault entirely?" he asked, looking at her searchingly.

She shook her head again. "How can I love any one who wrongs you so cruelly?"

The words burst from her before she could stop them.

"Is it really so?" he said; and something in his eyes, like a delight he seemed in vain to try to conceal, came for a moment and was gone directly. "Do you still believe in me as much as that?—But why," he added, hastily interrupting himself, "why do you say *more* lonely? What could be sadder or more lonely than the state in which I found you?"

"Because," she cried, "to have had so much, and to have lost it, is worse than never to have had anything at all. Because when I returned to the darkness and the loneliness in which you found me, I found it all the darker for having known what the light could be. Because when *you* left me you took all that *made* my life with you, and without you, life it has not been; only a slow bearing of existence from day to day. I always told you I could not live without you. Oh, Godfrey! why did you go?"

"Yet some say," he answered gently, without apparently noticing her last words, "some say the memory of bygone happiness is a blessing beyond price; a possession which is theirs for ever, which none can take away."

"*I* do not think so!" she exclaimed. "The contrast between the brightness of the past and the darkness of the present increases the pain tenfold. I endured my lonely childhood because I knew no better; but this blank, lonely girlhood, this present with no future, this life with no love—I *cannot* bear it, Godfrey. It is killing me day by day. And the past was so sunny; our life of love and sympathy so fair!"

He was deeply moved, and turned his head away with a bitter sigh. "And I," he said mournfully, "I, who vowed, under the picture, to care for you, and to make up to you for all you had suffered, I can do nothing to help you—nothing! Fate is dealing very sternly with us, little Joan."

"Godfrey!" she cried, "what is the mystery that is lying on your life? Tell me your secret, and let me bear with you all the sorrow and the trouble it entails upon you. Tell me."

She waited, breathless, as if life and death hung upon his answer.

He turned his head away again, and his eye sought the pure blue sky above, so often his refuge and solace in the dark hours of his trouble, and his face grew visibly paler. Oh, God! the temptation was terrible!

"Yes," urged one voice within him, "tell her. Let her help you to bear your life. It is for her happiness as well as for your own. Tell her."

"What!" said another voice, "lay such a burden on this young girl! Soil the whiteness of her pure young hands with your guilty secret!"

Very sadly he looked down upon her, as he answered, in hardly audible tones, "*I cannot.*"

Mournfully the summer breezes seemed to wail

and whisper round them; the wind in the fir-trees
caught up the accents and echoed, "I cannot."

"You do not really love me as you used," she
said, weeping, "or you would trust me more. Young
as I was, there were then no secrets between us, and
now—— "

He looked at her wistfully, almost reproachfully,
as he answered, in words they had so often in the old
days read together—

> "'Yet this inconstancy is such
> As you too shall adore;
> I could not love thee, dear, so much,
> Loved I not honour more.'"

A sudden light broke all over her face, and was
reflected for a moment on his. Then, as if alarmed
at the admission he was making, his face grew grave
and sad again, and the light died away.

"Between you and me, little Joan," he said in a
dreary, far-away voice, "there is a great gulf fixed.
On our sad young lives the word is written—divided!
I can link no life to mine; ask none to share my
name. Yet, I am not like you. I would not part
with the memory of our happy days together. To me
it is all in all!"

"And must it always be like this?" she asked;
"must we live on a memory for ever? Is there no
future for us, and to our sorrow and separation is
there to be *no* end?"

"I see no end as yet," he answered. "God
help us!"

"But we are so young," she cried, "and life stretches before us so long and so drearily. How shall we face our lives? How shall we bear to be divided—we who, though so unwanted by others, are all in all to each other?"

"Oh, Joan!" he said, "little Joan, is it really so? Am I really all in all to you still?"

He spoke with a kind of despair, with which a secret joy and pride struggled.

"Surely," she answered simply. "Who have I ever had in my world but you? And without you my world is empty indeed."

He half put out his hand as if to stop her as she spoke, but the look of pleasure crept into his eyes again, and this time it did not go directly.

Passionate words of love and devotion rose to his lips, but he forced them back, and clenched his hands firmly together.

"And you," she said timidly, pained by his manner—"do you not love me still? Am I not all in all to you too?"

"God help me!" he groaned; "you are the day-star of my life, little Joan."

"Then, Godfrey," she said, holding out her hands to him, "do not leave me any more. Think of the life to which I shall this day return! Am I loved? Am I wanted? Why should not we take our lives into our own hands. Take me with you. Let me share your troubles, and bear your burdens with you. Let me go where you go, live where you live, die where you die!"

She was looking at him with the trust and adoration of her childhood, in and with which the deeper love of riper years was merged and mingled.

He turned his head away, and covered his face with his hands.

Much had he borne in the dark and lonely path to which he had vowed himself, and the strength of his purpose had carried him through.

More would he bear, if bear he must; but when it came to see another suffer—oh, God! it was hard—hard.

So easy, in comparison, was it to bear trouble for himself; but to bear it for her! What was he to do? What was he to say? What could be done to help her?

He cast his thoughts back to her childhood, to see if he could glean or strength or counsel from the past; some memory of his dealings with the *child* in her troubles wherewith to help the woman in this her hour of trial.

Down the long gallery he sees her again receding, bright, brave, and smiling still; bearing herself so firm and bravely that he may not weaken or fail. He recalls once again, with a yearning love and pity, the light, childish step that strove so hard not to falter, the proud and queenly bearing of the now drooping little head.

Could he only touch that chord again; once more awaken those noble feelings which had carried her so bravely through before; call up for a moment that martyr spirit that so readily and gladly sacrifices itself for the sake of the one it loves!

He turned suddenly to her, holding out both his hands. "Little Joan," he said imploringly, "you must be my good angel still. You must help and not hinder me in my difficult life. Otherwise no blessing can rest upon our affection; it will be idolatry, not love. You must be the day-star of my life, to whom I may turn for strength to go on in the hard path of duty. Say you will help me to be brave and patient, by being both yourself. Oh, say it for my sake, little Joan!"

He had struck the right chord at last. She was herself again directly—her true unselfish self; a brave, self-sacrificing woman, ready to lay any burden on herself, if by so doing she could ease him by a fragment of the load he bore.

She put her hands in his and whispered, "I will."

"God bless you for those words!" he murmured; "refreshed and strengthened, they send me on my way. Oh, Joan! little Joan! God knows, *you* know, how gladly I would take you with me; but it may not be! Some day, perhaps; some day. Now wish me God-speed before I go."

* * * * * *

The children came chattering back, with their baskets full of the nuts and blackberries they had been gathering, to where Joan sat, as in a dream, feeling as if she had lived her life out since they went away.

"Have you been dull all alone?" said Bertie, anxiously. "Have we been too long away?"

The touch of his caressing little fingers and his coaxing accents were almost too much for the poor girl's overwrought feelings.

She hid her face in his curly hair to hide the tears which came into her eyes. "No, darling," she whispered, "I have not been dull."

But something in her voice made him suspicious, and he peeped anxiously under her hat.

"What's the matter *wiff* you?" he said. "Let me see your face. I want you to look at me with your great big eyes."

Joan raised her head, and looked full at the little fellow with a smile.

"You've got such a pretty face!" exclaimed the child, struck with a sudden admiration. "I didn't never *know* before what a pretty face you'd got!"

The light which is reflected straight from heaven was shining in the eyes of little Joan!

CHAPTER VII.

MR. WAUKENPHAST.

WHEN Hester returned from Nice, on the evening of Colin's visit to the châlet, she met the three girls a little way from the house, and they all returned home together.

"Well, my darlings," she said, as they walked along, "and what have you been doing all day? How did you get on without me?"

"Oh!" exclaimed Olive, "we have had such a happy day, mamma! You have no idea how pleasant it has been!"

"Why?" exclaimed Hester, surprised; "what has made it so pleasant?"

"We have had a visitor," said Olive, "and he has been sitting with us all day."

"A visitor!" exclaimed Hester. "Who? What do you mean?"

"Yes," said Olive, with sparkling eyes, "it was a

gentleman from Monaco; and we've had such a pleasant time!"

"A gentleman from Monaco!" repeated Hester,
more and more bewildered. "Has your father been
home? Did he bring him?"

"Oh dear, no!" said Olive; "he came quite by
himself. And he *is* so nice, mother dear; it is a pity
you missed him."

"But who is he?" inquired Hester, "and what
brought him here? What is his name?"

"He is a Scotchman," said Olive, "and we call
him Mr. Waukenphast."

"Waukenphast!" said Hester; "that is not a
Scotch name. Oh, my dear children, you should not
have made friends with a stranger when I was away.
He may be a card-sharper from Monaco, or anything
else."

"Oh no, indeed, mother," said Olive, earnestly;
"he has been saying what a wicked place Monaco is,
and how he has been so dreadfully cheated himself
that he's never going to play again. I am sure when
you see him, you'll see in a minute he *couldn't* be a
card-sharper. His face is much too good and
pleasant."

"When I see him!" repeated Hester. "Why, is
he here still?"

"No! but he's coming again," said Olive. "We
begged and prayed him to come again soon, and he
promised he would. So you will see him, and I
know you will like him."

Hester now turned to her eldest daughter, and succeeded in getting a rather more definite account from her of the day's proceedings.

But the circumstance only sent her to bed with a heavier heart than usual, and a deeper sense of her children's unprotected position, both in the present and in the future.

From that day she fancied she noticed a change in Olive. She seemed restless, and as if always in expectation of something.

She could not settle herself steadily to her usual occupations.

The days, however, passed on, and Mr. Waukenphast did not reappear.

But one morning, when Olive and her mother were sitting together in the orange grove, Olive's work suddenly dropped upon her lap, and her eyes became fixed on some distant object, while a bright blush overspread her face.

" What are you thinking about, Olly ? " asked her mother, surprised at the change in the girl's face, and suddenly struck with her beauty.

" He is coming, mother ! " said Olive, softly. " Here he is ! "

" Who ? " said Hester, much puzzled, and she turned quickly round.

Colin was advancing, hat in hand—the impersonation of bright, frank, English manhood.

Hester felt there was no doubting that the young man before her was a high-bred English gentleman.

She held out her hand with a smile.

"This is mamma," said Olive shyly, as he came up and shook hands.

"I am so sorry," he said, addressing himself to Olive, after a few respectful words of greeting to her mother, "I am so sorry I could not come before, but I have had some business to attend to, and could not get away."

"Business at Monaco!" exclaimed Olive; "I did not know there was any business at Monaco. I thought it was all play!"

"Ah! Miss Olive," said Colin, "unfortunately, play at Monaco is business to which what *we* call business is only play. *Their* play is indeed a terrible business. But my business has been at Nice, not Monaco!"

His brow clouded over as he spoke.

"And what has your business been *there?*" she asked. "Not play, surely!"

"No!" he answered gravely. "I have been engaged in trying to bring an old fox to earth, and I mean to hunt him down, too."

"Him!" she said. "Who?"

"I don't know his name," he answered, "or care to; I know *him*, that's quite enough. These gamblers, Miss Olive, don't care to give their real names always, and——"

"My daughter," interrupted Hester hastily, and rather stiffly, "knows nothing about these things; you are talking Greek to her."

"I beg your pardon," said Colin directly; "I ought not to run on like this. But I was just following the course of my own thoughts on a subject of which they are just now full, and I quite forgot who I was speaking to."

"Forgot who you were speaking to?" laughed Olive. "Why, you never knew, did you?"

"Yes!" he answered. "If you remember, when I was here before, you told me your name, and I said I should never forget it. And," he added, half to himself, "I never shall."

"Ah! yes, but only my Christian name," she said. "You don't know my surname. Now I don't know your Christian name, but I do know your surname. That's just the difference."

"*Do* you!" he said; "I do not remember telling it to you."

"Yes," answered Olive. "You are Mr. Waukenphast."

Colin laughed. "*You* said that was my name," he replied, "but *I* never did."

Hester here joined in.

"My daughter told me," she said, "that your name was Waukenphast, and I quite believed her. At the same time she said you were Scotch, and I confess I—— "

"You thought I was an impostor," laughed Colin. "I don't wonder. No, Miss Olive," he said, turning to the young girl, "there is no clan Waukenphast, but there *is* a clan Fraser, and to it I belong—

22

> Colin Fraser is my name,
> Scotland is my nation,
> The little Glen's my dwelling-place,
> A pleasant habitation.'

Or, rather," he added, "it ought to be. Unfortunately, it is not. You must," he added, turning once
more to Hester, who seemed suddenly lost in thought,
"have wondered who **your** daughters' visitor could
be!"

"I did, indeed!" she said, looking at him, but
speaking as if her thoughts were far away.

"But now you know, mamma," said Olive.

"Yes!" said Hester, dreamily, and as if speaking to herself, "I hear. He is Colin Fraser. Most
extraordinary!"

"No!" put in Olive, "not yet; something extraordinary some day, but only unpaid attaché as yet.
But how did you guess that, mamma dear?"

Hester shook herself free from her thoughts, to
wonder how she was ever to teach a daughter brought
up in the mountains the manners of society.

"I don't wish to ask impertinent questions," said
Colin, "but may I, in return for my own confidences,
know the name of the lady to whom I am speaking, and who, as yet, I only know as Miss Olive's
mother?"

"No!" said Hester, hurriedly, "not yet. Later
on, perhaps; but for the present, I will only be Miss
Olive's mother."

Colin bowed assent, but looked disappointed.

" Mr. Fraser," added Hester, " will you stay here the night, if your business at Nice is concluded ? We can only offer you a very humble lodging, and very frugal fare ; but such as it is you are welcome to it. And as to clothes, etc., my husband's wardrobe is very much at your disposal. He himself is away just now."

Colin accepted the invitation with great eagerness.

The arrival of Hessie and Venetia on the scene then gave a fresh turn to the conversation, and the mother, after a time, left them all together, and went into the house to make a few preparations for the comfort of the guest, and as soon as she was gone, Colin and Olive strolled away together, and were seen no more.

When the hour of supper drew near, Hessie and Venice returned to the châlet, but the other two were wandering still.

And when they appeared, they were still talking gaily, as though they had not half finished all they had to say.

Colin will never forget that evening. After supper, they all sat out in the orange grove, and the three sisters sang glees without accompaniment.

The moon shone through the olives, and to his mind it was the fairest scene he had ever beheld.

Fain would he it could have lasted longer; but Hester broke up the party after a time, and seemed anxious to dismiss him to the smoking-room, and to send the girls to bed.

She took him there herself, and then went upstairs with her daughters.

But as soon as the lights were out in the house and all was quiet, she came down again, and returned to the smoking-room, where Colin was sitting, wrapped in pleasant thoughts.

Closing the door carefully and softly behind her she came forward, and said, that if he were not very tired, she should be glad to have some conversation with him.

Colin, whose thoughts were all on one subject who could not that night conceive of any other, felt very nervous.

He was afraid the unpaid attaché was going to receive a dismissal at the hands of an anxious mother.

He placed a chair for her, and waited anxiously for her to begin.

CHAPTER VIII.

THE CONVERSATION IN THE SMOKING-ROOM.

BUT her first words changed the current of his thoughts entirely.

"Colin Fraser," she said sadly, "we ought not to be strangers to one another. Do you not know, have you not guessed, ere this, who we are?"

But Colin only looked bewildered.

"When I refused to give you my name to-day," she continued, "it was that I did not wish you in the presence of my daughters to discover what I perceived at once myself. Tell me, were you not brought up at Seaforth, and were you not for a time thrown there with Lord Seaforth's adopted son?"

"Godfrey Seaforth!" exclaimed Colin, starting from his seat, and a rush of thought coming over him; "what of Godfrey Seaforth? What have you to do with him?"

"Alas!" she said, "I am his mother!"

"His mother!" cried Colin, almost knocked over with astonishment; "Godfrey Seaforth's mother!"

But his next feeling was the overpowering shame and regret which he always felt in connection with that part of his life; the feeling that his own dead mother had, in all concerning Godfrey, been deeply to blame.

Surely Godfrey Seaforth's mother could not but be thinking so too!

But when he glanced at Hester, he saw that no feelings of that sort were at work in her mind. Her attitude was one of deep dejection, and her eyes expressed nothing but pitiful entreaty.

"My boy!" she said in a broken voice, "what of him? Tell me something about him. Has anything been heard? Is anything known?"

Colin shook his head mournfully.

"I know nothing about him, Mrs. Seaforth— nothing."

She turned away, deeply disappointed.

"But you can, perhaps, throw some light upon the past," she said eagerly. "*Anything* you can tell me of his life at Seaforth will be a revelation to me; and may help me to understand the present. Tell me anything you can remember."

Poor Colin! It was a trying request, and a hard task, to go over the past with Godfrey's mother, retracing passages he would so gladly forget in the life of his own!

He screened her in his recital as well as he could;

but he could not help letting Hester see that he did not hold her entirely blameless.

" She is dead, is she not ? " said Hester softly.

"Alas! poor mother! " he answered, " she pined away and died. Hers was a difficult nature, and its pride could not brook mortification. She could not survive failure and banishment. But she repented bitterly, Mrs. Seaforth," he went on earnestly. " She told me and my brother on her death-bed that had she that part of her life to live over again, she would act very differently. She charged us both, if ever we met Godfrey Seaforth again, to tell him so, and to beg him to forgive her for her conduct towards him. But one thing," he added hesitatingly, " one thing I must say. I do not think any word or act of hers had anything to do with Lord Seaforth's alienation from his nephew. That was altogether a separate matter. All that is wrapped in mystery, which will, I fancy sometimes, never be revealed till the Judgment Day. I have, however, my own ideas about it."

Hester caught eagerly at his words, and begged him to tell her what those ideas were.

Colin looked terribly confused. He blushed scarlet, and answered hurriedly, "Oh no! indeed I cannot. Pray do not ask me. I entirely forgot who I was speaking to."

She looked searchingly at him for a moment, and said quietly, though with deep sadness, " Do not fear offending me. Say on. It will be kinder in the end. Do not mind me. Look upon me only as Godfrey's mother, and speak without a thought of any one else."

"If it is your desire," he said—but he looked away from her as he spoke—" I will. I have always fancied he had fallen into the hands of, and been led away by, his father !"

There was a silence, and he was afraid that after all she was hurt and angry.

But she was only thinking deeply. "It could not be," she said at last; "it could not be without my knowing it. No! he has never been near his father nor me. He has held no communication of any sort with us. He has not written a line to me for many, many years."

"Then what is your idea about him?" asked Colin. "How do you account for his conduct?"

"I will tell you," she answered, with a deep sigh; "I feel I can trust you, and that you will understand."

She then, to begin with, confided to him all her old fears and scruples about the way in which Godfrey had been brought up, with which the reader is acquainted, keeping as much in the background as possible his father's share in the matter.

"Think," she went on, "of the almost primeval life he led here, and then think of his sudden introduction into English life. Look at his sisters. You see its effect upon them. They are like children in their ignorance of the world. And he was taken away from here and suddenly plunged into English life, with an independent fortune in the present, and heir to thousands in the future. His uncle had no hold over him. He deeply resented his conduct in the matter of disinheriting his father, and so he neither liked nor respected him. How do I know into what bad hands he may have fallen, into what a life of reckless expenditure he, with no idea of the value of money, may have been led? But still, in spite of all this, I should not have felt so hopeless if it had not been for his refusing to meet me, for his taking flight from me. That is really why my heart misgives me so. That is why I feel he must know himself to be deeply to blame. He shrank from seeing me. He would not meet me face to face. Me! his mother!"

And she covered her face with her hands. "Then the long, unbroken silence of all these years since," she went on, a few minutes after; "there is to my mind another sad proof of his guilt. Why should he mistrust my love and hide from me like this! He must have changed very much, or else entirely forgotten, if he can think me so unforgiving. What sin could he commit that I would not freely forgive? What sorrow could the knowledge of his wrong-doing bring me that could be so hard to bear as this blank, cold silence, this never-ending suspense and uncertainty? Oh, if I only knew where he was! If I could only write to him, and assure him of my forgiveness, and beg him to come back to me! I still feel that if I could only meet him, only look into his eyes for a moment, I could make him tell me all. But I have never been able to do anything to find him. I have never had any one to whom I could turn for help."

She paused for a moment, and then went on more calmly. "When I discovered who you were to-day, my first thought was you would be able to tell me something. It seems you cannot; but at least you can help me to find out. Oh, Mr. Fraser! find him for me, I implore you! Tell him all I have said. Or, if you cannot go to England yourself, have you no friend who would try and find out *something* about him; find out, at least, whether he is dead or alive?"

"Mrs. Seaforth," answered Colin, deeply moved, "I cannot tell you how thankful, how grateful, I should be, if I could be the means of helping you; if, in God's mercy, I might in any way lessen the trouble by which you and yours have been overwhelmed. That my family should be associated in your mind with other thoughts than those with which I feel you must regard it, would be a joy to me which I can hardly describe to you. I would start off to England this very night if I could; but, alas! I am not my own master. Do not, however," he added quickly, seeing her face fall with disappointment, "do not despair. Much can be done by writing, and I can trust my brother to do all that I would do myself. He is a curate in Warwickshire, but I know he will go to London directly on such an errand as this, and put himself in communication with the necessary authorities, and do all he can to find out something about your son. I will write now directly, and say exactly what you wish, so that my brother's answer may reach me before the ambassador carries me back to Berlin. After that, Andrew had better correspond directly with you."

"God bless you, Mr. Fraser!" she exclaimed, suddenly filled with hope. "May God bless and reward you! I can never tell you what it is to me. I have longed day and night for an opportunity of enlisting some one's sympathy and assistance, but all hope of it was fast dying away. It is, indeed, marvellous that you, of all people, should have been sent to my help. It seems almost like a miracle. God-sent you are, you must be. I wish I knew how to repay you for your kindness."

"You can," suddenly exclaimed Colin, impetuously; "you can repay me a thousandfold; you can give me the hope of a reward out of all proportion to the poor services I am rendering you!"

"Can I?" she said, wondering. "How?"

"Can you not guess?" exclaimed Colin.

"No," she said. "What can it be? Tell me."

"The hope," he answered, "that you will one day give me your daughter for my own!"

"My daughter!" she repeated. "Which daughter?"

"Your daughter Olive," he answered.

"Olive!" she exclaimed. "Little Olly! Why, Olive is a mere child!"

" Time will cure that," he said eagerly; " and I am only asking you to give me the hope of it, when I have risen in my profession, and can offer her a home."

" Have you spoken to her ? " she asked hastily.

And, on Colin's earnestly answering in the negative, she added, imploringly—

"Do not speak to her yet! She is so young, so inexperienced. Wait a little longer. And indeed, even as far as *I* am concerned, you must not expect an answer to-night. I am so taken by surprise, so bewildered. Let me sleep upon it, and give you an answer to-morrow."

So saying, she wished Colin a kind good-night; and sought her pillow with a vague kind of undefined feeling that the future did not look quite so hopeless as usual, and that there was a glimmer of light on the darkness of her way.

For, if one child's future was settled, and in safe hands, there would be a refuge for the others, when those dark days came which were still ever present to her mind.

CHAPTER IX.

MUTUAL RECOGNITIONS.

DOWNWARDS, ever downwards, had been Godfrey Seaforth the elder's career. Gradually he had passed the narrow boundary line that divides honour from dishonour, truth from falsehood.

Lost now to all sense of principle, he stooped habitually to get by foul means what he could not always obtain by fair.

He had of late years frequented Nice more than Monaco, and it was here that he was the terror of the club, though as yet he was not definitely suspected. Vague rumours were heard sometimes as to the secret of his extraordinary and persistent luck; but they died away without any results, for no one could bring home to him their vague suspicions.

Intense was the excitement of the life Godfrey led.

At first, he had been in daily and hourly dread of detection, but he had got accustomed to the feeling now; and as he had never been in any danger of being discovered, he had got hardened in his evil course, and had lost the fear of exposure.

But soon after the arrival of the English ambassador from Berlin, he began to have an uneasy feeling with regard to a young Englishman, who, at about the same time, appeared at the club. He was a tall, fair, good-looking young man. At first he had been willing enough to become one of Godfrey's victims. But he now never played. All the same, he continued to frequent the club, and Godfrey had an uncomfortable consciousness that he was often hovering near him, and it suddenly occurred to him that the young man was watching his play.

As this dawned upon him more forcibly, he grew alarmed; and made up his mind to play fairly for a time to disarm suspicion.

But the consequence of this manœuvre was that he lost heavily.

Terrified at this result, he resolved to win back some part of his money in his accustomed manner, and then to go home for a while till this young spy should have disappeared. He ascertained that he was one of the attachés belonging to the Embassy, and he also ascertained that the ambassador's visit to Nice was drawing to a close, so that the club would only be for a week or so longer infested by this young and observant Englishman.

Godfrey was very little at the châlet now. His home was not to him what it had been in the days when we first found him in the orange grove, playing with his little daughters. He did not care for them as he used.

The girls were growing up, and he was often made to feel that they were sufferers through him, as he had felt long ago in his son's case. He knew Hester thought so, he could not help feeling it himself; and any one who caused him twinges of conscience was apt to become distasteful to him.

His life of hidden dishonesty, too, made him feel them far above him, and the incessant excitement in which he lived made the pure pleasures of his home insipid.

But a deeper reason was that he could never look his wife in the face now. He had so much on his conscience which he kept concealed from her, and he knew well how she would shrink from him, did she know all.

And, hardened as Godfrey was, he could not bear the thought of this even now. He could not bear the idea of her despising him, and holding him in contempt.

His old love and admiration of her and of her goodness was strong in him as ever. He dared not meet the glance of her pure eyes, or contrast her blameless life with the pit of iniquity in which he felt himself to be irretrievably sunk.

That she had some vague suspicion in connection with his play he felt almost sure, for whenever he had returned home with large sums, she had invariably refused to make use of any part of them.

She would never touch a penny of the money
Her own and her girls' personal expenses and those
of the household she managed entirely on the share
of the allowance proportioned to her use ; and that
she declared, was sufficient.

So, as we said just now, Godfrey's visits to the
châlet were few and far between. He had not been
there for at least three weeks, when the resolution to
which he had come, with regard to the importance of
being absent from the club for a little while, made
him suddenly leave Nice, and take his way home.

     *   *   *   *   *   *

The morning after Hester's interview with Colin
when they all met at breakfast, she watched Olive
narrowly, and she fancied there was a shyness and a
tremulousness in her manner to Colin, which she had
never seen her show to any one else. She found her
self wondering whether the child had already, and in
so short a time, surrendered her young affections.

Her reverie was broken by the sound of hasty
footsteps in the garden. They ascended the steps of
the balcony, and some one entered the room by the
window.

"Papa!" cried the girls.

"How are you all?" said a voice that Colin
thought he knew, and he looked round.

As the new-comer's eye met those of the young
man who was sitting so happily with his wife and
daughters, he started as if he had seen a ghost. He
turned white to the very lips, and clinging tightly for

support to the back of the chair nearest him, he breathed hard and fast, uttering something between a curse and an exclamation.

And at the same moment there burst upon Colin the appalling conviction that the gambler at Nice and Godfrey Seaforth were one and the same person, and that the man he was seeking to destroy was Olive's father!

CHAPTER X.

WHAT DOES IT ALL MEAN?

GODFREY SEAFORTH was the first to recover himself He put on his most civil and cordial manner, and advancing to the young man as if he had never seen him before, he bade him welcome to his poor châlet and declared with great warmth that any friend of hi wife and daughters must be his friend too.

Colin received these overtures as calmly as he could, but he was so overcome by the discovery he had made that he could only find voice to express his thanks in a confused and incoherent manner.

Godfrey then turned to his daughters, and told them to entertain their guest by showing him the surrounding country, and specially mentioned a certain view to which he wished them to conduct him and which was at some distance.

As soon as the door had closed upon the three girls and Colin, Godfrey's manner changed. He looked nervous and confused. He offered his wife no explanation of what had taken place; his chief object seemed to be to avoid meeting her eye.

"I am very tired, Hester," he said, in an odd, confused way. "I shall go and lie down in the smoking-room, and try to sleep. Will you see that no one comes there to disturb me for the next two or three hours?"

So saying, he left the room, closing the door after him. But he did not remain in the smoking-room an instant. He went out by a back door, and crept stealthily along till his footsteps could not be heard by his wife as she sat by the window in the drawing-room.

Then he set off running as hard as he could back to the station, which he reached just in time to throw himself, hot and exhausted, into the train. And, an hour after, while Hester was imagining him to be asleep in the smoking-room, he was sitting in his usual place in the club at Nice, taking advantage of Colin's absence to recover the money he had lost in his usual unprincipled manner.

Now, the mistake that Godfrey made was in supposing Colin to be the only one who was concerned in trying to detect his evil practices.

There were several others, and he was, in fact, the victim of a plot which only his sudden change of tactics had for a time caused to fall to the ground. Colin's temporary absence from Nice, therefore, made no real difference to the danger he was in of being

He went thus, unconscious and unarmed, straight into the jaws of the enemy; and, as he sat playing, secure in the feeling that the young spy was miles away, he was in momentary danger of exposure, surrounded on all sides by those who were ready and waiting to bring his double-dealings to light.

Meanwhile, Hester, alarmed beyond measure at her husband's manner and conduct, sat where he had left her, trying to think it out. That something dreadful was going on she felt sure. Her husband's dismay at seeing Colin convinced her that such was the case, and also the effect which his appearance had had upon Colin himself.

Godfrey's evident fear of the young man, his anxiety to be civil to him, and to make him remain at the châlet, filled her with misgiving.

What could it all mean! There came back to her, too, with a cold pang, the recollection of Colin's words to Olive as to the business which had detained him, and his intention of unearthing a plot, or words to that effect.

Could it be—oh, horrible thought!—that her husband had fallen so low as to——? and that Colin was one of his victims?

She shuddered and turned cold.

Slow lingering steps now came on to the balcony, and paused at the drawing-room window.

Hester looked up, and saw Olive standing there in an attitude which expressed utter dejection, and with all the radiancy gone out of her face.

"What is the matter, darling?" she inquired anxiously.

Olive's pride struggled for a moment with her wounded feelings. She tried to say, "Nothing," but it would not do.

"He has gone!" she said, in a faltering voice.

"He!" exclaimed Hester. "Who? Not Colin Fraser, surely!"

Her thoughts for the moment were all of her husband, and she was terrified for his sake.

Olive bowed her head; she could not steady her voice to speak.

"Where has he gone?" exclaimed Hester. "What did he say?"

"Oh, mother," answered Olive, "he said nothing! He gave no reason at all. He suddenly said he *must* catch the train to Nice, and he rushed off without saying good-bye, or telling me when he would come back again."

Hester looked pityingly at the poor girl's quivering lips and glistening eyes, and murmured to herself, "Poor Olive! Poor little Olly!" For it was clear, too clear, to her.

Colin was gone without a word of explanation, without a word of farewell, without coming to her for the answer to the request he had made her last night, and which she had promised to give him to-day.

Yes; it was quite clear. There was no doubt in her mind as to the reason of his abrupt departure.

He had recognized Godfrey, and would have

nothing to do with the daughter of such a man; he had no longer any desire to connect himself with the family.

But even while her thoughts were full of Olive, she felt her husband ought at once to know the guest had returned to Nice. Much might be hanging upon it.

"Go, my darling," she whispered to Olive, "go to the smoking-room, and tell your father I want him to come and speak to me directly."

"I don't think papa is there," answered Olive. "We saw him about an hour ago running with all his might towards the station."

Hester quickly turned away her head that her child should not see the effect of her unexpected announcement.

She hastily left the **room**, and went to the smoking-room. Alas! she found Olive's information was correct.

There was no one there; and she realised with a sharp pang that her husband had purposely deceived her.

Colin Fraser all this time was chafing at the little station, having missed the train by a quarter of an hour.

The moment Olive had innocently pointed out to him her father's figure tearing in the direction of the station he had abruptly left her side, and torn after him.

His intention was to warn him of the plot which

was being concocted against him at Nice, and to persuade him to remain where he was.

He strained every nerve to reach the station. But in vain.

Hard as he tried, he was too late; and arrived to find the train had started.

Detained thus for an hour or more, it was past mid-day before Colin reached Nice.

His plan now was to try, by all the means in his power, to persuade his friends to give up the idea of exposing Godfrey Seaforth; to announce to them his intention of withdrawing altogether from the plot, and to beg them do the same.

Should he find them unwilling, he intended to urge his request on the ground that it was to him now a personal and family matter, since he had made the discovery that the gambler was his stepfather's own brother.

He went straight to the club, but found he was too late.

It was all over.

Godfrey Seaforth had been detected, exposed, disgraced, and had disappeared no one knew where.

CHAPTER XI.

IN THE GARDENS OF MONACO.

STRUCK dumb with consternation, Colin left the club, and took his way back to the station.

He supposed that most likely Godfrey would return home, and the hope of being of some use to the unhappy family made him determine to return to the châlet also.

His supposition proved correct, for he spied a skulking form disappearing into a carriage of the waiting train, and he got into the next compartment.

But the glimpse he had had of Godfrey Seaforth's face filled him with vague alarms. The idea of that awful face appearing in the orange grove made him quite giddy for a moment.

It seemed to him like Sin entering Paradise, and blighting for ever the happiness of its pure and innocent inhabitants.

To Colin's surprise, when the train stopped at the little station, no one got out from the next carriage.

What could this mean? With a dread upon him of impending trouble, Colin determined not to leave the train. He would follow Godfrey Seaforth, and keep watch over him. He felt it was not safe to leave him, and that he ought, for the family's sake, to find out where he was going, and what he was going to do.

On the first head he was not left long in doubt. When the train arrived at Monté Carlo, Godfrey was out in a moment, and disappeared in the crowd so rapidly that Colin lost sight of him.

However, he got out also, and joined the crowd which swarmed up the steps to the gaming establishment, and took his way to the tables.

The *salon de jeu* was crowded; but all the same he soon spied the figure of which he was in search, seating itself at the *rouge-et-noir* table, and about to begin to play.

Godfrey Seaforth's eyes had a wild, unnatural look about them, and he seemed strangely excited.

Afraid of attracting his attention, and yet so alarmed by his appearance as to be more determined than ever not to leave him, Colin went on to the *roulette* table for about half an hour, and then returned to the *rouge-et-noir* board.

Yes, still there; still playing. Playing heavily, madly, desperately—losing heavily, too.

Colin then left the *salon de jeu*, went into the ballroom, and sat down there to await the course of events.

The band was playing in its usual entrancing

manner, and, carried away on the wings of the music, Colin's thoughts were soon set moving with a mixture of tremulous happiness and a dull sense of pain, when suddenly he sees him coming.

How awful he looks! There is a nameless terror on his face, and a look of despair in his eye.

Hurrying through the ball-room, gliding from behind one marble column to another, he passes through the hall, and, stealing past the tall, grave men in their blue and red liveries laced with gold, goes out through the open door into the gardens.

And here Colin, though he had followed him as quickly as he dared, loses sight of him.

But the reader can follow him still.

Stealing along, with that nameless expression of fear and horror on his face; skulking like a thief, through the public walks, till he comes to a more secluded spot, where he halts, and with nerveless, trembling hands feels in his breast pocket, and takes out a pistol. . . . .

All around, the gorgeous scene of Nature's beauty —the tall parasol pine, the dark cypress, the graceful palm, bright orange, and fantastic fig-tree; the luxuriant growth of wild geranium, myrtle, oleander, cactus, and Indian fig;—above, the cloudless sky; and below, the blue waters of the Mediterranean!

So fair the background! And in the foreground a dishonoured, despairing man, flying from ruin and disgrace into ruin and crime more disgraceful still.

The loveliest place in all the world—and the wickedest!

Never had the sky been more cloudless, nor the sea more blue;—never had the surroundings looked more pure and lovely;—never, amid the sin and discord of Earth, had they seemed more to speak of the peace and purity of Heaven—than on that day and at that hour when Godfrey Seaforth shot himself in the Gardens of Monaco.

CHAPTER XII.

THE END OF IT ALL.

It is Sunday in the little châlet. Mother and daughters have been reading the Church Prayers; and now the three girls are at the piano singing hymns.

They are singing the hymn to the dying year.

Hester, sitting by the window, gazing out, shudders, she hardly knows why, as the solemn refrain falls upon her ear—

> "As the tree falls, so must it lie;
> As the man lives, so must he die."

But a sudden change was given to her thoughts by the opening of the door, and the sound of the cry of joy with which Olive left the piano and sprang forward.

Surprised, Hester turned round, and saw Colin Fraser standing in the doorway.

But though he took Olive's hand in his, there was

no answering look of joy in his eye. He looked at Hester and said, " Send them away, and let me speak to you alone."

There was something in his whole aspect, in the look of horror which still pervaded his face, that made her feel that something fearful had happened. She came up to him as the door closed upon the girls. " You have come to tell me," she said quietly, as she laid her hand upon his arm, "that something has happened to my husband."

And, sitting down, as gently as he could, he told her all.

It had come, then ! The blow had at last fallen ! The fears and forebodings she had always had, the presentiment ever in her mind, had at last come to their fulfilment. The terrible lesson which she had always felt she must at last be called upon to learn;—here it was !

But, O God ! in her wildest moments she had never thought of such untold horror as this ! Never could she have believed him to have fallen so low. Never could she have believed him to be capable of this !

Such fearful rebellion against his Maker; no moral sense, no conscience—nothing ! No feeling for her even, nor for the disgrace he was bringing upon his family, and handing down to his children: the heritage of unutterable shame.

And so this was the end of it all ! It was always to end like this.

All her thought and care wasted; all her prayers thrown away; all her influence vain.

All her ceaseless endeavours to lead him into the right path, all her silent hours of agonising intercession; all to end like this!

A disgraced life, a dishonoured name, and death by his own hand at last.

God had indeed taken the pruning-knife into His own hand: the rock was disintegrated, but, O God! how could it grow anything *now*!

Gradually as she sped along in the train with Colin on her way to Monaco, she grew calm enough to be thankful that he had not died on the spot—had not been cut off in a moment; that, though dying, he was not yet dead.

Faithful to nothing, true to no promise, bound by no laws; yet still, in the old days, he had seemed sometimes to *listen* to her instructions, though he never retained or acted upon them.

Though he would talk and act the next day as if she had said nothing the day before, yet she had felt sure she had *at the time* made some faint impression. She had been able *sometimes* to bring to bear all her influence upon him, to rouse his conscience and to get at his best feelings for a transient fit of earnestness, under the power of which he would sometimes make promises and form resolutions.

Oh for a transient fit of earnestness *now*! which would not, dying as he was, have time to pass away; and under the influence of which he might pass repenting into the presence of his Maker. Oh that he may yet find a place for repentance, if he sought it carefully with tears!

Might she not, perhaps, find him changed by the awful catastrophe?

Might this horrible event be an answer to her prayers, after all?

Far from its being a proof that God had forsaken him, might it not be one of His purposes concerning him, that he *should* fall into the very depths; because nothing less than sinking into such utter vileness, and becoming such an object of horror and detestation even to himself, could rouse him to a sense of what he was, and of what iniquity he was capable?

Something she had heard or read of, and it had fixed itself in her mind, of God sometimes making use of a terrible fall to reveal a sinner to himself; that sin being a disease, the man is not always conscious of his state. That he goes on from day to day, and no one, himself included, is aware how sinful he is. That God then lets him fall to the very depths, to show him to himself and to others as he really is; that, realising by his fault all the wickedness of which he is capable, he may look to God to raise him up out of the pit into which he has sunk. And so, by his very fall, he rises!

A messenger was waiting at the station at Monté Carlo, with a note from the doctor to say his patient was still alive; and they proceeded at once to the hotel.

"*Il demande madame, à chaque instant,*" said the kind old doctor as he met her at the door, and held both her hands for a moment in sympathising pity. And then he led her into the chamber of death, and left her alone with her husband.

CHAPTER XIII.

HUSBAND AND WIFE.

Looking down upon him as he lay, wandering, muttering, unconscious of her presence, a shrinking fear came over her, and her hopes died away.

It was not that she shrank herself from the polluted and blood-stained man; it was no physical fear. It was the fear suggested by the words of the hymn her girls had been so lately singing, and which kept repeating themselves in her brain—

> " As the tree falls, so must it lie,
> As the man lives, so must he die;
> As the man dies, so must he be,
> All through the days of eternity."

It seemed to her the voices of his own children were ringing the knell of their father's hopes of salvation.

For it seemed so impossible he should be otherwise than he had always been, so certain that death in itself can work no sudden and mysterious change.

24

The conviction came over her more surely than ever that death is in no sense an end, but merely an event, an episode, a development, in the course of the life which begins here, and continues throughout eternity; that as it finds the man, so will it leave him : he that is holy, holy still; he that is filthy, filthy still.

Yet she could not but feel she had no right to murmur or complain. Whatsoever a man soweth, *that* shall he also reap. He had sowed to the flesh, and he had reaped the reward of his sowing.

Yes. Godfrey Seaforth's punishment was natural, not arbitrary. For God's moral laws and judgments are as fixed and unalterable as the unchangeable laws of nature.

To the infringement of every law, moral as well as natural, its own penalty; and man, even here below, can no more escape the penalty annexed to the infringement of God's moral law, than can he who puts his hand into the flame escape being burnt, or he who throws himself from the roof of his dwelling escape being dashed to pieces.

And Godfrey had not escaped the penalties of the godless life he had led. He had sown to the flesh, and of the flesh he had reaped *corruption*. He had shut out God and love from his life, and God's punishment for this was the hardening of the heart.

Corruption and hardness of heart; these were the penalties annexed to such a course, and they had led him to deterioration, and deterioration to dishonour and dishonour to disgrace, and disgrace to crime, till he had ended in this last mad act; this laying violent hands himself on the life God had given him, and which he had so wasted and misused.

She bent over him and listened, trembling, to what he was saying, dreading what she might hear. She caught her own name ; over and over again her own name.

As far as she could gather the meaning of his rambling and incoherent utterances, his mind had travelled back to the early and happiest days of their married life ; before Godfrey was born.

And, as his speech grew more intelligible, she realised with wonder and gratitude that he was recalling and repeating some of her own old words of warning and instruction. Earnest words of hers, unheeded at the time, seemed to come crowding back upon his mind, and fell from his lips in confused and rambling speech.

Presently, as his mind got clearer, it reverted to more recent events, and to the last dire scene. With this recollection, he seemed to be seized with mortal dread and terror, and he tossed about wildly, and called loudly upon her to help and save him.

"Is she coming?" he cried; but he was not wandering now. "There is no time to lose. *Will* she come to me now? Come to such a——"

"Godfrey," she said softly, "I am here."

He did not seem to hear or notice, but the sound of her voice must have affected him somehow, for he

burst out wildly, "Hester! I am lost! Save me! I
am lost for ever—blood-stained, guilty!"

Then there arose her soft voice in the silence:
"'Though your sins be as scarlet, they shall be white
as snow.' Godfrey, dear Godfrey, I am here."

"Hester!" he cried, suddenly perceiving her, and
trying to hold out his arms. "Angel of my life, have
you come to such a wretch as I? Oh, Hester! I
have spoilt your life for you, and do you love me
still? Save me, Hester! I am lost! lost for ever!"

He seemed in an agony of terror, and the cold
drops of perspiration stood upon his brow. He clung
to her, imploring her to pray for him, to save him
from the awful doom which was impending—to stand
between him and God's coming wrath. "You are
pure and holy," he gasped wildly; "all your life long
you have never erred. God will hear *you*. *Pray* me
into heaven."

And at her quick, though gentle, repudiation of
such praise, he burst out: "I know it! I have
always known it. Have I not watched you all these
years?"

Then she listened with almost terrified thankfulness to his incoherent assurances that he believed, he
always had believed, in God, and Christ, and goodness, though he had never acted on his belief; that
he could not but do so in the sight of a life like hers.
He had, he told her, had holiness ever in his presence;
her life had revealed to him a life hid with Christ in
God. She had acted the Bible in her daily life: not

talking about it, but habitually living out the truths and principles which it taught; by her gentle, Christ-like temper, by her untiring patience, by her forbear-ance under his sore provocation. By her bravery, too, her courage in resisting him when he wished her to act in a way her conscience could not approve; by her calm, grand continuance in the path from which he had tried to turn her.

She had not preached, nor nagged, nor lectured, but she had steadily and consistently *acted*. He had "not obeyed the Word, but without the Word he had been won by the conversation of his wife." Aye; there is neither speech nor language, but their voices *are* heard; the voices of such wives are heard at last.

Thank God! those years of thought, and care, and striving had not been for nothing after all! Her life had not been wasted, her prayers not thrown away. She had cast her bread upon the waters, but she *had* found it after many days.

It was almost worth her long life of sorrow and trouble for an hour like this, and as she sank upon her knees, she murmured, " O God! Thy power is infinite; Thy mercy is infinite, too!"

CHAPTER XIV.

GODFREY'S CONFESSION.

ALL through the night she knelt and prayed by his side, and sought, by dwelling on the simple foundations of our faith, to bring peace to his mind.

Gradually his face assumed a calmer expression.

But a troubled look came over it at times, and he seemed still to have something to say.

Was it physical weakness and inability to collect his thoughts, or the old moral weakness and vacillation of character keeping its hold on him still? Who shall say?

But as the cold grey of morning dawned, both were overcome, and he called her to his side again.

"Now, Hester," he said feebly, "let me make restitution before I go."

"It is not needful," she tenderly answered. "I have forgiven it all long, long ago."

"But I have still something to tell you," he whispered. "I have not told you all. I cannot die happy till I have told you. I know you ought to be told."

"What is it?" she whispered soothingly.

"Come nearer," he said. "Come here. Put your arm round me — so. . . . Now say you will still forgive me, in spite of what I am going to say. . . . Promise that you will not take your arms away . . . but let me die . . . feeling your kiss of pardon on my lips."

"Surely," she answered. "Why should you fear?"

He drew her head down, and whispered something in her ear.

*   *   *   *   *   *

Whiter and whiter grew her face as she listened, more and more rigid her form. Slowly her arms relaxed their hold of him, and a change came over her whole expression ; a look of horror into her eye.

He tightened his hold as he felt her shrink from him, but she shook herself free, and started to her feet.

Retreating from his side to the other end of the room, she wound her arms round one of the pillars that supported the ceiling, and there she stood motionless, speechless, trembling, with her head turned away.

"Hester!" he moaned; but she took no heed of him.

She only turned upon him for a moment such a look as Eve might have turned upon Cain when he confessed to her that he had slain his brother Abel.

And all this time he kept moaning, "Forgive me! Forgive me! Kiss me before I die!"

She turned away with a shiver, and, looking at anything rather than at him, said at last, in a hard, dry voice—

"I *cannot* forgive you, Godfrey."

She hardly sees him; is barely conscious of his presence. There is another vision on which her eyes are fixed.

A fair young life—blasted. A life of hope, and fame, and distinction—cut short! A proud and honourable career nipped in its very bud. And instead?—a life of ignominy, a name sullied, a fair fame stained, young hopes—shattered! And all for what?

To screen a forger and a gambler, who was to die by his own hand at last.

"May God forgive you!" burst from the poor mother in her agony. "I cannot."

Who can forgive sins but God only? True, poor mother; but you are disproving all you have been trying to teach. By turning away from the sinful man in the hour of his extremity you are darkening the hope of a dying soul.

Is not your judgment to him a reflection of God's, a type or emblem to him of coming wrath or coming mercy? Are you not, by your attitude of unforgiveness, making the hope of God's pardoning mercy, through Christ, which had dawned upon his soul, seem uncertain, and, at last, even incredible?

Alas! poor mother! She cannot think of it all yet. Let her alone. Wait till the first bitterness is overpast, and then she will think on these things.

But now her thoughts are far away. Let her alone. She is thinking of her boy's calm, grand continuance in the path of devotion and self-sacrifice.

She is thinking how the lessons taught him by the example of his Lord and Master have in his young life been worked out; how he has wrought the Christian dogma into his very being, and probed to their depths the sufferings which come of sacrificing self, and of bearing the punishment due to others. What he must have suffered! What he must have endured! What lonely, silent endurance! How grandly, how nobly borne!

The thought of his young courage and devotion, all founded on a mistake, affected her suddenly, and she burst into a passion of tears.

Let her alone. It will all come right now.

Shall she be less noble than he?

Ah! he has left her far behind. She is still struggling, sinful and earth-bound. And he? He has long ago turned his back on the struggle and joined, even on earth, the noble army of martyrs. Shall his devotion be fruitless, and his desire to screen his father in vain? Shall the father he has bled for die, after all, unblessed and unforgiven? Shall it be thus that she, his mother, shall repay him for his life of devotion, and his years of uncomplaining self-sacrifice?

"Oh, Godfrey! Godfrey!" she cried, suddenly throwing herself on her knees by the bed and hiding her face, "how *could* you? How *could* you?—— "

It has been a hard and terrible struggle, but it is over now. And the reward shall surely come.

She wound her forgiving arms round him and pressed her lips to his brow.

And as she did so it came.

"Hester . . ." faintly gasped the dying man, "I ask you to forgive me . . . *for our boy's sake. . . .*"

BOOK VII.

CHAPTER I.

GODFREY'S TWENTY-FIFTH BIRTHDAY.

AT last! At last the day has come: the day for which Lord Seaforth has been waiting these many weary months, these three long years.

It is Godfrey's twenty-fifth birthday. Everything is ready, and before the day is over Lord Seaforth will have set his hand and seal to the document which cuts Godfrey off for ever from the property, and makes little Joan one of the greatest heiresses in England.

It is about eleven o'clock, and Lord Seaforth is sitting in the library, busy with many thoughts, glancing every now and then at the unsuspecting heiress, who is busy to-day with many thoughts too.

Yes, the day has come! This day Godfrey is to reap the reward of his sowing.

Yet it is not a day of joy and triumph, after all.

He had hoped it would be, but now that it has come all his feelings are of sorrow and regret.

He has been hardening his heart against him all

these years; trying to shut him out from his life and
thoughts, steeling himself against him to the very
utmost.   In vain!   Just as he had persuaded himself
he was beginning to forget him, a sharp pang would
strike his heart, as his eye rested on the empty chair
where he had been wont to watch him for hours
sitting, his handsome face bent over his book, the
leaves turning at intervals; and a craving longing to
see him once more, to hear something of him, would
overpower him.   What was he doing?   How was he
living?

It would have been easy enough to find out.   The
lawyers connected with the entail of course knew; but
he had refused to allow himself to make any inquiries.   So much, at any rate, he could make himself do: he could *act* the hard and relentless tyrant;
though he could not feel any satisfaction in doing it—
though righteous indignation and love of retribution
had no place in his heart.

It was all forced: not natural.   No wonder.   He
was doing that hard and difficult thing — fighting
against his own nature.

Still did he imagine he could conquer it.   He did
not know himself yet.   He was an example of the
theory that we do not know ourselves as others know
us: for he had not yet gauged the strength and
tenacity of his own feelings, as his wife had gauged
them long ago.

His own intensity of affection and unchanging
fidelity were too much for him.

Here, now, on this long-looked-for day, he knows in himself that he loves Godfrey still !

Another glance at his daughter. He must not think any more.

He must speak to her at once, and get it over.

"Joan," he said, "are you aware that you have this day become one of the greatest heiresses in England ? This day, this twenty-sixth of January, the entail on the estate is by mutual agreement cut off, and Seaforth is settled on you."

Joan flushed crimson, and clasped her hands together. She realised, quick as lightning, what this meant, and a tumult of indignation overpowered her.

Her father took these signs of surprise and emotion for natural feeling at the thought of such a weight of honour and glory falling to her share.

He went on to give an account of his arrangements with the lawyers, whom he now proposed to summon; and tried to reassure her, by hinting faintly that she would not have to bear the burden of responsibility alone. He tried to convey to her distantly that there was a possibility of his receiving an offer for her hand from a quarter where he would be ready to bestow it.

Joan sat very still till he had finished.

By that time she had had time to control herself and to resolve upon a course of action. Meanwhile, her visit to Ainsbro' and all that it had been intended to bring about became clear to her.

"I shall never marry," she said, quietly and firmly.

Her tone attracted Lord Seaforth's attention, and he looked up quickly. He was surprised at the expression of quiet determination which pervaded every line of her face.

"Never marry!" he exclaimed; "and why?"

Joan folded her hands quietly together, but she made no answer.

He looked at her again, and, as he looked, for the first time it struck him how like her eyes were to his own, to Godfrey's, and to every other Seaforth's. For the first time he felt that this was his child, a part of himself; and at the same moment he read his own spirit of uncompromising determination in the eyes of his daughter. He felt his position to be very perplexing.

"You are very young," he said, rather nervously; "all young girls talk like that."

No answer.

"You are only eighteen. You will change your mind some day."

Still no answer; and Lord Seaforth was getting more and more perplexed.

"Supposing, then," he said at last, "that, for the sake of the argument, we say that you will, as you affirm, never marry—the fact remains the same. You are still one of the greatest heiresses in England; still this day the estate is settled upon you."

She slightly shook her head.

What did she mean?

"You can settle it on me if you please," she answered, in a low voice; "but it will only come to the same thing—I should only give it back."

"Give it back!" he exclaimed. "And to whom?"

"To him who alone has a right to it," she answered firmly; "to Godfrey Seaforth, your nephew and rightful heir."

She raised her beautiful eyes as she spoke, and looked her father full in the face. Her small head was erect now with pride and defiance. She stood revealed a champion for the rights of the man she loved!

Looking full into the depths of her dark eyes, and taught by his own experience, something electric communicated itself to Lord Seaforth.

In that moment he guessed her secret!

He read his own story in hers—something of his own unchanging, never-dying fidelity to the object once loved—and realised that history was repeated in her life, and that their love and fidelity was given to the same object.

His heart went out to his daughter, and his very soul was wrung with pity for her fate. Alas! that another should have to pass through a like furnace of suffering and disappointment! Alas! that his own child should, like himself, have misplaced her love and her confidence, and given her young affections to one so utterly unworthy!

He longed to help her and to comfort her. What

25

could he do? Across the gulf of their divided lives dared he stretch the bridge of sympathy, the hand of fatherly pity and fellow-feeling? No! Never.

That much he read in her eyes; in the proud reserve of a neglected child; to which the reserve of a woman's pride was now added.

No! there was no hope of that. No words of his could wring her secret from her; no help could by him be given.

He may not now break down the wall his own hand had raised between them.

Nothing can undo the past nor alter the relationship in which they stand to one another, and which he himself had instituted.

He had given her nothing in the past, and she will accept nothing from him now.

He gazed at her sadly, yearningly, and then turned away.

"Poor child!" he murmured; "poor girl! God help her! I cannot."

He tottered to a chair, and sitting down began to think what was to be done next. Here was Seaforth returned upon his hands again. He had actually lived to see it refused on all sides, and tossed like a ball from one to the other!

First Hester, then Godfrey, now Joan.

Alike!—how alike, all three! Each in turn had refused the greatness and the glory he had offered to shower upon them.

Hester, a pensioner on another's bounty, had

refused it all without a thought. Godfrey, equally penniless, had resigned all his pretensions, without making a single condition.

This young girl was ready to do the same.

What made them all so unworldly? How came they to value so lightly what he so highly prized? This will not do. He must not think. He must act. He must break through this train of weak and sentimental thought by at once ringing the bell and sending for the lawyers.

He rose and laid his hand on the bell.

Joan, who was moving away, glanced at him as she left the room, and thought how old and bent he looked; and marked the uncertainty of his gait and the trembling of his hands. The servant entered the room, bringing in the newspapers.

Joan was half-way across the adjoining room, when she was startled by a curious sound which fell upon her ear, followed by a heavy fall.

Alarmed, she hurried back, and, to her horror, found her father lying on the ground, stiff and motionless.

She rang the bell violently, and then, bending over his prostrate form, she strove to render him some assistance and to raise him from the ground.

But he lay like a stone, cold and rigid.

Horrified, she bent closer over him, and as she did so her eye fell upon the newspaper which was tightly clutched in his hand.

And there, at the head of a paragraph, she read the words, " Suicide of Mr. Godfrey Seaforth!"

CHAPTER II.

THE IRONY OF FATE.

TREAD softly in the darkened chamber, round the curtained bed, where lies the stricken and helpless form which is all that remains of the proud and self-willed man whose career we have followed for so long.

Tread softly in the darkened chamber, nor mock its sadness with a smile.

We have seen him like a proud ship sailing on life's sea, with sails set and pennon gaily waving in the wind; carrying, as we know, nor chart nor compass; secure in his own strength and wisdom, feeling he needed nothing to guide him safely. Did he not know the way full well?

And now!

Ruined, wrecked, shattered; drifting, mastless and broken, at the mercy of the winds and waves—whither? Into the dark and fathomless ocean which rolls round the world?

No! the doctors say he will not die: the merciful

gates of death are not to open to him yet; but death in life is to be his portion now.

Helpless, hopeless, paralysed; limbs nerveless, and speech unintelligible—there he lies! "*Je me suffis.*"

Oh, the irony of fate!

How merry she might make her over a scene like this! How she might say, like the prophet of old, "Cry aloud! call upon your gods!" and mock when no answer came.

His gods. Yes. Let him call upon them now. Time, habit, self-will, self-respect, the gods to whom he bowed, and in whom he trusted, will they not come to his help?

In vain!

The thunderbolt of heaven has *this* time fallen too hot and heavy.

This time he *must* recognise God's hand; this time he must bow to a higher Will.

No self-will, phœnix-like, can spring from such ruin as this; and from the ashes of *this* past there can be no rising again.

Joan, all her woman's heart now moved with pity, tends him with devoted care.

There is no doubt in her mind that, reading no further than the heading of the paragraph, he had jumped at once to one conclusion, and not had time to realise that the Godfrey Seaforth referred to was his brother, and not his nephew.

Day by day she waited for an opportunity of en-

lightening him ; but there had been no chance of it.
He had never yet been sufficiently alive to what was
going on around him for it to be of any use to make
the attempt.

As she watched and waited, her own thoughts were
very full. A wild hope would sometimes come across
her that the clearing up of the mystery in which
Godfrey's life was shrouded might follow on his
father's death.

But time went by and she heard no tidings.

Still day after day found her watching, waiting,
and hoping.

Within, there was no change in her father's condition, and no sign or sound from without.

BOOK VIII.

CHAPTER I.

LINCOLN'S INN FIELDS.

A SMALL dingy lodging in the neighbourhood of Lincoln's Inn, with fog up to the windows, and the remains of snow on the opposite roofs.

The very small fire, which is slowly dying in the grate, does not contribute much to the warmth of the little apartment, does not certainly extend its heat sufficiently to reach the young man who, evidently recovering from an illness, is lying in bed, reading.

A knock at the door, and an ill-clad woman-of-all-work comes in and announces that the doctor is below.

"Show him up, if you please," says Godfrey, for it is he who we find in this poor little place.

"And if you please, sir," added the woman, "there's been a clergyman after you more nor once since you was took."

"A clergyman!" said Godfrey, inwardly wondering. "Have I been so ill as that?"

"And how are you this evening?" says the cheery voice of the doctor.

"Much better, I think," answered Godfrey, extending a rather thin hand of greeting. "Tell me, doctor—for I get confused about dates—have I been ill long? And when shall I be able to begin my work again?"

The doctor shook his head. "You must not think of work for a long time. You want a thorough rest of mind and body. You have had a sharp attack of fever, brought on entirely by over-work. You must keep quiet and be very careful. I should like to make a bonfire of all your law-books; and by the way," he added, glancing at the fast-dying fire, "they would not come amiss to that poor affair. What a wretched attempt for a raw February day!" The good-natured doctor advanced to the fire and began trying to improve it; but the scuttle was nearly empty.

"We lawyers," said Godfrey, with a smile, "can't afford to be ill. No fees, no fuel. Idleness for some weeks makes the exchequer low and the coal-cellar empty."

"Well, you rest a little longer," said the doctor as he took his leave, "and you'll get back to your work and your fees all the sooner. And don't read more than you can help," he added, looking with disgust at the very dry-looking volume on which Godfrey had been engaged on his entrance.

Godfrey smiled sadly after the doctor was gone.

"I *must* read," he said to himself, as he took up his volume again: "anything is better than thinking."

He lay very quiet for some time, but gradually the book dropped from his grasp and he fell asleep.

Some time elapsed. The fire flickered a little, the room got darker; outside the snow began to fall again.

The door opens very softly, and Hester, arrayed in the sombre garments of her widowhood, comes in.

She first gazes round the poverty-stricken apartment, and then she advances almost reverently and kneels down by the side of the bed. He is lying sleeping, as she has often watched him in his boyhood, quietly, peacefully, like a child.

And as she gazed, her heart beat high with pride and wonder that anything so grand, so noble, should have been cradled in her arms and taught at her knee.

And it is still the martyr-brow on which she gazes; still does it bear the brand of suspicion and guilt.

She has learnt from the woman below that he has been ill three weeks, so she knows he can have seen no newspapers, and is therefore in ignorance of what has befallen.

She is almost thankful that it is so, glad and grateful that hers is to be the hand to remove the chain that binds him, hers the lips to speak the words which will set him free.

She glances again at the signs of poverty around

her, at the wretched, fast-dying fire, and the tears rush to her eyes.

He stirs in his sleep. The word "Mother" escapes from his lips.

Is he dreaming of the old days at home?

She bends over him, and he wakes with her kiss on his brow.

"Mother!" rang out his voice clear and joyful in the glad surprise of the first moment; and he started up and held out his hands.

But even as he spoke recollection returned to him. A change came over his face, his hands dropped, and he turned his face to the wall. He must be on his guard, be firm. She has come to wrest his secret from him, and that secret must not be wrested.

"Godfrey," she implored, "my own boy, do not turn from me. I do not ask you to speak, but only to look at me."

Slowly he turned at last, for his eyes were longing to rest on her face again. And his eye wandered wondering over her mourning garments, till they rested on the widow's cap which crowned, while it did not hide, her still lovely hair.

"*Is he dead?*" he whispered, while he clasped her hands in both of his and held them tightly.

"He is dead," she answered. "He has told me everything, and you are free, my darling, from the burden you have borne so bravely and so long!" . . .

CHAPTER II.

GODFREY'S HISTORY.

"And now," said Hester, when the first excitement had a little subsided, "tell me all about it. Let me hear the truth at last."

Holding his hands, she prayed him to speak to her quite irrespective of the dead man.

"It can do him nor good nor harm," she whispered. "And, oh! Godfrey, I am so weary of mystery and concealment. Henceforth I pray you, darling, there may be no secrets between us. Tell me all. In my turn I will tell you everything which in your early youth I withheld from you."

Thus urged, Godfrey could not but consent to her entreaty.

He began from the time when his allowance had been first settled upon him, which was the beginning of all his troubles.

It must have been very soon after he had so proudly sent his mother and sisters his first cheque that the idea of forging his name had entered into the mind of his father. It was done at first for small sums, and so it was some time before Godfrey had noticed any discrepancy in his accounts. But by-and-by a very large sum was drawn, and by that time he had become most bewildered.

Still it was a long time before the truth dawned upon him, and even then he could hardly believe the evidence of his own senses. How to act under the circumstances he had been for a long while unable to make up his mind. He did nothing for a time, hoping that perhaps it might not occur again.

But time went on—larger sums were drawn, and it was clear that if matters went on at this rate it would come to the knowledge of his uncle. He at last made up his mind to write to his father, to let him at any rate know that he was aware of what was going on, and to see whether he could not work upon his feelings by representing to him the disgrace into which he must shortly fall. While waiting for the answer to this letter he had had to return to Seaforth; and it had been forwarded to him there.

In this answer his father did not attempt to deny that he had drawn these large sums, but added that he considered he had a perfect right to do so. The money was his; he was the legal and lawful heir-presumptive, deprived of his rights by a freak of his brother's.

After receiving this letter hope left Godfrey's breast. He saw his father was determined to continue his practices; and as he knew the money was used for gambling purposes he felt there was no limit to the amount that might be drawn.

It was at this time that his first interview with his uncle took place. His primary care was to ward off all suspicion from his father. His feeling all through the conversation was the old antagonism against his uncle for his dealings with his father in his youth, which were the remote causes of all his present trouble.

On his return to Oxford he again wrote to his father, and offered to supply him with money himself, if he would keep within a certain sum. He implored him to discontinue his practices, earnestly setting before him what an offence forgery was in the eyes of the law, and what terrible disgrace would follow if he were discovered.

To this letter an answer was returned which showed Godfrey the case was hopeless. His father upbraided him with his words, and said that unless *he* chose to turn informant the discovery would never be made; repeated what he had said at first, that he had a perfect right to the money; and added that, as he was only writing his own name, he did not see how the act could in any way be constituted into a legal offence.

It now became necessary for Godfrey to resolve upon some definite course of action. Either all his own hopes for the future must be relinquished, or his father must be disgraced.

There was no alternative between the two.

What an opportunity was here presented to him of making up to his father for all, and at the same time sparing his mother the knowledge of her husband's guilt! If it were such a blow to him, Godfrey, to discover his father had fallen so low, what would it be to her! She, who loved him so devotedly, and believed in him so firmly; who had so often, in Godfrey's boyhood, told him of the injustice and harshness with which his father had been treated, and the way in which in early life he had been mismanaged and misunderstood. She should remain in that opinion still. At all costs the knowledge should be concealed from her. She should never know; she and his little sisters should be spared for ever the hearing of this tale of guilt and shame.

At once and for ever his mind was made up; and when his uncle announced to him his intention of sending for his mother he resolved at once to fly. The thought of her arrival hastened the crisis. To meet her was impossible; to keep up this deception face to face with her a thing too difficult to be attempted.

Painful as he felt his conduct would be to her, he comforted himself with the reflection that he was sparing her a yet more bitter pain.

The sacrifice he had resolved upon was thus promptly carried out.

Fair name and character he sacrificed at once; relinquished thus all hopes of a career of distinction, of earthly fame and usefulness; left Seaforth secretly, and went to London, without giving himself time to think.

Once there, in the long, objectless days that followed, alone in the crowd of London, he became a prey to a feeling of utter dejection.

" His sufferings will be intelligible to any one who has ever conceived a sublime mission with a warm heart, and felt hope and courage fail in the idea of executing it." He felt that it was "easy to do wonders when upheld by the sympathy of those you love, and the approval of those whose opinion you value ; but quite another thing to go out into the darkness of ignominy and isolation, and the loneliness of suspicion and misunderstanding."

His deepest regret was little Joan.

It was so hard that she should feel he had deserted her; so bitter that she should believe him guilty too. He grieved so at the thought that she should regard him in this light, and that he should apparently nullify by his practice all the precepts he had taught her. Could he communicate with her? Could he trust her with the secret ?

No ; it could not be. It was not to be thought of. He must not dream of laying on the shoulders of another a burden he found so hard to bear himself.

He could not, child as she was, let her into so guilty a secret ; and her love for him might lead her some day to proclaim the innocent and to expose the guilty.

26

No; she, alas! must be sacrificed to his father too. There was nothing for it but to leave her in complete ignorance, like all the world beside.

His outlook for the future was indeed overwhelming, and the loneliness and hopelessness of his position great. His life being all marred, he would never be able, as he had always hoped, to do anything for his mother and sisters. His chosen path, politics, was now quite impossible.

But the rebound of youth is very powerful, and after a time came to his help the feeling he had always had, that he had it in him, born in him, to do something, to be something, to make his own way.

And his spirit rose at the thought of the difficulty. The more difficulty, the more glory.

He had an obstinate feeling within him, which would not be kept down, that though that chosen path of his was certainly more difficult now, though it was put off probably for many years, yet that it would still be his one day.

His faith did not fail him at this crisis. He believed firmly in God's power of bringing good out of all this: if not to him, then to others; if not here, then hereafter. Feeling sure that out of this darkness light must come some day, he stuck steadily to the measure of light he had, and never allowed himself to sink into despair.

Besides, it was not all suffering. He was ever upheld by the thought that he was screening his father, and thus making many happy; and to bear pain instead of, and for the sake of, another, has in it a pure and ennobling happiness which none save they who have experienced it know.

But he felt he must have work. God would give it to him as a help. Without it the sadness of his life would have been too overpowering for him to bear.

He had his fellowship, and on that he felt he could live, while he gave himself up to reading and study.

Oh, work! God's blessing to many a weary-minded man.

It is the idle who are wretched. Godfrey firmly believed this. He had the fixed idea, too, which lives in the breast of many a noble and true man, that each man should live and work as if no one but himself could do the special work which lies to his hand, and in the full realisation that he has only a short and uncertain time in which to do it.

He now tried to drown, as it were, the sorrows and regretful longings of his life in work.

He began a course of hard reading for the Bar. He took a small lodging in Lincoln's Inn Fields, and there he read and worked night and day, living on the income his fellowship gave him, till he was called to the Bar.

In this life he became entirely engrossed.

His love of reading and study was its great alleviation.

"Nobody," as Lord Seaforth had once said,

" could be very unhappy who possessed the power of thus losing self and being independent of present surroundings and outward circumstances."

And it was in a sense true.

And yet, sometimes in the evening, sitting in his little lodging by the fire, such sad thoughts would assail him, and such a sense of the void and emptiness in his heart and life come over him, that his book would drop from his hand, and he sit gazing into the fire in mute and tearless despair.

Sadly across him at such times would come the thought of little Joan.

Stealing unawares into his presence would come the little figure; the great dark eyes, with their trusting expression, would look up at him once more.

How was she faring without him? Did she ever think of him she had trusted, who had responded to her trust so ill, and deserted her without a word of explanation?

How was it all to end? Would she be faithful to his memory? Should he ever see her again?

At this point Godfrey's voice grew so faint and broken that Hester had to bend over him to hear.

She caught his impassioned declaration of his ever-abiding love and devotion for his little cousin; and, bending closer, she gathered with joy and thankfulness that all his fears and misgivings concerning her had some time since been turned into rejoicing—that he had met her in the autumn stillness, and found that she loved him still.

We leave it to the reader to imagine how a mother would be likely to be affected by the tale just told.

All that we will say is, that Hester, probably more than most, was moved by it to the most vivid, almost reverent, admiration.

For, to her, the loneliness and strength of silent endurance had always seemed the grandest thing in life; and it was a most bewildering sensation that her own ideal of all that was most noble should have been worked out in the life of her own son.

CHAPTER III.

EXPLANATIONS.

HESTER felt that for the moment the past had been sufficiently dwelt upon. She therefore reserved her promised recital for another occasion, and gave Godfrey an account of more recent events. She explained to him that Andrew Fraser, prompted by his brother Colin, had never rested till he had discovered his abode, and had telegraphed to her that he was ill with a fever in this little lodging. That she and his sisters had at once started for England, and had been met on their arrival by Andrew and Mr. Cartwright. That the latter had most kindly taken the three girls down to his home in Warwickshire, where they were under the care of Lady Margaret for the present.

She was, she told him, much perplexed about the future, as Lord Seaforth had returned no answer to the letters she had written him. She added that Andrew Fraser had now gone down to Seaforth to seek a personal interview, and was to come straight here on his return; that, in short, she expected him this evening.

Towards night he arrived.

As he entered the room Hester drew back to allow the young men to meet alone. She could see how warmly they grasped one another's hands, and how Andrew, bending down, spoke for some time in a low, earnest voice, to which Godfrey replied by another warm grasp of the hand.

Andrew then placed a chair for Hester, and, sitting down also himself, informed his astonished listeners that Lord Seaforth was lying stricken with paralysis, and that Godfrey was now, to all intents and purposes, absolute master of everything.

"How can that be?" hastily inquired Godfrey. "The entail was cut off on my twenty-fifth birthday, and I have no more to do with Seaforth than you have."

"*L'homme propose, Dieu dispose*," answered Andrew. "It was on that very day, just as he was about to summon the lawyers to sign the documents, that Lord Seaforth was suddenly seized with paralysis, and he has never spoken since."

So from the couch in the dingy lodging where he had laid himself down, a needy struggling lawyer, Godfrey was to rise the lord of all.

And as the three sat together in the gathering twilight, their thoughts were very busy with the intricate windings of the path of life which had led at last to this.

"My sister," said Andrew at last, addressing himself to Hester, "has desired me to beg you and your daughters to come at once to Seaforth, as she knows her father would have done long since had he been able. And your presence," he continued to Godfrey, "is very necessary. There is a great deal of business to be done, and many unopened letters—all of ours among the number."

It was then definitely arranged that as soon as Godfrey was sufficiently recovered he and his mother and sisters should all go to Seaforth.

The doctors there were of opinion that the sudden shock of a glad surprise would be more conducive to the recovery of Lord Seaforth's powers of speech and movement than anything else.

"What I want to know," said Godfrey, "is, what caused my uncle's stroke of paralysis?"

Andrew looked confused, but answered quietly, "My sister told me all about it. I will either explain it all to you in private or to Mrs. Seaforth; but you will not, I hope, ask me to do so in presence of you both."

Hester accordingly retired into another room with Andrew, and after some minutes' conversation he took his leave, and she returned to Godfrey's bedside.

"Can you bear to hear?" she said, as she sat down and took his hand in hers. "Oh, my darling, you have always misjudged him so; you have never valued his deep affection. It was my fault, I know; but you will perhaps realise a little what the love must have been to cause such a catastrophe as this. For he thought, he thinks still, that it is you of whose sad and terrible end he read quite suddenly."

She then proceeded to give the whole early history of the two brothers, and to show how Lord Seaforth had been made to suffer.

And as his mother proceeded with her tale, pity and gratitude at last woke up in Godfrey's heart.

He saw how he had failed to appreciate his uncle's good qualities, and, biassed ever by a deep-rooted prejudice, founded on a misconception, failed to give him his due.

Godfrey's convalescence now proceeded rapidly, and in the course of a week he was well enough to leave London and to proceed to Seaforth.

The day before his departure the three girls arrived, and joyful indeed was the meeting which took place between the long-divided brother and sisters.

CHAPTER IV.

LET us return to the bedside of the stricken man, to whom, though he had no power to make others aware of the fact, consciousness of what had passed, and of what was passing around him, was now returning.

He had no wish to make others conscious of him. He shrank from every one, more especially from his daughter, of whose watchful form, sitting not far from his bed, he was fully aware. How came she to be there? Why did she care to watch and tend him? What mattered it whether he lived or died; least of all to her? He had driven the man she loved to a cruel death. By him, by his harshness, Godfrey had been hunted to a terrible end; and now what mattered anything?

How quiet she sits—always so quiet and silent! How can she sit there at all? How can she bear to be near him?

He wondered sometimes if it were really Joan or only a figure.

Such a longing to hear her say she forgave him his part in the terrible transaction came over him, that he tried one day to attract her attention. He tried to say "Joan." But no sound came.

He tried again—an unintelligible murmur, which he heard himself, but which did not attract her attention.

Good God! was his power of speech gone? Was he never to be able to express his contrition, never to ask her pardon for his share in the sorrows of her life?

Oh, wretched man that he was!—wretched life, wretched end!

"This was how God had dealt with him:" laid him on a bed of helplessness, unable to move or speak, and said, "Lie there face to face with God and think."

And he did.

Like a map unrolled before him, his past life rose before his eyes, and he realised at last what a fiasco it had been.

What a long course of self-will and failure! What wheel within wheel of wilful mistakes, and their inevitable consequences! As husband and as father how wilful, how hard he had been!

How determined he had been, and how proud of being determined, about many things which now seemed unimportant!

Revenging himself all his life long on his wife for her early deception by his systematic neglect of her sons. How proud he had always been of his consistency in that matter, and what a waste of life it seemed now!

Then his daughter. Revenge again. And for what?

First, for the fact of her sex, and then for an accidental likeness.

How senseless, how wicked it was!

And the inevitable consequence, the just retribution? He had irretrievably alienated his only child. Her confidence and her affection were lost to him for ever.

Wife and child both hardened against him! Poisoned for ever those pure sources of affection.

Yet they *could* love.

How his wife had loved her boys! And his daughter—ah! how lovely her eyes had looked that day when she spoke of him who was gone; when she stood champion for his rights so boldly!

Poor child! There she sits, so quiet and silent. He fancied he could move his arm a little. He lifted it up, and tried to make a sign. He took hold of the heavy curtain; it moved—it shook the hangings above.

And Joan moved too. She started and looked up.

She is coming! O God! how shall he bear the grief, the reproach in her face, the mute sorrow and despair in her eyes?

She is coming. She is quite near now. She is bending over him to speak. How is this? Her face is beaming with joy, her eyes suffused with happy tears.

"Dear father!" she is saying very softly, "do you know me at last? Can you listen, father, to what I have to say? Godfrey is alive and well. It was your brother's death you read."

After that nothing is very clear to him for some time. Confused figures swim before his eyes; young, girlish forms flit in and out of his room.

Hester comes sometimes and smiles upon him— Hester as he remembers her on the night of Godfrey's flight; and then again sometimes another Hester—a young, girlish Hester, the Hester of old, with the light step of youth and its gay, dancing expression in her face. What does it all mean? Perhaps Joan will tell him.

He motions her once more to his side, and tries to express in his eyes the question his poor maimed tongue refuses to utter.

And in a low, thrilling voice she tells him at last the meaning of it all; tells him such a wondrous tale of self-devotion and self-sacrifice, that in his bewilderment and agitation he tries to put out his trembling hands to stop her, that he may have time to think of it awhile.

But she goes on. With all a loving woman's pride and joy in the noble conduct of the man she loves she tells the tale to its very ending, and then her figure disappears from his bedside and her place is empty.

Who is this standing where she has so lately been? This tall, noble figure, with the beauty of manhood added to the grace of youth; this well-known face, from which all sternness has departed; these dark eyes from which every trace of coldness and antagonism has fled; whose deep, rich voice sounds in the silence with the old familiar name, unheard so long? "Uncle Harold!"

A wild struggle for speech, an unintelligible sound; another—one more effort, and there bursts from his lips a word, stammering, indeed, incoherent, but still a word—"Godfrey!"

"Thank God, dear Uncle Harold," says the beloved voice of his darling, "your speech is restored to you. We shall all be happy now!"

CHAPTER V.

THE MEETING OF THE LOVERS IN THE OLD PICTURE-GALLERY.

COME we to the old picture-gallery once more, where, in the moonlight which floods it from one end to the other, the reunited lovers are standing hand in hand : to be parted this time never again !

Here, again, as once before, with " Godfrey, Earl of Seaforth," looking down upon them, and the groups of children round, he vows himself from this moment to devote his life to her, and to the endeavour to make her happy; to atone to her, not only for those early sorrows of which he had been the innocent cause, but for that added suffering which his peculiar life and circumstances had entailed upon her—for the long, long years of loneliness, for his seeming desertion, for his broken vows, for his enforced leaving her in ignorance, and apparent want of trust and confidence.

What the temptation had been in that interview

in the meadows to trust her with his secret he could never tell her; what it had cost him to refuse her entreaty to reveal to her the mystery lying on his life he could never say—what the longing had been to hear her say she still believed in him, in the teeth of all the evidence against him.

But he had felt bound to resist the temptation, feeling it would not be right to put her into such a false position—to make her, as it were, a participator in a fraud.

It had been, he told her, the most bitter part of all the bitterness his chosen path had entailed upon him to feel that he was deserting her, that he was leaving her to her fate. He had felt, he said, like the captain who deserts the sinking ship, leaving the women and children on board. And yet, at the time, it was the only thing to be done. There was no help for it.

But now! With clean hands and a vindicated character he stands before her; and now he may take up the vows he had broken, take up for ever the loving task he had once been forced to lay down. Now may he take her life into his own safe keeping, into the shelter of his own love and care. Now may it be his to devote his life to flood her path with love and sunshine, and to make its radiant light atone for all past darkness.

Now may their young dreams have a bright fulfilling; fame and distinction for one, tender devotion for the other, love and happiness for both.

Now may they reap the harvest of happy memories; golden days of light and love may be theirs once more!

And as the full realisation of the dream of joy he painted burst upon the vision of little Joan, she shaded her eyes with her hand like one dazzled, while she murmured, "I am not worthy of such happiness. Oh, Godfrey! how is it that you love me so?"

"Could I help it?" was his loving answer, as he clasped her in his arms and poured forth new vows of love and devotion.

The sound of the old familiar cry that she had been wont to address to the picture beneath which they stood, caused for a moment the memory of her forlorn childhood to sweep like a cold blast over her soul; but it was quickly succeeded by such a rush of gladness as made the present and the future, by contrast, seen almost overpoweringly bright—

> "Some moments may
> With bliss repay
> Unnumbered hours of pain."

And from that moment the very memory of her past troubles grew dim in the eyes of little Joan.

CHAPTER VI.

ONCE again is Seaforth alive with rejoicings; once again made bright for feasting and hospitality.

A year has passed away, and it is Godfrey's twenty-sixth birthday.

All our friends are congregated to celebrate his coming of age. Colin is there, now openly affianced to Olive; and Andrew is there, a mere shadow on the flitting form of pretty little Venetia; Mr. and Lady Margaret Cartwright, and their sons; Lord and Lady Ainsbro'; Edward Manners; and last, though not least, the little pair—Marion and Bertie.

Lady Ainsbro's eye rests with pride and satisfaction on her eldest son and the lovely girl with whom he is talking; for, in the year which has gone by, he has sought and won the hand of Hester Seaforth, Lord Seaforth's eldest and favourite niece; and Marion and Bertie are consoled for their previous disappointment by the reflection that Joan will be a " sort-of-kind-of-sister," after all.

It is a joyful day, and will long be remembered by all who took part in it.

Towards evening Lord Seaforth sent for his two stepsons to the library, and, in the faltering, stammering language which was all he had now at his command, he declared his intention of paying off all the burdens on Colin's estate in Scotland, and of giving his niece Olive a dowry of £60,000 on her wedding-day. He further expressed his wish that Colin should stand for his own county at the approaching election, and his hope that he would allow him the satisfaction of paying his election expenses.

Turning to Andrew, he informed him that the present incumbent of Seaforth had been appointed to the head-mastership of one of the great public schools, and that the living was now vacant. He begged Andrew, therefore, to accept it, adding that he would rather have him as rector of Seaforth than any man in England.

He concluded by a touching allusion to their mother's love for them and her deep interest in their welfare.

The young men wrung his hand in silence. They were too much moved to speak.

Lord Seaforth has learnt at last the hardest and severest lesson which man here below is called upon to learn—submission to the will of God. Godfrey's course had first impressed him with the reality of

religion, its beauty, its manliness, and its power.
And as he lay on his bed of helplessness, during the
long months of convalescence, the conviction had
come to him that his nephew's character was his
own, ennobled, exalted, and purified by religion.

Godfrey had made a hard life easy by submitting
to it, while he had rendered life doubly difficult by
rebelling against it.

How religion would have softened and beautified
his character, drawn out and made noble all that
had been either repressed or, worse still, perverted!
Drawn out the good in those who came in contact
with him, too; while he, on the contrary, had drawn
out everything that was bad. Medusa-like, he had
hardened and turned to stone every one who had had
anything to do with him; and in his wife's case he
had, alas! had the fatal power of drawing out and
intensifying all the faults of her character.

And in the sorrow of his spirit he had compared
himself with Godfrey, and had realised that it was
religion which had been the moving spring of all
his actions, and that it was this which had constituted
the difference in characters by nature alike, and had
resulted in one in a life of self-will, and in the other
in a life of self-sacrifice.

And he had cried in the loneliness of the night
"Give me this strength! Show me this power!
Teach me how to gain this peace!"

Many were the resolutions he had made that
everything should be very different if he were spared

to begin again; that he would for the future be content to be a mere cypher—as no doubt his physical infirmities would, to a great extent, necessitate—and resign all power into Godfrey's hands; give himself no quarter, but bit by bit atone for every hard act of his past life, and make everywhere restitution and satisfaction.

He expected to find it hard; but he found it easy. He came armed to the fight, and found no foe to contend with!

For he had by that time realised that the hardest taskmaster a man can have is his own unbending pride and self-will, when he lets them master and overcome him; "that of whom a man is overcome, of the same is he brought in bondage;" and, standing fast now in the "liberty wherewith Christ has made him free," he will be entangled in that yoke no more.

BOOK IX.

CHAPTER I.

A PEEP INTO THE FUTURE.

AND now let us take a peep into the future, at Lord Seaforth's quiet and happy old age.

He lived long enough to see his grandsons playing on the green lawns of Seaforth, making the old place ring with their young voices from morning till night; and to rejoice in the thought that, under the wise and loving control of such a father and such a mother as theirs, there was no fear that a graceless *vaurien* would ever again darken the pages of the family history.

He lived long enough to see his beloved nephew and son-in-law the brightest ornament in the House of Commons, and to hear, as he sat in the Gallery, trembling with pride and delight, some of those bursts of oratory which soon made his name famous.

It was a familiar sight to all the *habitués* of the House to see the old man, leaning on the arm of his son-in-law, being settled comfortably in his seat

before the debate began; and it was well known that
he would remain there for hours, contented and absorbed, till his son-in-law was at leisure to come and
take him away again.

With his hands crossed on the top of his stick,
and his chin on his hands, he would sit, his eyes
intent on the figure in the scene below, his ear
strained to catch every word which fell from its
lips.

It was his pride and joy to see how, the moment
Godfrey rose in his place and the rumour spread that
he was on his feet, members came flocking in from all
directions and the House was soon filled. It was his
to be an exultant witness of the power wherewith
Godfrey held all hanging on his words with the most
eager attention, while the deepest silence reigned in
the House, so that his clear, quiet voice was distinctly heard in every part.

His speeches were as rare as they were beautiful.
He was ever ready to make way for others, and to
resign the task of speaking to them. He cared little
who had the credit of bringing the subject forward,
provided only it were brought forward as it should
be.

He considered two qualifications indispensable for
speaking: to have his subject at his fingers' ends,
and to be deeply and thoroughly interested in it.
Except under these conditions he never spoke: never
for a useless display of oratory.

Living thus to see the realisation of all his dreams

and ambitions, and to receive from those he loved all
the affection and devotion for which he had so long
vainly craved, Lord Seaforth experienced, in

" Evening's calm light,"

all that he had never found in

" The wild freshness of morning."

Then, tended by loving hands, and surrounded by
loving faces—he died.

Let us look a stage further ere we close ; and see
Godfrey a Cabinet Minister and one of the greatest
statesmen of the day.

He is known far and wide as an earnest and true-
hearted man ; one on whose judgment all rely, and
of whose uprightness and right-mindedness there is
no question.

Friend and opponent alike value him as much for
his singleness of purpose and large-hearted liberality
as for his powers of oratory and all his many gifts.

He is ever ready to make himself acquainted with
all shades of political opinion, and to give each its
just weight and consideration.

Such is our hero in his public life. Let us follow
him now into his private life, into his own happy home,
into the old picture-gallery, where " Godfrey, Earl of
Seaforth," looks down upon the living Godfreys and
Harolds, and Joans and Bridgets, romping and playing hand in hand.

The old place rings now with glad young voices.

and merry shouts of laughter, where once it rang sadly to the cry of a neglected child.

And dearer to Godfrey's heart than all that group of happy children is that once neglected child.

A feeling akin to envy of his own boys' and girls' happy childhood will come over him sometimes as he sees them at their play, thinking how their young mother's early life was spent.

Again there will arise within him the longing to atone to her for all the sorrows of her life, the desire to keep the wind from blowing on her too roughly, to strew the path of her life with flowers.

Is it only a vague longing, or does he carry it out? We will put our hero to the test. We have heard his vows in the picture-gallery—we will see how those vows have been kept.

For in the wear and tear of life there is not the flash, and the fire, and the excitement which in such hours bring words of love and devotion so easily to the lips.

Many a lover's vow has in this world been spoken, deep and sincere in its meaning at the time. But wait till the words have been tested, wait till the love has been tried; wait till the cares of life and its troubles, and the wear and tear of existence, have worked their canker into the fair bud of life's promise.

Holy, and true, and enduring is the love which comes out strong from the trial.

So we will put our hero to the test.

We will watch him in the daily routine of domestic

existence, which is, after all, the arena where lovers'
vows are tried and tested, where self is met and vanquished, where noble deeds are done. What do we
see ?

The eye that ever on her fondly lingers, the heart
with which the thought of her is ever full, the tender
and thoughtful consideration which reads her wishes
almost before she knows them herself, and, antici-
pating thus her every thought, strives to give her all
of which he thinks she is desirous, and to keep far
from her all that he deems may give her pain.

While it is his will that every joy shall with her
be divided, he would take the cares of life on his own
strong shoulders and let her go free.

Yes, he can stand the test. Not lightly those
words were spoken ; nobly have those vows been kept.
Love is not worthy the name unless there enter into
it the element of self-sacrifice ; and his is a love with
which no thought of self is ever mingled ; a tenderness which, by sharing, softens every sorrow, heightens
and increases every joy.

A love which, come what may, and arise what
will—as in the happiest domestic existence the cares
and trials of life *must* sometimes enter ; mistakes,
misfortunes, and their attendant worries *will* sometimes come—never suffers the shadow of blame to
rest upon her. In his eyes she can do no wrong. Let
who may be in fault, never her.

No ; she is for ever sacred, for ever guarded and
sheltered, for ever shielded from anything which could

give her pain, or mar for a moment the flood of sunshine with which it is his joy to encompass her, in which it is the aim of his life she should dwell.

Surely such love as this must make amends even for a lonely and a loveless girlhood, even for years of seeming neglect and desertion, even for a childhood branded with the words " Not wanted."

THE END.

PRINTED BY WILLIAM CLOWES AND SONS, LIMITED, LONDON AND BECCLES.

S. & H.

www.ingramcontent.com/pod-product-compliance
Lightning Source LLC
Chambersburg PA
CBHW030948110726
47900CB00004B/1173